Sisters Red

Sisters Red

by Jackson Pearce

LITTLE, BROWN AND COMPANY

New York   Boston

Little, Brown and Company

Hachette Book Group
237 Park Avenue, New York, NY 10017
Visit our website at www.lb-teens.com

Little, Brown and Company is a division of Hachette Book Group, Inc.
The Little, Brown name and logo are trademarks of Hachette Book Group, Inc.

The publisher is not responsible for websites (or their content) that are not owned by the publisher.

First Paperback Edition: April 2011
First published in hardcover in June 2010 by Little, Brown and Company

The characters and events portrayed in this book are fictitious. Any similarity to real persons, living or dead, is coincidental and not intended by the author.

Library of Congress Cataloging-in-Publication Data
Pearce, Jackson.
    Sisters red / by Jackson Pearce. — 1st ed.
        p. cm.
    Summary: After a Fenris, or werewolf, killed their grandmother and almost killed them, sisters Scarlett and Rosie March devote themselves to hunting and killing the beasts that prey on teenaged girls, learning how to lure them with red cloaks and occasionally using the help of their old friend, Silas, the woodsman's son.
    ISBN 978-0-316-06868-0 (hc) / ISBN 978-0-316-06867-3 (pb)
    [1. Werewolves—Fiction.   2. Sisters—Fiction.   3. Supernatural—Fiction.]
I. Title.
    PZ7.P31482Si 2010
    [Fic]—dc22   2009044734

10 9 8 7 6 5 4 3 2 1

RRD-C

Book design by Tracy Shaw

Printed in the United States of America

FOR MY SISTER

PROLOGUE

A Fairy Tale, Seven Years Ago

Strangers never walk down this road, the sisters thought in unison as the man trudged toward them. *Certainly* not strangers in business suits — there was just no reason for them to be out here in the middle of nowhere. Yet here one was, clouds of dirt rising around his feet with each step before settling into the cuffs of his impeccably pressed slacks. The older sister raised an eyebrow and stepped up to the white fence, while the younger sister finished a cherry Popsicle already half melted from the afternoon sun.

The man nodded his head in greeting as he finally came to a stop in front of them. "Hello, little ones," he said, voice smooth. The sunlight glinted off the man's slick blond hair and created thin shadows on his face where wrinkles were just beginning to form.

"I'm *eleven*," the older sister answered boldly, lifting her chin high.

"My mistake! *Young ladies*," the man corrected with a chuckle.

The older sister twirled in response, pretending not to study him as her party dress bloomed like a red mushroom around her. As the man watched her, his smile faded. His eyes grew darker, his smile more forced, and he licked his lips in a way that made the older sister's stomach tighten. She stopped midturn and grabbed her sister's sticky hand, snatching away the Popsicle stick and gripping it tightly, like a weapon.

"Is your mother home?" the man asked, the pleasant expression sweeping over his face once again.

"Our mother doesn't live here," the little sister declared, kicking at a dandelion. "You have weird eyes," she added, squinting in the sun to look at the stranger's face. His irises were dark sienna, the red-brown shade of autumn leaves.

"Shh, Rosie!" the older sister scolded, backing away.

"Ah, it's all right," the man said, stepping forward. "The better to see your lovely faces with, my dears. Your father is home, then? Brother?"

The older sister shook her head, black curls scattering over her shoulders. "Our grandmother is here, though."

"Would you fetch her for me?"

The older sister hesitated, sizing him up again. She finally gave a curt nod and turned toward the little cottage behind her. "Oma March! There's a man here!"

No answer.

"*Oma March!*" she yelled louder.

The door swung open, slamming into the rows of gerbera daisies planted just outside the cottage. Oma March stepped outside, her daisy-patterned apron dusted with flour from the cake she was making for a neighboring boy's birthday party. Sounds from the television drifted through the yard, the *Price Is Right* theme intrusive against the songs of sparrows in nearby trees.

"Scarlett, love, what's wrong?" she asked calmly, never one to be easily riled.

Scarlett yanked Rosie toward the house. "There's a man— a *stranger*—here," she said, a note of warning in her voice as she brushed past her grandmother in the doorway. Rosie plopped down in front of the tiny television in the kitchen, but Scarlett lingered behind Oma March's broad back, fingers still gripping the red Popsicle stick.

"Oh," Oma March said as she regarded the stranger in surprise and tugged her apron off to reveal blue jeans underneath.

"Good afternoon, ma'am. I'm here as a representative of Hanau Citrus Grove. We're trying to expand our business by selling citrus fruits door to door. Pay on delivery in three to six weeks. May I show you our catalogue?"

"Citrus? You mean like oranges?" Oma March asked in her German accent. She waved the man forward; he unlocked the white gate and strode toward her, hand outstretched.

"Yes, ma'am. Oranges, grapefruits, tangerines—" The

3

man clasped Oma March's palm in his, the sleeve of his navy suit jacket sliding back to reveal a curious black mark on his wrist.

Scarlett narrowed her green eyes to get a better look. It was an arrow that didn't look so much like the tattoos the woodsman down the road had, but rather as though it was a true part of his skin.

Oma March followed Scarlett's gaze, and suddenly her mouth became a firm line. The air stilled. The salesman's sparkling eyes clouded with the same eerie expression they'd held when he'd regarded Scarlett outside.

"We don't need any. Thank you, sir," Oma March said, her voice suddenly hard.

No one moved at first, and it reminded Scarlett of the way dogs stand perfectly still before lunging in to fight. The salesman licked his lips again and stared at Oma March for a long moment before a slow, creeping smile pulled at the corners of his mouth.

"You're sure?" the salesman said as Oma March shut the door.

As soon as the latch clicked, she wheeled around to face them, face blanched and eyes pale green disks. Scarlett backed up, afraid to see her grandmother wear such a foreign expression. The Popsicle stick clattered to the ground.

"*Versteckt euch!*" Oma March whispered hoarsely, pointing urgently toward her bedroom in the back of the cottage. *Hide. Hide* now.

Rosie abandoned the television, grabbing her sister's

hand nervously. Scarlett opened her mouth to ask Oma March to explain, but before she could find the words, a guttural, ragged howl erupted on the other side of the front door. Scarlett's blood ran cold.

Oma March slammed a wooden beam across the door, then swung one of the bright yellow kitchen chairs over their heads and propped it up at an angle against the doorknob just before the knob began to turn furiously.

"*Schatzi,* my treasures, I won't let him have you!" Oma March murmured under her breath, like a prayer. She dashed for the telephone and began dialing.

"Charlie? Charlie, one is here. Outside," Oma March whispered frantically to Pa Reynolds, the woodsman who lived down the road. "Oh god, Charlie, hurry," she pleaded. She slammed the receiver of the avocado-colored phone back down and threw her weight behind the couch to slide it in front of the door as well.

Another low, growling howl, followed by frantic scratching at the door.

Oma March snapped her head toward her granddaughters, eyes watery and pleading. "Scarlett! Don't worry about me. Take Rosie and *hide,*" she begged.

Scarlett nodded and squeezed Rosie's hand, yanking her into Oma March's room and slamming the door behind them. A tangle of legs and arms, they scrambled into the corner between the bed and bookshelf, breathing in the cool scent of laundry detergent and musky old philosophy books. They heard scraping from the other room as Oma March

5

struggled with the couch. Another low, growling howl, then a sharp bang and a rainlike sound as splinters from the door poured down onto the floor.

Oma March shouted frantically in German, but her voice was cut off by loud thuds of furniture crashing to the ground, upholstery ripping, pans clattering. Scarlett bit her bottom lip so hard it began to bleed.

And then silence: eerie, thick silence that poured over the little cottage and drowned out the yammering of *The Price Is Right* contestants.

The sisters clung to each other, near mirror images with their chests pressed together until it seemed as if their hearts were one single organ beating between them. Rosie tangled her tiny fingers into Scarlett's thick black hair and hid her face by her sister's neck. Scarlett stroked Rosie's head comfortingly with one hand, while the other groped under the bed for something—anything—that she could use to defend them. Something more than a Popsicle stick. Scarlett shuddered when a shadow appeared in the line of light under the door. Finally, her fingers found the smooth handle of a handheld mirror beneath the bed.

The shadow began to pace back and forth on the other side of the door, every few steps punctuated by a breathy growl and the scraping of talonlike nails on the hardwood floor. Scarlett watched, hypnotized, and when the pacing suddenly stopped, she gasped. The shadow pressed against the wooden door so hard that it looked as though the door might splinter under the weight. Rosie cried out, and Scarlett struck the mirror hard against the nightstand, cracking the glass. Trembling, Scarlett pried the largest shard from the mirror's frame.

The aluminum knob turned so slowly that for a moment Scarlett thought perhaps it was just Oma March coming to check on them like she often did just before she turned in for the night. Scarlett squeezed her eyes shut. *Just Oma March. I am not here, Rosie is not here, we are in bed.* But as the door cracked, Scarlett forced her eyes wide, gritting her teeth when she saw Rosie's chubby cheeks still shaking in fear. The door opened a little farther, a little farther, the stream of light hunting them down in the darkness. The single heart between them pounded as the door finally swung fully open and they were exposed to the light, helpless to hide from the form silhouetted in the door frame.

It was *him,* the salesman, but it was also...not. He still had shiny blond hair, but now it was speckled across his body like patches of disease. His eyes were enormous and hollow, his mouth twisted and stretched as if his face had been pulled apart at the corners, revealing rows of long, pointed fangs. His back arched as if it were broken, hunching his shoulders and turning his feet in. And his feet...the horrible claws were as long as fishing hooks and left deep gashes in the floorboards as he inched closer to the girls.

He ducked to fit under the door frame and, in one fluid transformation, lost the last few characteristics that had made him look even remotely like the blue-suited salesman. That had made him look remotely *human.* His nose became long and canine, his lips spread even farther. He lurched forward and planted his two hands—no, *paws*—onto the ground, thick, greasy hair clinging to his entire body. And the *smell*. A rotting, corpselike stench emanated from the thing—the *wolf*—making the sisters retch. He watched them hungrily, evil adoration in his eyes.

Scarlett swallowed hard, gripping the mirror piece so tightly that it cut her hand. She pushed away the impending tears, the energy in her legs screaming for her to run, and the sound of Bob Barker shouting about dinette sets as if nothing were wrong, as if she couldn't see her grandmother's form slumped on the ground just behind the monster.

She stared into the monster's hard sienna eyes and it cocked its mangy head. Before Scarlett knew what she was doing, she shoved Rosie under the bed and leapt to her feet, wielding the shard of mirror like a knife. Scarlett took a step forward, then another, until she was so close to the monster that the rotting stench emanating from his throat choked her. The wolf opened his wide, long jaws, rows of teeth and bloodstained tongue stretching for her. A thought locked itself in Scarlett's mind, and she repeated it over and over until it became a chant, a prayer: *I am the only one left to fight, so now I must kill you.*

CHAPTER ONE

SCARLETT MARCH

HE'S FOLLOWING ME.

About time. I had to walk past the old train depot five times before this one caught the scent of my perfume on the wind. I feign obliviousness to the sound of his dull footsteps in the darkness behind me and tug my crimson cloak tighter around my shoulders. I give a fake shiver as a breeze whips through my glossy hair. *That's right...come along, now. Think about how badly you want to devour me. Think of how good my heart will taste.*

I pause on a street corner, both to be certain that my stalker is still behind me *and* so I can appear confused and scared. There's nothing like a lost teenage girl on the bad side of town to get their blood pumping. The street lamps make the wet pavement glittery, and I avoid the light as best

I can. It would ruin the whole charade if he saw the bumpy, jagged line where my right eye should be. The eye patch covers some of the mark, but the scar is still obvious. Luckily, the wolves are usually too focused on the red cloak to care all that much.

I turn sharply and head down an alley. My stalker turns as well. This side of town reeks of stale beer from the restaurants that have become bars now that the sun is down, but I suspect the man following me can smell my perfume above the booze. If you can call him a man. They slowly lose their human souls when they become monsters. I walk faster— one of the first tricks I learned. Run from an animal, and it chases you.

My fingertips skim the worn handle of the hatchet hanging at my waist, hidden by the flutter of the red cloak. The cloak serves multiple purposes—the color of passion, sex, and lust is irresistible to wolves, and the fabric hides the instrument of their death. And perhaps most important, wearing it feels *right,* as if I've put on a uniform that turns me into more than a scarred-up orphan girl.

"Miss!" my stalker calls out just as I emerge from the alley's opposite end.

Gotcha.

I gasp and turn around, careful not to let the red hood slip off my head. "You scared me," I say, clutching my heart—the only part of my body untouched by Fenris jaws. My hands are scarred, just like my face, but the marks are so small that I count on him overlooking them in his fit of hunger. It's easy enough to make a wolf notice my hair, my long legs, my waist, but hiding the scars took practice.

"So sorry," he says, stepping out of the alley. He looks normal. Nice, actually—mahogany-colored hair and a firm jaw speckled with facial hair, like a high school football star in his prime. He's wearing a pale blue polo shirt and jeans. If I didn't know any better, I'd easily believe he just stepped out of one of the bars. That's all part of the illusion, of course; it's hard to lure young girls to their doom if you look like a psychopath. You have to look kind, put together, clean-cut. Show them pretty hair and stylish clothes, and most girls won't look close enough to see that your teeth point in a very canine way or recognize that it's *hunger* your eyes are lit with.

He glances down the road. There are a few shady characters hanging out on the street corners several blocks away, small-town thug-wannabes smoking, shouting at one another. No good—he doesn't want to kill me where people can see, and I don't want to fight him where someone might intervene. The wolves and I both prefer to stalk our prey under the cover of darkness—if possible, anyhow. I'll take killing a wolf in daylight over letting one escape alive any day.

He takes a step closer. He can't be much older than I am, really—twenty-two, absolute tops, though they stop aging once they change, so it's hard to tell exactly. Once they've transformed, they're ageless—unless, of course, someone kills them. He smiles, white teeth dazzling in the night. A normal girl would be drawn to him. A normal girl would think about touching him, would think about kissing him, about wanting him. A normal, stupid, ignorant girl.

"A lovely girl like you shouldn't be out so late, alone and all," he says calmly, though I can hear the panting in his voice as his eyes run across the red cloak. I notice that the hair on his arms has started to grow; he's too hungry to totally control his transformation for long. I'll never kill a Fenris if he hasn't transformed. It's not worth the risk of killing a person, putting someone through the same agony that my sister and I went through. I'd be nothing more than a murderer, so even though I've never been wrong, I always wait.

I shuffle my feet with pretend nervousness. "I'm lost," I lie. I meander across the street, swaying my hips. "I was supposed to meet a friend here…" Just a little farther, and the row of pawnshops on the cross street will hide us. He laughs, a deep, growl-like sound.

"Lost, huh?" he says, walking toward me. "Why don't you let me show you the way back?" He extends a hand. I look down. There's a black tattoo-like mark on his wrist, a flawless image of a coin. A member of the Coin pack, out this far? Odd. I take another step away from him. I'm hidden from the civilians' view now, and if he comes just a tad closer, he'll be as well.

"I…I'll be okay," I mutter. He grins. He thinks he's scaring me, and he's relishing it. It's not enough to just slaughter and devour girls. They need to frighten them first. I turn my back to him and start to walk quickly, letting my cloak billow out in the wind, taunting him. *Come along, follow me.* Time to die.

"Hey, wait," he calls out. His voice is dark now, almost guttural. He's fighting the transformation, but his hunger is winning—I can *feel* it somehow. His bloodlust hangs in the air like a fog. He wants to tear me apart, to dig his teeth into my throat. I stop, allowing the hood to slip down and my curls to wave in the breeze. I hear him groan with disgusting delight as I grip the familiar grooves of the hatchet's handle. *Don't turn around, not yet.* He hasn't changed, and if he sees the scars on my face, my cover will be blown. Can't risk him running and getting away—he has to die. He deserves to die.

"All I'm saying is"—he chokes on the words as the mutation begins to overpower his vocal cords—"people might get the wrong idea, a pretty girl like you out alone on a corner like this."

My lips curve into a grin as I draw the hatchet from my belt. There's a swish as his clothes hit the ground, then the clicking sound of claws on pavement. "I'm not worried," I answer, unable to suppress a sly grin. "I'm not that kind of girl."

When I spin around, there's no man behind me, only a monster. Some call them werewolves, but they're so much more than wolves. This Fenris's fur is dark and oily looking, fading to gray-mottled skin by his enormous feet. He growls and brings his long snout to the ground, tensing his jaw and clacking his yellowed teeth. The streetlight illuminates his enormous frame and casts a shadow that overtakes the ground at my feet. I raise an unimpressed eyebrow at him, and his eyes find the gleaming hatchet in my hand.

He leaps.

I'm ready.

His powerful shoulders launch him through the air at me; he snarls, the sound like rocks being shredded. I whip around toward him, low to the pavement. He begins to sail over my head but twists back in midair. I snap the hatchet up at the last possible moment. The blade makes contact and skims his front leg, and then I spin the hatchet to the left and manage to slice into the top of his back leg before the Fenris even hits the ground. Blood showers me.

The Fenris howls and collapses onto the pavement behind me. *Try again, wolf. Don't run away yet.* You can't let them run, once you've started a fight. They'll be starving from the expended energy, slaughter twice as many in half the time. It can end only one way: with the wolf's death. This one isn't a runner, though. He still wants to devour me.

Saliva drips from his lips, and his eyes narrow. The Fenris paces in front of me, shoulders rolling with every step. He curls his black lips back and bares his fangs.

The Fenris darts at me again. I sidestep and swipe at him — miss. He doubles around. No time to draw the hatchet back. I lift it like a shield in front of me and let my body relax. When the Fenris slams into me, I hit the pavement — hard — but he's run his chest into the hatchet, the weight of his body driving it in. I brace my legs against his abdomen and kick up, sending the monster flailing away behind me. Back to my feet. I grimace as a wave of dizziness rushes over me, as blood runs down the back of my shoulders, scrapes from hitting the asphalt. *Get it together, come on.*

I blink. The wolf is gone. No, not gone—I can still smell him in the air. I hold my breath, ears straining.

Wait for it. He's here. *Wait for it*—

The Fenris crashes into me with all the force of a bus. My right side, my blind side. His claws pop through the skin on my waist, sharp, stinging pain that makes my eye water and my vision blur. I hit the ground again and lose my grip on the hatchet. The wolf's weight bears into me, his breathing heavy and labored. I don't struggle—it makes them happy. Blood from his chest wound pools on my stomach, and as he presses his face closer to mine, I can see only one raging eye.

Wait for it. He'll relax. He'll make a mistake. You get only one shot to get them off you—make sure you take the right one. Flecks of his fur catch in my nose and mouth, and grime from his body sticks to my sweat. I could try to reach the hunting knife on my waist, but both of my hands are locked in place by his front feet. I choke as he lowers himself even farther against me, heavy on my lungs, gagging as he exhales almost directly into my throat.

Then a thick, dull sound echoes through the night, surprising enough to distract both me and the wolf. Footsteps? Before either the Fenris or I can react, a solid hit to its side throws the Fenris off my body, and I gasp for air as though I'm surfacing from water. *Get up, get up, quick.* I roll to my

15

stomach. Out of the corner of my good eye, I see a man, shadowed by the night but with a familiar lanky gait. He turns his head from me to the Fenris, who prowls a few yards away.

"You'd think after all these years, you'd know to keep a Fenris from getting to your blind side," the intruder says. I grin, standing up. The Fenris growls at us; I lean to one side as it leaps forward and swing my hunting knife into his front leg. The wolf manages to shred part of my cloak as he stumbles away.

"I could have gotten him. I was waiting for my moment," I answer. The boy laughs, eyes sparkling gray-blue even in the darkness.

"Would that moment have come just after we carved 'Scarlett March' on your tombstone?" the boy snickers.

The Fenris rears back and snarls. It knows it's too late to run. It's kill us or be killed. I join the boy, grabbing my hatchet off the ground. He licks his lips nervously. He's rusty at hunting, obviously. I wonder how long it's been.

"You know," I say, smirking, "if you aren't up to all this, I can handle it for you. You know, if you aren't man enough."

He narrows his eyes, but a smile tugs at the corners of his thin lips. We turn toward the Fenris as the wolf lowers its shoulders to the ground, eyes focused and furious. The boy draws two knives from his belt. I flip my hatchet in my hand.

"He's gonna come at you first," the boy says.

"I know," I answer. "You go to his—"

"I will," he replies, grinning. I shake my head. Nothing's changed. We don't need words, not when we're hunting together.

The wolf charges us just as we take the first few running steps toward him. The boy reaches it first. He leaps high over the Fenris's arched back and sinks both knives into his sides. That should do the trick, but I won't let him take the credit. I skid to a stop and release the hatchet toward the Fenris. It lassos through the air before sinking into his chest with a squelching thud.

The Fenris collapses to the ground, its eyes glimmering in a mix of hunger and hatred as I step toward it. It snaps at my legs once or twice uselessly. There's nothing human about it now, nothing canine, only a dying creature both bestial and disgusting. Its rotting-garbage-meets-sour-milk scent makes me gag. I've lost track of how many Fenris I've hunted, but the smell gets to me every time.

"When did you get back? And where's your ax?" I ask the boy without taking my eye off the Fenris. Best to wait until you know they're dead.

"About an hour ago, and I didn't exactly expect to be hunting straight off—hence, no ax. Figures I'd find you out here before I even get back to my house. You need some hobbies, you know?"

I shake my head as the Fenris takes a few final raspy breaths. Its tongue lolls out of its mouth, and with a final growl, it dies. The dead Fenris bursts into darkness, an explosion of nighttime. Shadows flit over walls, into the cars, between blades of grass like coal-colored fireworks scattering across the world. I look toward the boy.

"Good to see you, Silas."

Silas grins and shakes the Fenris blood off his knives before sheathing them. "You too, Lett."

"Good to see a *real* hunter in action again, you mean," I quip.

He steps forward and hugs me. I tense—I *like* being hugged, but it doesn't happen too often. Something about a girl that's missing an eye turns people off to touching her, I guess. Silas has known me since before the scars, though. I give in and put my arms around him.

Silas releases me and frowns at the bloodstains on his jeans. "There are some parts of hunting that I really didn't miss," he grumbles. "Are you okay, by the way?" he asks, motioning to the wound on my waist.

"It's nothing," I say, waving it off. "Are you saying you didn't hunt the entire time you were in San Francisco?" I run my hatchet along the hem of my cloak. The Fenris's blood barely shows up on the crimson fabric.

"Forgive me for trying to spend some time with my uncle!"

"Yeah, yeah," I sigh. It's hard to understand how he can just *not* hunt for such long periods of time, but the subject has always been a losing battle for me. "So how is Uncle Jacob these days?"

Silas shrugs. "Okay. I mean, for a forty-year-old man who's practically a hermit."

"That's not his fault, though," I say as we meander back through the alley. "Your brothers and sisters still riled up about your father giving Jacob all the inheritance money?"

"Yep. Even angrier about him giving me the house here," Silas mutters. Silas finished high school instead of taking a woodsman apprenticeship, something his brothers found fairly dishonorable and his triplet sisters found emasculating. Combine that with the fact that Pa Reynolds gave him and Jacob his worldly possessions before going senile...they can really hold a grudge, it seems.

"I'm sorry," I offer. I try to imagine my life without my sister, but it's impossible; if she were gone, my life would stop. I give Silas what I hope is a sympathetic smile. He nods in response.

At the end of the alley there's a car without hubcaps or a front bumper, the driver's-side door flung open. The back is piled high with duffel bags and fast-food cups.

"That thing made it to California?" I say, frowning.

"Not only that, but I managed to make it run off vegetable oil while I was there," he answers.

"All the way to California and not a single Fenris..." I sigh.

Silas grins and wraps an arm around my shoulders. "Lett, really, you've got to get a hobby. Come on, I'll give you a ride home."

I climb into the passenger seat, knocking a few empty soda bottles to the floorboard. I have the window rolled down before Silas can even get to the driver's side—maybe it's because I don't ride in them often, but cars make me claustrophobic. Silas slides in beside me and fiddles around with a few wires that stick out by the ignition, and the car grumbles to a start.

"What about here, though? I didn't realize packs were starting to prowl around Ellison again," Silas says.

I shrug. "It's been kind of recent. That one had been here awhile, I think. He was Coin. No sign from Arrow or Bell," I answer. *What are packs like on the West Coast? As large as the ones in the South, as fierce? Is there anyone there to destroy them like I do here? How much more could I accomplish if I were in California instead of small-town Georgia? I can't believe he didn't hunt even once...*

"Also, thanks for saying happy birthday," Silas interrupts my thoughts.

"Oh, wow, Silas, I forgot. I'm sorry. So you're old enough to drink finally?" I ask.

"It's not as exciting as you'd think." He grins. We sail past the edge of town and into the night. A few scattered farmhouses glow like stars on hills, but other than that, there's nothing but the dim glow of Silas's single working headlight. I double-check that there's no blood on my hatchet or hunting knife, then wrap both up in my cloak. I flip down the sun visor and grimace. I lick my fingers and try to smooth my hair, which is shooting out as if I've been electrocuted.

"Well, looks like Ellison hasn't changed much—hey, since when do you care about your hair?" Silas asks.

"Since now," I answer quickly. I adjust my shirt and tuck

the cloak and weapons under my seat as we turn down an unpaved road. Tall grasses line either side, and the shrieks of crickets and locusts become deafening through the open window. I wipe away the moisture on my forehead.

"Wait, are you...you're trying to hide the fact that you were hunting!"

I sigh. "Look, I told Rosie that she could go hunting on her own for the first time, but that Fenris—"

"You *stole* a solo hunt from your sister?"

"No! I mean, *yeah,* but it's a good thing I did. That wolf was harder than I predicted. I don't know. She's not ready and I had to go hunting or lose my mind..."

"Scarlett..." Silas begins in a serious tone. He started using "the tone" when we were kids to remind me that he's older than I am. It annoys me just as much now as it did then, only now it's less acceptable for me to push him into the mud for it. "She's supposed to be your partner."

"No, she's supposed to be my sister. *You* were my partner, before you up and abandoned us—"

"Hey, I still am, I've just been away—actually, *no,* I'm not getting into this argument again. Why can't Rosie be in on this partnership too?"

"Look, I'm not going to wait for my sister to finish grocery shopping while the Fenris slaughter people left and right," I snap as we take the right fork in the road, toward Oma March's house. It doesn't matter how long she's been dead; I'll always consider it *her* cottage. The left fork goes to Silas's house. The only other thing close to us is the back

21

side of a massive cow pasture. "It's our responsibility," I add. "We know how to kill them. We know how to save people's lives. We don't take nights off or vacations to California for a year."

"Ouch," Silas says, but I can tell my words roll off him. It's hard to get Silas riled up, unfortunately. "All I'm saying," he continues, "is that you can't keep Rosie locked up forever."

I sigh in annoyance as the cottage appears in the distance like a lit oasis in the dark. "She's just not ready," I mutter. "And I don't want her to end up like me." Silas nods knowingly and traces his thumb over the scars on my arm as the smell of jasmine flowers wafts in through the air. We ride along in silence for a few moments.

Finally, Silas's car growls up to the edge of the gravel drive. The cottage's front door swings open, sending a long stripe of light through the yard.

"Wow," Silas says softly as he kills the ignition. I follow his stare out the windshield—Rosie is standing in the kitchen doorway, arms folded and eyes sparkling in anger. "Rosie looks...different."

"Yeah. 'Different' as in *mad*." I sigh, throwing the car door open. "Stay here for a second."

CHAPTER TWO

❀

Rosie March

She's back. I pace in front of the door, trying to build up strength. *You have every right to be upset,* I convince myself. *Don't let her out of this one.* I blink furiously, trying to keep myself from choking up. I can put up with a lot. But it's hard to just shrug when your sister thinks you're incapable.

I inhale deeply, throw the old wooden door open, and step outside.

It slams shut behind me, destroying the tiny ray of kitchen light that had spilled into the darkness. My face is hot and probably bright pink, and my hands are balled into fists. If Scarlett wants to think I'm a child, I'll act like a child. I storm forward, pretending the crunchy gravel isn't slicing into my bare feet. Silas Reynolds's car looms in the driveway — he was probably hunting *with* her. I'll deal with him next. Scarlett sighs, holding out her hands as if she's calming a wild animal.

"You *promised!*" I snarl. I throw a bundle of red-violet fabric to the ground at her feet—my cloak, almost the exact same color as Scarlett's.

"Rosie, look—" Scarlett begins. I grab at my waist and yank two daggers off the belt. Their bone handles clunk together as they tumble onto the rocky drive. I cringe and try to hide it; Scarlett's always nagging me about dirtying the blades, and it's a measure of how angry I am that she doesn't call me on it now. It's silent for a moment, other than the occasional hoot from a nearby owl. I fold my arms and glare.

Scarlett groans. "Oh, stop pouting." She bends over and grabs the daggers and my cloak. The moon reflects off the shiny scars on her shoulders, evenly spaced lines that disappear under her tank top. She shoves my things toward me, but I don't budge.

"I'm not pouting!" I snap back, realizing how pouty that sounds. "I can hunt too, Scarlett. *You* don't have to go running out into the dark every time."

"It was just one Fenris, and he was on the prowl. Someone might have died tonight if I'd waited for you. You want that on your head?"

"All you had to do was tell me you were going! How am I ever supposed to hunt on my own if you keep going after every wolf that sets foot in Ellison?"

"Look, Rosie, I'm sorry. Really."

"Just because you're older doesn't mean you get to treat me like I'm some kind of lame sidekick!" I shout, emotion betraying me on the last word. I mean for it to be furious, but instead the hurt creeps in, tiny squeaks of impending tears slipping through my lips. I hate that — it's as though I have an anger threshold, when suddenly the rage turns into hurt. It never happens to my sister — her body is always hard, firm, perfectly trained and controlled. Her body could never allow tears — it isn't trained for it.

"Um, if I may add," a male voice calls out. The driver's side of the Chevy squeals open and Silas leans out, face still shrouded in darkness. "I helped her. I'm just saying. If it makes you feel any better . . . she needed help. So, you know . . . that'll teach her." There's a hint of humor in his voice, and somehow, it makes my anger dissipate the smallest bit.

"Thanks, Silas," Scarlett mutters. "Get my things out from under the seat, will you?"

Scarlett sidesteps me and throws open the front door, dashing the yard in light that illuminates Silas's face for a fraction of a second before the door shuts. I squint to get another look — Silas looks different from what I remember. But what, exactly, has changed? The line of his jaw, or the length of his hair, something in his eyes — were they always that shade of ocean gray? I can't pinpoint what exactly is different about his face, his body, *him*.

Upstairs, Scarlett's bedroom door slams, interrupting my thoughts. I roll my eyes and turn to hobble back inside. The jagged edges of the gravel hurt a lot more now that I'm not on an adrenaline rush.

"So, Scarlett hasn't changed much," Silas says from behind me. I nod and then wince as a particularly sharp rock lodges itself in my heel. "You need some help, Rosie?"

His footsteps quicken behind me, and before I can respond, I feel his calloused hands on my waist. I accidentally slide back against his chest and inhale the scent that has always clung to his whole family—something like forests, damp leaves, and sunshine. I suppose when your father is a woodsman you're bound to carry the scent of oak in your veins. One breath is all I get the chance for, though; he kicks the door open and sets me down on the front stoop, then takes a step back. I turn to face him, hoping to thank him for the help and in the same sentence admonish him for carrying me like a little girl.

Instead, I smile. He's still Silas—Silas who left a year ago, the boy just a little older than my sister. His eyes are still sparkling and expressive, hair still the brown-black color of pine bark, body broad-shouldered and a little too willowy for his features. He's still there, but it's as if someone new has been layered on top of him. Someone older and stronger, who isn't looking at me as if I'm Scarlett's kid sister... someone who makes me feel dizzy and quivery. How did this happen?

Calm down. It's just Silas. Sort of.

"You're staring," he says cautiously, looking worried.

"Oh. Um, sorry," I say, shaking my head. Silas shoves his

hands into his pockets with a familiar sway. "It's just been a while, that's all."

"Yeah, no kidding," he replies. "You're heavier than I remember."

I frown, mortified.

"Oh, no, wait. I didn't mean like that, just that you've gotten older. Wait, that doesn't sound much better..." Silas runs a hand through his hair and curses under his breath.

"No, I get it." I let him off the hook, grinning. Something about seeing him nervous thaws some of my shyness. "Do you want something to eat?"

"You're sure you and Lett don't need...sister time?" He glances up the stairs warily.

"No," I answer, stepping backward into the kitchen. "In fact, I really don't want sister time right now."

"Hey, now. Appreciate the sibling time."

I cringe. "Sorry, I forgot. Your brothers and the triplets still aren't talking to you?"

"Lucas is coming around, slowly. I'll manage. But hey—when did you start to cook?" He changes the subject as he follows me inside and plops down into one of our mismatched dining room chairs.

"I don't, really. I just picked up a few of Oma March's old recipes because I got tired of eating Chinese delivery."

"Ah yes. I'd forgotten Lett's love affair with Chinese food," Silas says, grinning affectionately. "She's been stressed lately?" It's a measure of how tense Scarlett is—when it gets really bad, cheap Chinese is her only comfort food.

"She didn't exactly handle you leaving that well," I say, frowning. I missed Silas too, but not the way Scarlett did. Did he miss her, his partner, that way? Do I want to know if he did? Guilt flashes over Silas's face, so I hurry to continue. "Cooking is nice, though. You know, something to do that isn't quite as hunting-centric..." I blush, afraid I've said too much.

But Silas surprises me by waving his hand dismissively. "No, I get it. I just spent a year doing non-hunting-centric things. Sometimes you need a break."

"Yeah, well, don't tell my sister," I mutter, glaring at the ceiling. "She wants me to be a hunter but won't let me solo. I just can't make her happy."

"I didn't know you'd grown to love hunting so much," Silas notes, sounding genuinely surprised.

I backpedal. "I...I mean, it's not about liking hunting. It's about the fact that I spend hours training every day for solo hunts she won't let me do. If I have to live the life of a hunter, I'd like to actually, you know, hunt."

"Ah," Silas says, though I'm pretty sure I didn't make any sense. "Well, not that I'm in favor of her stealing hunts from you, but I'll confess it's hard to think about little Rosie March on her own, killing wolves, and not get overprotective." He pauses, and he seems to be choosing his words carefully. "Even if you aren't exactly 'little Rosie March' anymore."

My eyes find his, trying to analyze the meaning of his words, of the change in his tone. But just as I finally take a breath and will myself to speak, the pipes from the upstairs shower rattle above us. I turn back to the oven, out of my trance. I'm overanalyzing things, as usual.

"What are you making, then?" Silas asks, voice back to normal.

"Um...meatloaf." The sexiest of foods.

"It smells great," Silas replies kindly. I look over my shoulder at him and smile. Out of the corner of my eye, I see a gray blur dart from the stairwell to the living room couch, accompanied by the tinkling of bells.

"Is that my arch-nemesis I hear?" Silas asks, turning toward the blur.

"Screwtape? Yep."

"I wonder if he *still* hates me," Silas says as the cat edges out from the couch, pale green eyes like little limes in the dark. As if to answer Silas's question, Screwtape takes a flying leap onto his lap and begins to purr wildly.

"I'm not falling for this anymore, cat," Silas says firmly. He moves to push Screwtape away, but as soon as his palms are within a few inches of Screwtape's wild fur, the cat extends his claws into Silas's thighs. Silas winces and muffles a yelp.

"Need some help?" I say, trying to hide my laughter.

"That'd be great," he answers tensely. I hurry over and scoop Screwtape into my arms. The cat instantly melts against me and rubs his face against mine, the scent of catnip on his breath. I crinkle my nose.

"Thanks." Silas sighs in relief. "I can hunt wolves, but it's a cat I can't handle. Not terribly manly of me, is it?"

"I won't tell anyone," I answer with a soft smile that he

returns. The oven buzzer rings out behind me; I hurry over to whip the Sexy Meatloaf out of the heat.

Scarlett trudges down the stairs, fresh from her shower. If you don't take one right after a hunt, the scent of the Fenris somehow gets into your skin and sticks around for ages. Her hair is pulled off her face and the eye patch is gone. There's a long, diagonal scar where her eye would be that slices from the crown of her head across her high cheekbones. She'd never admit it, but I know she's self-conscious about the scar. In fact, I can remember her taking the eye patch off only around me and Silas. She gives me a sort of apologetic look, but I glance away.

"TV?" Silas asks her. Scarlett nods in response and Silas turns on our tiny television to the news, as if he'd never left.

We begin to eat while Scarlett watches the television intently until a story about a rash of Atlanta murders is over. Most of the world isn't on to the Fenris, even though they've apparently been around for centuries, but you can learn more about them than you'd expect by watching a newscast. Some people see a string of murders or a strange disappearance as a lunatic on the loose, but we see a Fenris being sloppy. But the truth is, usually a Fenris attack in disguise doesn't even *make* the news, unless the girl is particularly beautiful or her family particularly rich; it's just written off, another statistic of a missing young woman.

When the report turns to some political sex scandal, Scarlett turns the set off and looks at Silas. "You want to start hunting with us again, now that you're back?" The question carries a heavy intensity, and if I were Silas, I'd be afraid to say no.

I'm not sure what answer I'm hoping for. I've gone hunting with Silas a thousand times before, but in the past, I usually ended up standing in the background while he and Scarlett fought together, a blur of movement and ferocity that I've never felt able to match. Will that have changed, as Silas has?

Silas shrugs. "Sure. Especially if you're finding them in a place as small as Ellison. That must mean there are too many wolves in all the nearby cities."

Silas talks about San Francisco, so avidly that I think he's trying to fill the air with words before it can be consumed with awkward silences. I don't know *why* I feel those silences lurking all around us, but every time Silas and I make eye contact, I can sense them there, waiting to slip in and make me blush. I try to avoid his eyes, stealing glances at his arched brows and bow-shaped lips whenever he's looking away. Trying to avoid the awkwardness mostly diverts me from feeling jealous—Silas got to see other cities, travel across the country, do things, while I sat here in Ellison.

"You can stay here tonight if you want," Scarlett offers as she sets her empty plate by the sink. "I mean, I imagine your house is coated in dust."

Silas laughs, deep and honey-toned. "I slept in a car for two weeks on the drive back here. And before that, on Jacob's couch. Trust me, dust is fine." He stands and pushes his chair in. "Thanks for the offer, but I do need to go."

"Hunting tomorrow, then?" Scarlett asks.

"Maybe. I think I'll be taking care of house stuff all day tomorrow, to tell the truth. Inheriting a giant house sounds like a great idea until you realize you have to replace shingles and everything. I have a sinking feeling that Pa Reynolds is laughing it up in that nursing home, if he remembers it."

Scarlett and I grin simultaneously. Pa Reynolds—the man who took care of us, who gave Scarlett the information she needed to begin to hunt, the man who raised us when our mother wasn't around after the attack—now has Alzheimer's and, as best as I can tell, scarcely remembers anyone who comes to visit him. It's painful to think that Pa Reynolds, who was a veritable encyclopedia of information about the Fenris and the forest, has no memory of who he is. But we smile, as does Silas, because it's the sort of thing that you'll cry about if you don't treat it lightly.

Silas turns to me, exhaling. "Thanks for dinner, Rosie."

"Anytime," I reply. Silas waves and leaves; a few moments later I hear the rumble of his car pulling out of the drive. Scarlett sits down beside me and doesn't speak for a moment. I avoid her eye. Just because I'm sort of dazzled by Silas doesn't mean I've forgotten how mad I am at her.

"Rosie? Come on. Don't be mad."

I don't answer. Screwtape leaps into my lap; I scratch under his chin until he erupts into purrs.

"I couldn't help it," Scarlett says sincerely, folding her

arms. Her voice is softer than normal. I sigh, set Screwtape on the ground, and turn to go to my bedroom. My sister knows I'll forgive her. I'll always forgive her. I have to. It's one of those things that's just necessary when someone has saved your life.

CHAPTER THREE

SCARLETT

I WAKE UP AT DAWN, EVEN THOUGH I DIDN'T FALL INTO bed till close to four. I lie in bed staring at the faded flower wallpaper, tracing the little line of bluebells from floor to ceiling with my eye. I didn't pick it out—this was our mother's room and is far too country and girly for my tastes. I sigh and try to fall back asleep, but there's no use. I've always been able to function just fine on three hours of sleep. If I sleep any longer, I have nightmares. Not *nightmares*, I suppose. Flashbacks: The Fenris breaking down our door. My grandmother screaming in German. The feeling of his teeth on my arms, my legs, my face.

It's enough to make anyone an insomniac.

I roll over and crinkle my nose. I should shower again. I can still smell the Fenris on me. I think. It's hard to tell, at times, if the scent is really there or if it just somehow haunts me.

The Fenris. I sigh. The only thing worse than making Rosie angry is knowing I have to make up for making Rosie angry. Otherwise, something is wrong. It's hard to explain, but when she's angry, it feels as though someone has put me together incorrectly, like a bookshelf with a row of upside-down books. I can't help being protective, though—I can never shake the mental image of Rosie making one little mistake. One slipup, and it's all over. What kind of hunter would I be if I couldn't keep the one surviving member of my own family safe?

That's *why* I hunt: to kill the monsters that destroy lives and ruin families. I don't know when it will end, exactly—there's not really a finish line, unless I somehow kill every Fenris in existence. That feels like dreaming to win the lottery, but it's still a dream. All the fear, the darkness...gone.

I throw my feet over the side of the bed and tiptoe across the worn hardwood floors, stepping over the floorboards that I know will creak. Periwinkle sunshine pours in through the tiny octagonal window at the end of the hall. It casts shadows off the ceiling beams and doorknobs that dapple the ground in light, like a forest floor. The house is silent, but outside, the earliest birds are calling out in the brush and I can hear the low, rumbling sounds of cattle. I love this time of morning; being inside is like hiding out behind some secret screen in the middle of rolling southern farmland.

I creep closer to Rosie's door, stepping over Screwtape. He claws my leg in annoyance, all gray fur and teeth. I shake him away, and he scampers off with an indignant look. I pause, hand wrapped around the doorknob.

One, two, *three*.

I fling the door open, letting it slam into the wall behind it. I sprint forward, leaping through the air at the very last moment and pouncing on Rosie in her tiny twin bed. She screams and leaps up, hair frazzled and eyes only half open, pink quilt clutched to her chest.

"What the hell are you doing?" she demands groggily. She falls back onto the bed beside me and yanks the quilt over her head.

"I'm apologizing for the…uh…'thing' that happened last night."

"By jumping on me? Your apology sucks."

"Not this—this is just me being your annoying older sister. The apology is that…we can have a movie night tonight. And you can pick the movie."

Rosie sits upright and eyes me cautiously. "*Any* movie?"

I press my lips together to hide my distaste at the idea of Rosie's movie selection. She likes *love* stories. I can't help but think they're a waste of energy.

Rosie folds her arms. I nod reluctantly.

"*And* you let me have the solo hunt next time?" she adds.

"I promise…I promise to try."

Rosie rolls her eyes, but we both know it's as good as I'll do. "Okay. But then you also have to promise you won't back out of the movie again."

"I promise."

"And promise me you'll get out of my room and let me sleep like a normal person," she says as she melts back into her mattress. I laugh and retreat just as Screwtape leaps onto the bed and nestles in beside Rosie's legs. I yank the door shut behind me, snickering as it crashes closed and I hear Rosie groan in annoyance. What are older sisters for? The upside-down books are righted again, though. I can go on with my morning.

I duck back into my bedroom just long enough to throw on a pair of jeans and pull my hair into a ponytail, then slip out the downstairs screen door.

Our backyard is bordered by the cow pasture and tall grasses and mostly consists of a garden that Rosie and I attempt to tend. I peer at the soil. Nearly time to plant snap peas, which I'm supposed to do by moonlight, according to my grandmother. I'm not sure that it matters, but I'll do it anyway. It was always difficult to tell when Oma March was imparting wisdom and when she was merely storytelling. More than once she replaced our nightly fairy tales with something clever inspired by her philosophy books or a rhyme intended to help us learn German. We absorbed it all, never realizing she was teaching us.

The German didn't really catch on beyond a few phrases, but there were bits of philosophy that stuck with me. Descartes, Hume, Plato...I look at the sun, squinting. My favorite was a story she told several times before I realized it was more than a fairy tale:

"Once upon a time," Oma March said, her singsong voice carrying across the bedroom Rosie and I shared.

"Once upon a time, there was a man who lived in a cave—"

"What was his name?" I interrupted.

"It doesn't matter."

"He has to have a name!"

"All right, his name was John. And he lived in a cave with his sister, Mary," my grandmother continued as Rosie and I snuggled close to each other beneath fleece blankets. "John and Mary were born in a cave and lived in the cave their entire lives. They always stayed far back in the cave in the near darkness, because if they tried to leave, they saw giant dark monsters on the wall. John and Mary didn't know it, but the monsters were only shadows."

"Why were they scared of shadows?" Rosie cut in.

"Because they didn't know that the monsters were merely shadows, schatzi. They thought they were real, live monsters that would hurt them if they got too close. Anyhow, one day their grandmother came into the cave. She grabbed John and Mary by the hands and led them to the monsters, then explained how the monsters were only shadows, like the ones on the walls in here," Oma March said, pointing to the far wall where the branches of a nearby crape myrtle cast fingery shadows on the paint.

"Then," she continued, "their grandmother took them outside into the bright, bright sunlight. It hurt *and burned their eyes because it was the first time they'd ever seen the sun after living in the dark for so long. In fact, it hurt so badly that John thought he must be dreaming. He decided that the sun and the shadows were only a dream and that the cave and the monsters must be real. So John ran back inside the cave, sure that the grandmother was just playing tricks. But Mary stayed outside, and even though it hurt, she waited until her eyes got used to the bright sunshine.*

"So, schatzi, who made the wiser choice? John, who refused to believe in the sunshine because it was strange and new, or Mary, who let her eyes get used to the light?"

Of course, I didn't realize that Oma March was talking to us about Plato at the time, but it forever changed the way I saw the sunshine. I look down at the shadow I'm casting across the rows of carrots that Rosie and I planted together a few weeks ago. Even in shadow, you can see the raised scars on my arms. My scars are my sunlight: I know the truth about the Fenris, while so much of the world still lives in the cave, in total, blissful ignorance.

God, sometimes I envy them, the freedom to go on with life without knowing about the monsters lurking in their midst. But I can't be John. How could I possibly try to pretend the sunlight doesn't exist, now that it's taken so much of me?

And I'm not stupid—I realize what I'm giving up. At first it was just a drive to kill all the wolves in Ellison. When that was done, Rosie and I started camping in nearby towns, taking the occasional night trip to Atlanta to fight them there. The farther we traveled, the more successful we were—until they returned to Ellison. I inhale, letting the cool morning air swirl through my lungs, then return to the cottage.

I pause as the screen door slams shut behind me. Something is different. I furrow my eyebrows and scan the room, my senses on high alert. There—the door to Oma March's bedroom is cracked.

I step forward, muscles tensed and ready for whatever lurks on the other side. I grab a kitchen knife from the block and slink across the room, eyes locked on Oma March's door. I reach it and listen for a moment, waiting for the sound of haggard breathing to reach my ears or a corpselike stench to reach my nose, to let me know about the wolf on the other side.

But there's nothing. No scent, no sound, nothing to do but open the door and prepare to fight.

I ready myself. Count to three. And fling the door open.

Rosie screams as I charge forward, stopping me in my tracks. "God, Scarlett, you scared the hell out of me."

I sigh, heart still pounding, and lower the kitchen knife.

"Screwtape chased a mouse toy in here," she explains, annoyed. Her bare feet are brushing the exact spot where it happened. "I didn't mean to scare you."

I shake my head; my hair clings to the sweat on my forehead.

"You don't need to explain. This is your house too—you can go where you want," I reply. I smile as best I can. "Except my room, of course."

"Why, you'll stab me with a kitchen knife if I do?" she jokes as I set the knife down onto Oma March's bedside table.

"Maybe," I answer.

Rosie laughs, but it's cloaked in melancholy. It's hard to *really* laugh in here; the room is like a tomb, thick with dust and trinkets and still, heavy air. All the shades are drawn, the bed is made, clothes folded in the drawers. We don't come in here. At least, not often. Rosie clutches a silver picture frame. She looks up at me from Oma March's squashy mattress like a doe uncertain if she should flee.

I lower myself to the bed and lean over her shoulder to see what picture she's looking at—it's an old black-and-white shot of our mother and grandmother, taken just weeks before our mother literally ran off to join the circus. Who'd have thought that a country girl from Georgia could become a star trapeze girl? The photo is like looking into a mirror—Rosie and I look uncannily like our mother. Dark hair, grass-colored irises, sharply tapered eyebrows, and bodies straight like boards.

"I like that picture. It's like a before shot," I say aloud. "Before they started fighting and Mom started, um...dating." That's putting it kindly. It's never been a secret that Rosie and I likely have two different fathers. In fact, we suspect we may have another sibling somewhere, but since Mom hasn't been here in more than two years, it's hard to know for certain. She came back after we were attacked but couldn't handle it—couldn't handle Oma March's death, could barely *look* at my scars... It was easier for her to skip out of town for a week, a month, a season, now years. Easier to leave her daughters to carry the weight of death alone.

Rosie exhales, a discouraged sigh. She sets the picture in her lap and looks around the rest of the room. "How long till we have to start selling off this room?"

I sigh. "Not for a while. There's still plenty of Mom's things in the attic to get rid of."

Rosie and I have sold everything from antique clocks to vegetables from the garden to make extra cash; she tried working at a coffee shop once, but it's impossible to have a job and hunt. We had college funds, but our mother drained those on liquor and drugs just after Oma March died. We've hardly touched this room, though I know that there will come a day when we'll have to decide to keep Oma's things or hunt Fenris. And of course, we have to hunt; it's our responsibility, now that we're out of the cave.

That doesn't make seeing our dead grandmother's things disappear hurt me any less. What if I lose my memory, like Pa Reynolds has? Will there be anything left of Oma March to remind me she existed at all? Anything left to remind me why I've dedicated my very being to the hunt?

"I guess it doesn't matter. I hardly remember some of this stuff anyway. It's like I know it's important, though," she says.

"It is important." I lean into her a little. "It's important *because* you can't remember."

Rosie shrugs. She stretches her toes to the floor and flips up the corner of the woven blue and white rug. I look away. The rug is the only thing in the room that Oma March didn't put here. We had to buy it to cover the rust-brown stain that no amount of bleach or hot water would remove. I don't like to look at it, but Rosie brushes the rug away every time we're in this room, as if seeing the mark where blood puddled— some mine, some the Fenris's, some Oma March's—will make her remember the attack better. It's all a haze, from what she's told me. She remembers the Fenris, him charging us, and his teeth.

I remember more. I don't need to see the stain to remember the sound the Fenris's teeth made when they popped through the skin on Oma March's stomach. Or the way it felt to see out of my right eye for the last time, the image of a claw careening toward my face, the exploding sensation. The strong vengeance and turmoil that rushed through my body, the desire to be the last thing the monster *ever* saw. The blur of red blood and crimson rage that changed me forever. I wait until I hear the soft swish of the rug hitting the floor to turn my head back to my sister. Everything about this room *aches* somehow, as though it's one of my scars being reopened whenever the doorknob is turned.

"Sorry," she whispers. She rises from the bed and sets the picture frame back on the nightstand, in the exact spot where it came from. I rise and smooth the quilt where we wrinkled it, then follow her to the door. She shuts it quietly, as if there's someone on the other side whom she doesn't wish to disturb.

"Why don't you go into town to rent the movie for tonight? And we need more gauze," I add, swinging open the refrigerator door. Rosie nods and grabs a canister off the countertop, rooting through a few layers of cookies to find a plastic bag filled with twenty-dollar bills. She removes two and reburies the bag.

"And take your knives." Rosie looks at me skeptically but straps the belt that holds her hunting knives around her waist. I'm overprotective, I know. But then, I know that the Fenris are everywhere.

CHAPTER FOUR

Rosie

My mother is the only one in our family who ever learned how to drive, and for all her faults, I have to admit I sort of admire her for it. Oma March insisted that cars were a waste of money, and once she was gone, Scarlett adopted the sentiment, so I'm used to a lot of walking. Downtown Ellison is only a half hour or so by car, but it's a good two hours by foot and bus. I trudge down our gravel road, two canvas shopping bags in hand—I learned the hard way that plastic store bags can break during a long trek.

The hills and farmland surrounding our cottage are the very definition of "rolling." Everything rolls endlessly—the trees into forests, hills into the horizon, clouds into mountains. Nothing really seems to end here, like we're situated on the roundest part of the earth. Whenever they show clips on the news of cities or deserts or steep-pitched mountains, it almost feels as if those places couldn't possibly exist — nothing can truly be that jagged, or that flat, or that sharp. The scattered few times I've been to Atlanta were even stranger, as though I were walking inside a storybook that couldn't possibly be real.

I find a rock and tap it with my foot as I walk. Halfway to the bus station. Scarlett would rather walk than ride the bus on the rare occasions she goes into Ellison; she says when she sits with people for that long, they begin to feel comfortable staring at her. Once, someone slipped her a card for a plastic surgery consultation. People don't understand that Scarlett is who she is *because of* the scars, because of the bites and wounds and pain.

When we were little, Scarlett and I were utterly convinced that we'd originally been one person in our mother's belly. We believed that somehow, half of us wanted to be born and half wanted to stay. So our heart had to be broken in two so that Scarlett could be born first, and then I finally braved the outside world a few years later. It made sense, in our little pig-tailed heads — it explained why, when we ran through grass or danced or spun in circles long enough, we would lose track of who was who and it started to feel as if there were some organic, elegant link between us, our single heart holding the same tempo and pumping the same blood. That was before the attack, though. Now our hearts link only when we're hunting, when Scarlett looks at me with a sort of beautiful excitement that's more powerful than her scars and then tears after a Fenris as though her life depends on its death. I follow, always, because it's the only time when our hearts beat in perfect harmony, the only time when *I'm* certain, beyond a shadow of a doubt, that we are one person broken in two.

I finally reach the bus stop and check my watch—I'm right on time, if the buses are running exact today. I sit down in a patch of soft clover and hunt for a shamrock with four leaves while I wait, using one of my knives to pick through the leaves. I wonder what Silas is doing, in that big empty house. I could go visit him...but the bus rolls up, a fog of dust and exhaust, dashing the prospect away. The driver gives me a curious look as she opens the door. I can tell she always wonders where I come from, but she never asks. Right after the attack people were concerned, but Mom and Pa Reynolds were enough to quell their worries. I imagine people just think one of them is still watching out for us. If they think of us at all.

I take a seat toward the back, one of only a few riders. It takes fifteen minutes for the long grasses to give way to freshly plowed fields, then scattered neighborhoods, and finally to downtown Ellison. The bus comes to a hard stop, the air brake shouting out, and the driver opens the door and slumps back in her seat. The knitting lady hobbles off, followed by a couple mountain-man-type passengers, and finally I step out onto the warm street.

The town's not bustling, by any means, but a few families push strollers, and groups of middle-aged women window-shop along the sidewalk. Ellison is the sort of place that

47

people move to when they want a slice of Americana, though the entire place turns rather shady after the sun sets: BBQ restaurants become bars; coffeehouses transform into dance clubs; and, of course, the monsters come out after dark.

I stop in the grocery store first and grab eggs, milk, and ramen noodles, then pick up a bar of Baker's chocolate and some flour to make cookies for our movie night tonight. The video store is next, and then the drugstore. I want to rent *My Best Friend's Wedding,* but I don't want to be that cruel to Scarlett. At least she'll like the fight scenes in *The Princess Bride.*

The Ellison drugstore used to be a little family-owned thing, but a few years ago CVS slapped a giant red logo on the ancient wood and it went from basic drugstore to something closer to a mini-mart, complete with automatic doors and little customer-care cards. I hit the first-aid aisle and then head straight for the checkout counter. It's amazing, really, that the clerk hasn't called the police about me. Who else buys eleven packages of gauze every two weeks? There are a few essentials if you're going to be a hunter: peroxide, make-shift sutures, and *lots* of gauze. Fenris know to aim for the spots that bleed the most, so something to clot the blood is crucial. I fumble in my pocket for the two wadded-up twenty-dollar bills.

A rash of bubbly laughter distracts me halfway to the register; a group of girls about my age are clustered in the makeup section. They cast wayward glances at the cashier as they sample pink and purple bottles of nail polish, giggling to one another and holding their hands up to the light. I recognize one of them: Sarah Worrell. We were friends in middle school the year before I dropped out, just a few years after the attack. I couldn't bear leaving Scarlett home alone, training . to fight wolves, so I just didn't go back after the summer was over. I told a few friends I was being homeschooled, dodged bullets when concerned parents and the county checked up on us, and tried to keep in touch with everyone, but it's amazing how quickly friends become strangers when you take textbooks and school socials out of the conversation.

I linger near the scented soaps longer than necessary, listening in on their discussion.

"This one won't match the beads on the dress, though," a girl with perfectly highlighted chestnut hair says brightly.

"They don't have to match. Try this one—it's called Second Honeymoon. Oh, or maybe Hawaiian Orchid!" Sarah offers, adjusting her glasses. I carefully watch the highlighted girl for a moment, trying to imagine what the dress looks like and where she might be wearing it. Not prom—it's not the right season, is it? I imagine all four of them in floor-length Hawaiian Orchid–colored gowns in a ballroom straight out of a Cinderella story. Is nail polish what I'd be talking about, if things had gone differently?

Sarah makes eye contact with me as she reaches for Second Honeymoon—I see flickers of recognition on her face. Maybe I should say something. Ask how she's doing, if she remembers me, what event they're picking out nail polish for. I smile at her a little, waiting to see if she'll break the ice and wave or something. But no—instead she just gives me a polite smile back, like she probably would anyone, and returns to her friends' discussion. I try to busy myself with a shelf of soaps but listen in closely; their voices carry, even at a whisper.

"I think she used to go to school with us," the blonde to Sarah's left says quietly. The others respond in hushed voices, before the blonde continues. "I don't remember. I wish I had hair like that, though. Do you think she uses that volumizing shampoo?"

"I know, right? Though her clothes could use some help—who wears pink like that? Oh yeah, her sister was *that* girl that got all torn up!" Sarah mutters, answering someone else's whispered interjection.

The torn-up girl and her sister. I know I should feel bad for Scarlett—she's been relegated to the worse title—but a wave of self-pity hits me anyhow. I turn and block out their conversation. Why should I care what they think? They're concerned with parties and clothes and a variety of vain, stupid things. I run my hand over the columns of soap before tossing a coral-colored bar that reeks of flowers into my basket, where it clatters against the bottles of peroxide and boxes of gauze. Heavy perfume appeals to the Fenris. It draws them to you, makes them hungry. *Second Honeymoon nail polish wouldn't make a difference to a Fenris,* a Scarlett-like voice in my head reminds me. *It's a waste of effort.*

I grab a few more bars of the flowery soap when a clear woodsy scent sweeps over me, overpowering the soaps. I know this scent, though it's not the sort that would rein in a Fenris. I hold my breath, afraid to be the first one to speak.

"Those girls have nothing on the March sisters," Silas says, leaning in so close that I can feel his breath on my shoulder. A strange shiny feeling ripples through me and I wheel toward him, accidentally ramming my shopping basket into Silas's side. A few Ace bandages topple to the floor and the girls look up from their polish dilemma to snicker at me. *Nice one, Rosie.* I can feel the blush starting as I duck to grab the bandages, and when my hand brushes against Silas's legs, the heat spreads down my neck. *Calm down. It's just Silas.* I rise and force a smile that I hope doesn't look as goofy as I suspect.

He smiles back, bright-eyed, and reaches forward to take the basket from my hand. "Weekly supplies?"

"We might get a month out of it," I answer. I meander toward the register and he follows, basket in hand. I breathe slowly, willing my heartbeat to return to something of a normal rhythm as the cashier swipes each package of gauze over the bar-code reader.

"So what brought you to town?" I ask.

"Guitar lessons, actually," Silas responds. "I sort of got into experimenting with new things while I was up at Jacob's. I kept meaning to sign up for a guitar class before I left, but I put it off. So I made myself come down here first thing in the morning. Just had my first lesson."

"Wow. That's impressive," I reply as I hand the cashier the two twenties.

Silas laughs, rich and smoky—Sarah and her friends stare our way, regarding Silas as if he's some sort of dessert tray and me as if they're sizing me up for a fight. He doesn't even glance their way, his eyes firmly on me. "Not hardly. After an hour and a half my fingers are killing me and all I can play is the first part of 'Twinkle, Twinkle, Little Star.' Slowly."

Silas takes my bag from the cashier and we exit the store. The street is even busier now; people with shirts that read "City of Ellison" are hanging red and green streamers from the lampposts in preparation for the Apple Time Festival this weekend.

"Still," I continue, "guitar lessons. I wish I did something like that."

"What do you mean?" he asks as we pause at the crosswalk.

I shrug, turning to face him. "Just that you *do* something. Something other than hunt and the whole woodsman gig, I mean."

Silas laughs again. "Yeah, well...I was never that into the whole woodsman thing. It was just sort of the default for our family. And hunting...I'm happy to hunt, but that doesn't mean I'm chained down to it. I do it because it's the right thing to do. The guitar lessons and all are just for fun."

I frown. "I suppose..." I can't think of an argument that doesn't somehow cast Scarlett in a bad light, so I close my mouth. Silas nods toward the green crosswalk sign and lightly places his hand on the small of my back to urge me forward.

The touch sends shivers up my spine and the swoozy feeling takes over. *Walk, Rosie, walk. Don't be stupid.*

Silas points several blocks away as we arrive on the opposite curb. "I can give you a ride home, if you don't mind waiting for a few hours. I've got to go see the power company about getting my lights turned back on."

"I, um..." Sit with Silas for a few hours in the power company office? And then for another half hour on the ride home? I want to. I really, really want to. But what will we talk about? How long will it take me to start giggling like a moron? I can lure a Fenris — sway my hips, giggle lustily, bat my eyelashes — but I have no idea how not to look like a bumbling idiot in front of Silas Reynolds. Though in all fairness, it isn't often I see guys who aren't Fenris. How am I *supposed* to know what to do?

"No, it's okay. I'll take the bus," I respond.

I think I catch Silas's face fall a little. "Okay, no problem. I'll walk you to the stop, though?" he asks with a hopeful ring to his voice. I nod a tad too emphatically.

We walk to the end of the street and linger beneath the bus stop sign silently for a few moments. *Think of something to say, Rosie. Anything.*

"You can come to dinner again tonight," I say. Silas shakes his head.

"I'd love to, really. But I actually have plans. Catching up with an old friend from school for an elegant meal at Burger King," he says sarcastically. "Though any other time — are you okay?"

"Me? Oh, yeah. So you have a hot date?" I tease him, hoping he can't detect just how far my voice fell. Of course Silas has a date. Silas always had a date. He stuck through high school, unlike his siblings, Scarlett, or me, and was the type never to be short of female company by the time his senior year rolled around. It frustrated Scarlett to no end, hearing that he was out on a date instead of hunting with her.

"No. Not a date at all," he says firmly, as if it's important I believe him. "Just a friend from high school. Named Jason. And come on, Rosie, don't you think that if I were going on a date, I'd go somewhere better than Burger King?"

I laugh in both relief and amusement. "I don't know. You always had a girlfriend before you went to San Francisco."

"Not hardly. I lost touch with most of my high school friends a year before that, right after they all went to college. Couldn't you hear me crying at night from the loneliness?" he teases, shouldering me.

"Oh," I say dumbly. I guess I wasn't paying attention, but then, it had never occurred to me to pay attention to Silas Reynolds before. "Why did you lose touch?"

"Well," Silas says thoughtfully, "when it came down to it, we had nothing in common."

I raise my eyebrows. "I know how you feel."

"Lucky for me, I seem to have enough in common with the March sisters to keep me afloat without...you know, friends or family," he says.

"Hey, we count as your friends," I interject.

"Also my family, it seems. Er, sort of," he adds quickly. The bus rounds a far corner and rumbles our way.

"Anyhow, I have to admit, Rosie—you're a better cook than the guys at Burger King, so I'm sort of sad that my non-date is tonight. Or rather, that my non-date is with someone else, or . . . right. Never mind," Silas says.

I smile as the bus's air brake squeals and the door opens, a rush of AC casting my hair back. "You *should* be sad—I'm making cookies. Though it's just ramen for dinner, so you aren't missing out on much there."

"Cookies? Damn—" He's cut off by the bus driver's impatient glare. "I'll see you later, though, right, Rosie?"

"Right," I say softly, trying not to trip as I'm getting on the bus. I slide into a seat by the air conditioner and close my eyes so I don't stare at him as we drive away.

I can make only eight things, if you don't count ramen noodles and sandwiches. One of them is meatloaf. Another is Oma March's chocolate cookies. I smash the chocolate into one of her green glass mixing bowls and beat it carefully. I like using Oma March's kitchen things; it makes me feel closer to her somehow. Scarlett is nowhere to be found, but I suspect she's running again. I think she's trying to become as fast as a Fenris or something. Good luck.

I lean against the oven, waiting for the cookies to bake. I made too many. So many that I could probably take some over to Silas's house.

Would that be weird? It's just bringing cookies to an old family friend. No big deal. *Yes, do it now, before you change your mind.*

The oven buzzer sounds loudly, and I dump the hot tray of cookies into the basket, then fold the corners of the cloth over the edges. They probably won't stay warm, but still, they look prettier this way. I stop in the bathroom to brush my hair behind my ears and adjust my shirt. *It's just Silas,* I remind myself.

I'm secretly both afraid and hopeful that I'll hear his car coming up the street behind me as I walk to his house. He lives in the middle of the forest that seems to start all at once, the road going from sunny and hot to dark and cool in a matter of moments. With the limbs swaying together in the breeze, it's almost like being underwater. Birdcalls seem to echo off the trunks, all of which are wide and impressive.

Silas's house emerges like a castle built by nature itself. The logs surrounding the front door are heavily carved with lifelike images of bears and rabbits and turtles, almost as if they were once real animals that were frozen here. One of Silas's brothers carved them—Lucas, I think, or maybe Samuel—one of them was good with a rifle, the other at carvings, but it's hard to keep the Reynolds boys straight. It's obvious the cabin was originally small, but now rooms stretch high into the trees and off to the sides. That was Pa Reynolds's rule: if you want your own bedroom, build it yourself. The top rooms of the house have broad decks that reach out into the upper tree limbs, a few with sketchy-looking tire swings hanging off the railings. Even Silas's sisters, who *weren't* in training to become woodsmen, had to haul timber to have their own space before they went off to boarding school. I barely got the chance to know them, but Pa Reynolds was scared at the prospect of raising three girls alone after Silas's mother died.

His car isn't in the driveway, but I knock on the door anyway. No answer. I run my hand along the back of a carved wooden bear and then place the basket of cookies in front of the door. I linger for a moment longer...

Someone is here.

Behind me, I hear faint breathing. I spin around, hands darting to my waist, and I'm instantly grateful for Scarlett's obsession that I always carry my knives.

"So sorry, miss. Didn't mean to frighten you," a young man says calmly. He looks at me from heavy-lidded eyes and presses his perfectly shaped lips together. He's not alone—another man stands silently behind him, hair hinting at gray, face mature and chiseled, something like an older movie star. The younger man is in an artistically torn T-shirt, his hair tousled like some sort of rock star. I'm suspicious, though—most people don't come out this far, unless they're bill collectors or Fenris.

"You didn't," I lie. I lean against one of the carved rabbits and try to look casual, though I keep my hands near the handles of my knives. If they *are* Fenris, I want to be ready. "Are you guys looking for someone?"

"Sort of," the young one says. "But it doesn't look like

there's anyone home." He grins at me kindly, moving to brush his shaggy hair from his face.

"I don't think there is," I answer cautiously. "Maybe try back later?"

"Yeah…yeah, we'll do that," the older one answers. "Thanks for your help."

"No problem," I say a little too quickly.

"Hang on," the younger one says. He steps toward me, thrusting his hands into his pockets sheepishly. "Can we walk you home at least? Seems dangerous for a girl to be out here all alone."

"I…" I hesitate. His eyes are beautiful, a golden color that reminds me of autumn leaves. "I'm okay, really."

"Really. We'd love to," the older one interjects. His voice is smooth, granite-like. He moves to slick his hair back.

I clench my teeth. On the wrist of the older man I can see a pack symbol. Something circular—Bell, maybe? The younger man's would be hidden by the star-studded wristbands he wears, but surely he's a wolf too, right? I can never tell immediately the way Scarlett can. I still see the human first and have to find the wolf by way of the pack mark. She sees the wolf, and only the wolf.

"Okay. Sure, walk me home," I reply, a little too boldly. I shrug my shoulders and force myself to flip my hair in what I hope is a carefree way. Alone. It's just me, no Scarlett. *You can do this, Rosie. You've fought dozens of wolves. Lead them in, draw them to you, kill them.*

I walk down the cabin's front steps, letting my hips sway a little more than usual; the older Fenris looks at me with what has become a sickening grin. I react exactly how I'm supposed to — by looking nervous. It forces the animal to take over, to hunt. But genuine goose bumps race up and down my arms as the younger Fenris takes a step closer.

"So why did you walk all the way out here instead of drive? Not old enough?" he asks, his voice more guttural than when we first spoke.

"I'm sixteen. How old are you?" I reply as we walk back toward the main road.

The older Fenris laughs loudly, and the younger one's eyes sparkle with dark mischievousness. "He's forty-nine. I'm twenty-one."

"A big age gap for friends," I say. The younger Fenris shrugs but doesn't say anything. I'm gripping the handle of a knife so hard that my hands have started to go numb, but I can't do anything until they change.

I'm surprised that they haven't made their move by the time we reach the main road. If they attack here, I'll have them in open space. If I let them pull me into the tall grasses that line this section of the road, we're both at a disadvantage. They'll want to stay out here in the open, where I can't hide.

"Uh, miss?" one of the Fenris says from a few yards behind me, though the voice is so snarled that I can't tell if it was the older or younger wolf. I whirl around and the older

59

wolf is half transformed, his dashing gray hair now snarled in greasy patches of gray fur, chiseled features now muscular jaws and wide-set ocher eyes.

"Oh my...um...what?" I stammer.

"My friend seems to be sick," the younger Fenris says, stepping closer as if he hopes to feed off my fear. The handsome indie-rocker look has transformed into a grin that's just a tad too wide for a normal human. I take a step back and fold my arms over my waist, trying to tremble as I secretly wrap my fingers around the handles of my knives. "I think there's something in the water here. But you know what I think would make him feel better?"

"What?" I ask timidly.

The younger Fenris races toward me, moving like a flood over dry earth. His nose starts to speckle with fur, and when he speaks, the scent of decomposition and death is so heavy on his breath that I almost choke. He stops only a foot or so from me and leans forward, clicking his long incisors together when he answers. "Eating *you*, my dear."

He changes in one fluid motion, his human disguise melting away. I leap back and yank both knives from my belt just as the older wolf howls and steps forward. Both lower their heads and growl, baring their teeth and digging at the dirt with thick claws.

Everything is still—the wolves, me, the wind. None of us wants to make the first move.

Then, in the distance, faintly, I hear a familiar rumble. The bus, making another round. Both Fenris and I glance down the road in frustration. No one wants a fight in plain sight of the bus; the wolves'll have to make the choice to take a large handful of humans or run. And Fenris hate to run, but they aren't stupid.

The decision is made—the older Fenris propels himself at me, bounding off his back legs. I spin to the left, avoiding him, hands held out so that the tips of my blades skim his body. The younger Fenris growls and the older one grunts in response, a conversation I don't understand. I take advantage of his distraction and fling a well-aimed knife at him. He shies away at the last instant, but it still grazes the side of his face, shearing enough skin off to reveal raw pink muscles underneath. The bus rumbles closer—we all know time is up. I can't let them get away. Scarlett would never forgive me.

While the older Fenris shakes his head as if he's trying to throw the pain off his wound, the younger one runs forward. He darts side to side, and when I try to follow, I become unbalanced. He lunges for my left just as I lean to the right, and I hit the ground so hard that I feel bits of gravel sinking into my cheeks and the hilt of the knife I threw underneath my hip. I roll onto my chest and see the younger wolf whipping around, jaws open. I yank the knife from underneath my hip and thrust it upward. He avoids it narrowly. I sit up as the older wolf rejoins the fray, just as the first hints of the bus's dust cloud creep our way.

Stand up, stand up. I spring to my feet and spin around, kicking the older wolf solidly in the side of the head, then turn just in time to drive my heel into the chest of the younger wolf as he leaps for my neck. The gray-blue top of the bus breaks through the horizon. *Come on, it's now or never,* Scarlett's warnings repeat in my head. If they run, they'll be starving, they'll have to eat, someone will die. I wheel toward the old Fenris and throw a knife at him with all the strength I possess. It sinks into his chest with a sickening squelch, and the wolf collapses to the side.

The younger wolf howls angrily, looking between me, the dying Fenris, and the bus. The bus is only moments away, and the driver might even see us by now. The young Fenris snaps his jaws at me and then leaps into the grasses. I hear his heavy claws padding through the briars and weeds. I could go after him, I could find him—no. I can't outrun him. He'll be long gone or he'll know enough to jump me. *Think, Rosie, think.*

The bus starts to slow, and I realize there's a blue hatchback driving along in its shadow—Silas's car. I run to the fallen Fenris and yank my knife out of its side. I can't leave till I know I've killed it. *Come on, die already.* Its red-brown eyes are lined in hatred as it glares at me. The bus driver sees me, and her eyes widen at the sight of a girl looming over a dead beast, knife above her head. My eyes dart to Silas's car. We see each other at the same instant.

And the Fenris vanishes. He bursts into a cloud of black shadow that seems to scream in the sunlight before sliding under the pebbles in protest. I dash into the thick grasses in the opposite direction of the Fenris. I could have killed him sooner, should have killed them in the woods. What if I just

62

ruined our cover? What if the bus driver recognized me and calls child services? I'll have destroyed it all.

Scarlett is going to kill me.

The grasses whip past me and my eyes begin to water, in both frustration and pain from the leaves slapping against my cheeks. Silas's horn wails behind me and I hear him shouting my name, but I don't stop, far too ashamed to even consider seeing him right now. He's wrong about me. I haven't grown up; I'm still the stupid little girl I was a year ago.

My heart is pounding and my skin sticky with sweat by the time I make it through the field. I trudge slowly toward our cottage, trying to breathe and get the tearstains off my cheeks. I should be proud. I just soloed, just killed a Fenris on my own.

And also let one get away, one who will now be starving after trying to attack me.

Also, let someone see me hunting.

Also, I'm pathetic.

I creep in through the back door, relieved to hear the dull thuds of Scarlett slamming the punching bag in the cellar-turned-training-room. I hurry upstairs, peeling away my wet and bloodied clothes. Once I'm in the shower with Screwtape standing guard on the bathroom rug, I cry. Silent, choked sobs of inadequacy. I have to tell Scarlett about the Fenris that got away. I have to warn her that a bus driver and social worker could come pounding on our door in a few days. I'll have to tell her, and then she'll scold me and insist on hunting down the other Fenris immediately. Selfishly, I'm angry because I know this means that the night I made cookies and picked out movies for is now shot to hell. God, I'm so stupid.

I can stall. I can wait to tell her. We can have our movie night, I can get her in a good mood, and then we'll go out and hunt together. Just like always. Her anger will fade like it always does. If a social worker shows up, we can hide, Scarlett can insist Mom is around, we can stall...it will work out.

"Rosie!" Scarlett shouts. There's fear in her voice, mixed with fury. I grit my teeth. My sister flings the bathroom door open, a hazy form behind the white shower curtain. "What happened? Are you okay?" she demands, voice dark enough to intimidate a wolf.

"I...Scarlett," I say, cutting the water off. I sigh and reach for a towel.

A voice interrupts my movement. "Look, Scarlett, come on, it was an accident—"

Silas rounds the corner. I freeze, arm outstretched and still a few inches from the towel, body half exposed around the curtain. His mouth drops, cheeks flush, and he immediately whirls around to face the hallway.

"Sorry, Rosie," he says quickly. He puts his hands into his pockets and bounces on his heels. My face turns bright red, goose bumps scattering across my arms from both the cold and the shivery feeling Silas is giving me.

"Rosie, what *happened?*" Scarlett asks again through gritted teeth, seemingly oblivious to the fact that I'm still naked and Silas is still incredibly close. She grabs a towel off the rack and thrusts it into my outstretched hand.

"I was taking cookies to Silas's house," I mutter, wrapping the towel around myself hurriedly. I ignore the stream of water that runs from my hair down my back as the steam begins to fade away, leaving the room wet and muggy. I glance at Silas's back for a moment and then look at Scarlett. "I left them there when these two wolves jumped me. They were prowling together, I think. I took the older one out, but..."

"Go on," she says in a steely tone. Silas shifts uncomfortably.

"The young one got away." I sigh, guilt swimming through my head.

Her jaw tightens. "Got away?" she says lowly, dangerously. "You couldn't go after him?"

"I couldn't. He ran because the bus was coming up the road."

"You fought... The bus? A bus full of people?" she snaps. "Did they see you?"

"I..." My eyes well up with tears, and I'm very grateful Silas's back is still turned. "Yes. The driver saw me. So did Silas—he was coming from town and driving behind the bus. But the old wolf shadowed pretty quickly and I ran into that field of grass, and they didn't come after me—"

"The bus driver didn't even get out of the bus," Silas interjects without looking at us. "She just drove on. I think she was hoping it was all in her head."

"Wait, wait," Scarlett says, brushing past Silas and into the hall. She begins to pace. "So you let a Fenris get away *and* got spotted? Do you have any idea what could have happened to you?" Her voice is careful, something simmering just beneath the surface.

"I...yes," I reply glumly as tears run down my cheeks.

And then Scarlett erupts.

"Don't you remember what that might mean, Rosie? What if she decides to call the cops? Are you going to explain why you were stabbing things in the middle of the highway?"

"I—"

"Lett, come on," Silas says calmly. "I thought you were finally letting her solo. And she did solo. Shouldn't we congratulate her?"

Scarlett glares at him. "She—you *both*—let a Fenris get away! Now he's out, he's hungrier than before, and he's got something to prove. So yeah, Silas, let's congratulate my sister here, for sentencing some poor, stupid girl to death."

Silas doesn't answer, and I wonder what he's thinking.

"Come on. We're hunting. *Now*," Scarlett demands.

"You won't find him now, Scarlett. After a fight like the one Rosie put him through, he'll sleep it off. He'll be out tomorrow morning, if I had to guess," Silas says matter-of-factly. Scarlett pauses. She doesn't want him to be right, but she's always respected Silas where hunting is concerned. She trusts him in a way she's never trusted me.

"And I did kill one, Scarlett," I mutter halfheartedly. "I still did a solo hunt."

Scarlett's face is still tense, but she nods at me shortly. I take that as her congratulating me and have to admit I'm totally satisfied with even that small act at the moment.

"We'll go out tomorrow morning, then. First thing," she ventures, more to Silas than me. "Though how the hell are we supposed to hunt? The Fenris certainly can't see my face, and he'll recognize Rosie. We've got no bait, unless you think you'll look pretty in a dress, Silas."

"Okay, one, I would look great in a dress," Silas begins. He turns to lean against the bathroom door, seemingly forgetting that I'm still in a towel. When he sees me, he averts his eyes and flushes a little. "And two," he continues in a forced voice, "you've been luring Fenris on your own for ages, Scarlett. The Apple Time Festival is tomorrow. Perfect place for a Fenris to hang out, even if you don't take into account all the red people will be wearing. We'll go there."

Scarlett nods curtly. No one moves for a few moments as water continues to trickle off my back and onto the shower floor. Finally, Scarlett gives me another cold look, turns on her heel, and storms down the hall.

"Sorry I got you in trouble," Silas whispers guiltily, his voice the only sound other than the steady pattering of water hitting the tile floor. "I was worried about you when you took off, and then I realized it was probably your first solo…"

I shake my head. "I had to tell her eventually."

"For what it's worth," he says, eyes still averted respectfully, "I thought you did great."

"Thanks, Silas." He finally meets my eyes, keeping his gaze firmly on my face. I tug the towel a little tighter.

"You're welcome. And I'm sorry for barging in. I didn't… um… *see* anything. I promise."

"It's okay," I say, smiling a little. Our eyes stay locked, and the tiny bathroom seems to close in on us. I bite my lip, feeling something between nervousness and anticipation, and Silas leans toward me, as if he might close the gap between us.

Instead, he clears his throat suddenly, then looks down. "Well, I, um . . . I guess I'll see you tomorrow morning, then?" he says quickly.

"Oh. Yeah. Okay," I answer, snapping out of my stupor. "Have fun on your non-date," I add.

"Right. Jason . . . I think I'm late, but he'll live," Silas replies, voice a little edgy. He lingers a moment, then turns and leaves, shutting the door gently on his way out. I hear him sigh before starting down the stairs.

I exhale and lower myself to the edge of the bathtub, dropping my wet head into my hands. The shame floods back in, fills my veins in wordless screams, relieved only by the small fluttering in my heart that Silas left behind.

CHAPTER FIVE

✦

SCARLETT

I WAKE ROSIE UP AT SIX IN THE MORNING. SHE CRAWLS from her bed in a bleary-eyed fog, and I hurry around her, anxious to start the hunt as soon as possible and get our wolf before he leaves a trail of dead.

"Eat," I tell Rosie as she collapses into a kitchen chair. Best to use single words with her before eight o'clock. I slide a plate of toast covered with strawberry jam toward her. She reaches out hazily and takes a piece as I prop my foot up on the counter and lean forward.

I stretch, tightening and releasing the muscles in my legs and arms, flipping my hatchet from hand to hand. Despite the fact that I'm still angry, I can't help but be excited. Hunting isn't *fun,* per se, but it's *right*. And I have to admit that there is something undeniably fulfilling about hunting with

Rosie. Somehow, it makes me feel as if the long list of differences between us doesn't exist. We're dressed the same, we fight the same enemy, we win together...It's as though for that moment I get to be her, the one who isn't covered in thick scars, and she gets to understand what it is to be me. It's different than hunting with Silas—he and I are partners, not part of the same heart.

"Ishapen nines," Rosie finally says. I turn to face her, one eyebrow raised. She clears her throat and leans back in the chair, toast in hand. "I sharpened my knives," she repeats, tugging one of her bone-handled daggers off her belt. The blade gleams as a ray of morning sun darts through our kitchen window.

"When?" I ask.

"Last night. I stayed up," she replies. "Watched the movie again, sharpened my knives, washed both our cloaks."

"They look great," I answer sincerely. I know her actions are a peace offering—it's unlike Rosie to sacrifice sleep for much of anything. Rosie nods through an enormous yawn.

It's seven thirty before she finally shows a few signs of life—spinning the knives between her fingers, throwing a few at a target we painted on the back of the front door. She could never handle the hatchet well, but she's deadly with a dagger, I have to admit. She throws each one several times, her sleepy stupor fading.

My sister sprays a few pumps of a sickening cotton candy–scented perfume over each of us, then helps me pin one side of my hair to cover my missing eye. She puts on heavy makeup—dark eye shadow, violently red lipstick, and bright blush—in an attempt to make her unrecognizable to the Fenris. We stand and silently inspect each other: weapons, cloaks, hair, glittery lip gloss, perfume. All part of the lure. Rosie signals for me to spin around. She knows where each and every scar is and tugs at my clothing to hide the largest ones. I motion for her to turn to check that her top is pulled low enough and her hair curls in the right places. We play the same role—we just do so differently.

Silas's car grumbles into our driveway. Rosie beats me to the front door, and when she flings it open, her face lights up. I hurry to see what she's grinning at. I sigh and smile at once.

"Just because we're there to hunt doesn't mean we can't be spirited about the whole thing," Silas calls out mischievously. His car windows are painted with bright red and green pictures of apples and apple trees. On the back windshield are the words "Feelin' fine at Apple Time," which has been the festival's slogan for as long as I can remember.

"How much time did you waste painting apples?" I ask, but I don't try to hide my smile. That's Silas. No wonder I missed him, despite how angry I was that he left.

"About thirty minutes. Which is valuable time I could have spent hunting," he ends in a serious voice.

"Yeah, yeah. Let's leave. Wouldn't want to miss the parade," I tease.

Silas's car is hot and sticky inside, and every now and then it lurches forward like a runner in the last desperate leg of a race. We rumble along the country roads in silence, windows down and the blurred sounds of birds chirping filling the car.

Finally, the gravel road stops and we emerge onto the paved drive, leading to where Silas helped me hunt just a few nights before. The seedy, dangerous bits of Ellison seem to vanish during the day — though apparently the wolves we're after aren't as deterred by daylight as the local thugs are, so things aren't as shiny as they might look. Cars are parked along the street, with housewives ushering children into stores, fathers and sons dipping into a coffee shop, young couples walking with their fingers intertwined. Everything is bright and cheery. And if we're successful, by this afternoon there will be one less Fenris in the world to change that.

The Apple Time Festival is held in Ellison's only park, a wide parcel of land that's little more than a forest with nature trails and a giant picnic area. All the surrounding roads are blocked off, and parking is hell; we finally find a spot in a row of cars just as heavily decorated as Silas's. Rosie and I put our cloaks on, though I'm not sure how well we'll stand out in the sea of red and green. Silas swings a tattered black backpack onto his shoulders. The ax head is hidden inside so that only the handle sticks out a hole in the zipper.

"Any thoughts on where to start?" I ask Silas as we join a pack of people being led across the street by a cop. A little girl with apples painted on her cheeks nearly runs over my feet with her tricycle. I turn my face away when she looks back at me, all innocent blue eyes and red cheeks. No sense in scaring the poor thing.

Silas scans the thick crowd several times before answering. "Go around the back, cut through the trees, maybe?"

I peer in the direction he's pointing. "No good. They built a new road out that way. I think the wolves avoid it."

Silas gives me a pointed look. "Why do you ask me if you don't want my opinion anyway?" he questions, smiling despite himself.

I snicker and shake my head in response.

Silas rolls his eyes. "How about we go through the festival once before picking a spot?"

"Why?" I ask.

"Because I enjoy apples," he replies. Rosie giggles. "Because then we can know if there's a spot that would be particularly easy to grab a girl from," he answers again, voice serious this time.

The picnic area is full of booths of people selling wooden apples, apple jelly, apple butter. A few grungy-looking carnival types dole out candy apples or invite people to knock down a pyramid of green apples with a wooden ball for the low, low price of five dollars a throw. I study them carefully... no, they're harmless.

A crowd of laughing women wearing glittery apple-themed T-shirts brushes past me, glancing away when they see my scars. I think a few recognize me—they don't remember my name, maybe, but they remember "that incident with the March girl." The news they got was that a wild dog attacked us. Which still makes me laugh.

Silas buys caramel-and-peanut-covered apples for all three of us just as the parade begins. It mostly consists of local dance studios tap-dancing through the grass and debutantes waving from convertibles, but people cheer wildly. Silas takes Rosie's hand to lead her to the front and she blushes. I linger in the back, where I can go unnoticed a little easier—though I'm not sure if I'm avoiding the wolves or sideways glances. Most of the debutantes are girls I went to school with. Would I be up there with them, had things turned out differently? I look at my feet and try to imagine them in high heels, try to imagine myself in a ball gown on a float with friends who know nothing of wolves and have gorgeous, unmarred faces. Things can change so swiftly, so easily.

It's impossible—no matter what, the Fenris lurk on the edge of my thoughts. Besides, I don't *need* an entourage of friends when I have Rosie and Silas. They'd just get in the way of the hunt. I sigh and scan the area around me and finally see it—the perfect spot for a Fenris to prowl. A row of picnic tables back behind the booths, far enough into the woods that they're darkened by the canopy of leaves above them and isolated enough that it would be easy to snatch a girl or lead her farther into the forest. When Silas and Rosie return, their hands full of candy that the high school cheerleaders were tossing out, I nod toward the tables.

"What do you think?" I ask Silas. He nods and drops his candy into Rosie's bag.

"That looks perfect, actually. I'll circle around on the trail?" he says. Silas has this amazing ability to go from a guy catching candy to a serious hunter in a matter of heartbeats. I have to admit I'm a little jealous sometimes. My mind seems locked on hunting.

"Yep," I answer. Rosie and I push through the crowd to the side of one of the apple-jam booths.

We walk slowly toward the picnic tables. I sit down on a bench and pull my shoulders back, pushing my breasts out, and Rosie sits on the mossy table, leaning back on her hands.

"Keep your head down," I remind her.

"I know," Rosie mutters, swinging her legs back and forth. She sighs after a long pause. "We came here with Mom once."

"How do you remember that?" Mom hung around— without the drugs—only really for the first five years of Rosie's life. She could never be chained down for much longer than that; Oma March used to call her a *Ruhelose*. Of course, Oma March also called her a whore when she was particularly angry. Both are pretty accurate.

Rosie shrugs and leans forward. I scan the crowd and give her a meaningful look—*come on, we're supposed to be hunting*—and she tosses her hair enticingly before answering me. *Come on, wolves. Don't we look delightful?*

"I remember that the car we rode in was painted like Silas's," my sister says. "And I remember that Mom stapled paper apples all over my shirt."

"Wow," I answer. She's dead-on. I wouldn't let Mom staple apples to me but regretted it once I was at the festival and saw all the other kids were dressed just as ridiculously.

A branch pops in the forest behind us. Rosie and I make brief eye contact.

And then we laugh. Loudly. Bright, bubbly, ignorant-girl laughter. Rosie's wolf-lure laugh isn't all that different from her normal one, but I raise my voice, drop my usual snickering, and giggle. *Yes, wolf, we are stupid, giggly little girls. Devour us.* Another branch pops. I lower my head so my hair spills forward, then peer through the strands to catch a glimpse of Silas milling around in the parking lot. Casual, all casual.

Rosie leans back on her hands again and swishes her legs through the air like some sort of pinup model. Steady footsteps begin to tromp through the woods, crushing leaves and twigs as they grow closer. We pretend not to hear it, pretend not to see the movement of the person approaching. I rise, head low, and let the wind pick up the edges of my cloak, casting my perfumed scent into the forest.

"Finally, civilization!" a male voice cries out triumphantly. Rosie and I give each other a secretive smile.

The man coming out of the forest looks like a college frat boy. His hair is sandy blond, his eyes deep and wide-set, and his frame thick, broad-shouldered. He springs toward us, a grin on his face. I try to sneak looks through my hair without revealing my eye patch or scars. Something is odd about this one—he smells like a Fenris, and I can somehow feel the wolves' presence nearby, yet this man's eyes are reddened, the

76

way someone's look after weeping. Wolves don't cry—the soulless have nothing to mourn.

"Where did you come from?" I ask, laughing. At times like these, I often pretend to be Rosie, though I've never told her. I may be the better hunter, but there's no question that she's the better bait. I look at the man's nails—not claws, but then, bits of greasy Fenris fur cling to the leg of his pants.

"I somehow lost the trail I was on," the man says, all grins and boyish charm. "Thought I'd be stuck out in the middle of the woods for the rest of my life."

"You'd have missed all the apple festivities," I answer brightly. He nods hungrily, crescent-shaped blue eyes sparkling. He *must* be a Fenris—I'm clearly just misreading the evidence of tears in his eyes.

"I know, which would have been a bummer. I got turned around because I was actually following this fawn in the woods that I think might be lost," he says, nodding back toward the forest.

You've got to be kidding me. The baby-animal route? Wow. It's hard not to sigh.

"A fawn?" Rosie squeals, though I detect a hint of sarcasm in her voice. She glances up at him, letting him see her face for a split second so he doesn't get too suspicious about me hiding my own. I hold my breath, waiting for him to recognize her despite the layers of makeup. Rosie meets my eye briefly and shakes her head—a tiny movement, so slight that I don't think anyone but me would have caught it. This is not the Fenris she let get away yesterday. This is a new one.

He'll need to die just the same. I turn back to the man, his sandy blond hair straying in the slight breeze. I wonder how old he was when he turned. He doesn't look much older than Silas. I imagine he rarely goes hungry, with that age and that voice full of charm. He's just as good at baiting his prey as Rosie is.

"Do you want to see it? I was going to go call animal control, but I'll show him to you girls first if you want," he says, motioning in the direction he came from.

"I want to see it! Let's go." Rosie nods to me emphatically. The man licks his lips as we rise, and then turns and retreats back into the woods. We follow several yards behind him.

"How far in is the deer?" I ask cheerily.

"Oh, not far," he answers, flashing us a bright grin. How has he not started to transform yet? Usually they can't keep up the charade this long. I move to try to see the pack sign on his wrist but somehow can't find it amid his movement. The man swallows hard—nervously? No. Wolves are never nervous. Something isn't right.

The sounds of the Apple Time Festival fade into the sounds of the forest. Only the occasional honk of a parade car's horn reaches our ears. I listen to the forest sounds to focus: twigs breaking, birds calling, the slight trickle of the creek that runs through the park's center. I have to look to the right constantly, whenever the Fenris looks back, so he sees only my still-present eye.

We trudge farther into the woods before the man finally stops.

"So...here it is!" he calls out, oddly loud. He whirls around and points to a spot on the forest floor.

Rosie lets out a horrified gasp. I force the same sound, though I think it sounds rather overacted.

Is it wrong that part of me is used to seeing the things a Fenris will do to make a girl squirm, make her tremble or cry, before he plans to devour her? The Fenris is pointing to what seems to be a deer, but only barely. It's a carcass, bloodied and eviscerated. Tubes of purple intestines splay about the forest floor like worms, and its tongue lolls out of its mouth near dead gray eyes. It's nearly torn in half, and the marks are all wolf: shredded skin and broken legs that lie like a pile of twisted sticks underneath the doe's body. Rosie throws her hand to her mouth, but I don't think it's part of the act — she genuinely looks as if she might get sick.

"I said, 'Here it is!'" the man repeats. His voice quavers.

I've killed dozens upon dozens of wolves in my life and never, ever has one's voice quavered. I look up at him, ignoring the fact that I've given away my cover and he can now see my scars. And I suddenly begin to understand why there were tears in his eyes. He's not a wolf. He's a human. A stupid, foolish human, staring longingly at something just over my shoulder.

"Two?" a low, growl-like voice says behind me. "I said five."

Rosie and I whirl around. The Fenris is younger, with disheveled hair and ripped-up jeans. Rosie ducks her head down, which tells me all I need to know: this is the Fenris she faced yesterday, and she can't let him recognize her. I step in front of my sister, trying to take the focus off her—I want to fight him on our terms, when we say it's time, not when the wolf says it is.

"And this one's damaged," the Fenris hisses, staring at my face with disdain. His head is partially transformed, giving him the look of a human whose facial bones have been cracked apart and hastily glued back together.

"Please," the man behind us begs, voice choppy and broken. "I tried, but I got lost in the woods. Two is all I could get in thirty minutes."

"So you don't care about her, then?" the Fenris mocks. It takes me a moment to understand whom the wolf is talking about, but then I see her—a young woman with corn silk hair, quivering near a tree trunk. She has her knees tucked into her Apple Time T-shirt, like the jersey fabric will provide some sort of shield against the monster.

"I do!"

"Not enough to win her freedom," the Fenris says with a shrug. His nails start to lengthen into claws, his eyes darken. The man behind us begins to weep again.

Pa Reynolds said wolves do this occasionally—blackmail humans when they're too weak to hunt for all the prey they need. After all, who wouldn't be willing to sacrifice others for the one he loves? Clearly, Rosie gave this one a run for his money yesterday if he wants five girls. It's the first time I've fought a Fenris with a hostage, though, so I scan the wolf carefully, trying to plan my attack.

And then I see it. My eye, my mind, my throat—everything feels dark and dry. On his right wrist, the clean, crisp mark. A pack sign I recognize, a pack sign I've seen only once before. I saw it for a brief moment on the wrist of the man who came to my grandmother's cottage selling oranges. My skin leaps up in chill bumps and something powerful races through me. I don't know if Rosie sees the sign or not, but she takes my hand as soon as my nerves peak as if doing so is instinctual. I exhale.

An Arrow, back in Ellison. Hunting is mechanical for me—my body and mind just do it as if it's what they were created for. But the Arrow makes me rage with emotion, my heart pounding in fury and frustration and memory. I want to kill him—not just him, the entire pack. I want them to pay more than I want any other Fenris to pay, and the drive to act now, before he's transformed, clouds my better judgment. *Focus, Scarlett. Stop this pack from doing to others what it's done to you.* The crying man behind us takes a step toward the terrified girl, but the wolf inhales sharply enough to stop him in his tracks.

"You still owe me three," the Fenris says, slinking across the ground with a gait more lupine than human. "But we can start with these," he finishes with a dark grin. He gives me another disgusted look, then turns to Rosie, who keeps her head down.

"You don't like the deer, darling?" the Fenris asks her, his voice both sweet and horrifying. "That's not very kind of you. Perhaps if you pet it."

He moves, far too fast for a human. His right hand, the one bearing the pack sign, darts out. It grabs Rosie's wrist so tightly that I know she'll bruise later. She squeals uncomfortably and looks away.

"Give it a pat," he says in a dark singsong voice, leaning so close to my sister that his breath blows her hair back. He tightens his grip on her wrist and draws her hand downward toward the deer's grotesquely twisted neck. Rosie winces in pain, which makes the Fenris grin and makes my rage intensify a thousand times over. No one hurts my sister. Her fingers tremble as he presses them forward and her nails finally glance across the animal's carcass. Only then does she finally raise her face and boldly make eye contact with him.

"*You,*" the wolf hisses accusingly.

"Hey!" I snap. The Fenris's eyes turn to me, and his lips curl in an angry snarl.

"Don't touch my sister," I sneer.

"Oh, I will," he growls. "And then you—" He doesn't finish the thought as Rosie suddenly sinks her foot into his crotch, then delivers a left hook to his ear. He howls in surprise, his breathing heavy, labored, like an animal's. I reach under my cloak to draw my hatchet, but before I can swing at him, he leaps out of my reach. Rosie grabs for her knives, and the Fenris's eyes dart between us.

Then he turns and bolts.

Rosie and I race after him, ducking under branches and briars. I signal to my sister: *Go right!* I cut to the left. The Fenris's footsteps still sound like two feet instead of four. I slide down a ravine of wet leaves as if it's a wave, never stopping. My heart thuds loudly in my chest, pushing me onward, faster, faster. He's got nowhere to go; Silas is in one direction, Rosie in the other, and then me. He's mine — I don't care how strong Arrows are, he's mine. I run faster, leaping over a rock formation and scanning the forest. They're good at camouflaging themselves, but years of hunting have taught me to look for their shape among the dead leaves. There he is. Half monster now. I can see scraggly fur begin to creep down his back, burst through his shirt. He looks up and sees me just as I jump down from some boulders, and his teeth lengthen to yellowed fangs.

His fast and heavy footsteps pound toward me, all anger now. I flip the hatchet in my right hand and look behind the Fenris to see Silas darting toward me, quick like a fox around trees and over plants. Rosie won't be far behind.

I roll to the side just as the Fenris lunges at me with a bloodcurdling growl. As he turns around, I send my hatchet through the air toward him. It sinks into his side, and I catch a glimpse of white rib bones. He howls in anger and pain, eyes flashing in fury. He darts at me again, but I'm faster, and I take a swipe, knocking his front feet out from under him. His long snout crashes into the ground as I jump away, yanking my hatchet up from the dirt as I do so.

A sharp whistling cuts through the air. As if it merely

materialized in the Fenris's haunches, Rosie's knife appears, sunk in all the way to the hilt. I look right and see her breaking through the underbrush. I swing out with my hatchet, catching the wolf's shoulder. He leaps up and tries to flee, wounded body crumpling beneath him every few steps, but still faster than any man or animal. He makes it through only a few patches of trees before Silas jumps out from behind a thick oak and delivers a swift kick to the jaw. The wolf launches himself forward and manages to sink his front teeth into Silas's arm, but by now I've reached them. Just as Silas cringes and knocks the wolf away, I swing the hatchet down, ramming it firmly into the wolf's back. The pack mark still lingers under sparse fur near the monster's ankles, a black arrow.

Things flash — Oma March's wide eyes, the shadow on the door, the clicking of nails on hardwood, the feeling of Rosie clinging to me. I withdraw my hatchet and plunge it deep into the Fenris's back again, just like I did with a shard of mirror years ago. The wolf reacts swiftly, pushing me away, trying to regain its strength.

I won't let it.

I dive back toward it, the forest a blur around me. I want it to suffer, I want it to feel ripped apart, I want to take its eye like one of its pack took mine. I slice forward at its face, but it rears back and strikes me with a heavy claw. My mouth fills with blood, and Rosie or Silas — I'm not sure who — grabs at my cloak and tries to pull me away.

No, no — I shake the person off and dart toward the

wolf. It's breathing heavily, trying to survive, but the dark hatred and hunger still lurks in its eyes. It dashes forward, long jaws outstretched to take a bite of my waist. I spin and thrust the top of my hatchet upward, into its chest. It roars in anger, but no, I'm not done. Arrows don't just let people die—they fight every inch of life from their victims. And I'll do the same. I take a step forward, rousing up what's left of my energy for another blow—

"Scarlett, *stop!*" a voice shouts, and Silas steps in front of me. He pushes me gently, but I'm so exhausted that it's enough—I collapse against a tree, panting. "It's dying. Don't risk getting hurt to fight a dying Fenris."

I gasp for air, scanning the forest for my sister. She steps up behind me and puts a hand on my shoulder. Her touch soothes the rage still swirling around my heart like a storm. I killed the wolf already, killed another Arrow. That's enough.

"Right," I finally answer Silas, nodding. "Sorry, I just…" I don't even know what to say. I shake my head and look over Silas's shoulder, where the beast uselessly struggles to get back to its feet. He catches my eye and snarls, then gives Rosie a long, hungry look.

Silas storms over to it and yanks Rosie's knife from the creature's haunches. The wolf shudders, and the fur on his back begins to creep back into his skin. Transforming? Now, when he's moments from death? Why waste what little energy he has left? I trudge forward as Rosie links her arm with mine. He snaps at us with a horrible human mouth lined with wolf teeth. Silas kneels and holds the edge of the knife to the beast's throat.

"Why is the Arrow pack hunting in Ellison?" Silas asks in a low voice.

The Fenris grins, lips spreading too wide for a human, blood flowing through the sparse fur on its face. Silas pushes the blade closer.

"The phase is about to begin," the Fenris responds hoarsely without dropping the evil smile.

And then it dies. The Fenris explodes into shadow that scatters across the forest floor, skittering under leaves and fallen branches as if it's terrified of exposure.

The sound of a parade car horn echoes in the distance.

"Where did that guy and his girlfriend go?" Rosie breaks the silence, peering back through the forest carefully. She has a kind look on her face, as though she's hoping they'll come out of hiding and she'll be able to comfort them.

"The one we fought the night you got back was Coin," I remind Silas quickly, ignoring my sister.

He answers Rosie first. "They ran back together right after the wolf took off—I think they'll be fine, once they convince themselves it was a nightmare. And Scarlett, that means there's been one Arrow, one Coin—Rosie, did you get a chance to see the other one you killed yesterday?"

"I think it was a Bell. I'm not sure—I guess it could have been another Coin?"

"You didn't make it your business to find out?" I snap harshly.

"Sorry, I was a little busy fighting two Fenris. Maybe if I'd had a chance to solo before then, I'd have been able to relax long enough to pick up on pack signs," Rosie whips back.

"It's the pack mark, Rosie! How could you not know for certain—"

"Both of you calm down!" Silas interrupts. He wipes Rosie's knife on his jeans and hands it to her, then stoops to toss my still-bloody hatchet to me. I give him a dark look as I clean my own blade on my cloak.

"Arrow, Bell, Coin. A representative of each pack. Phase—he means the moon phases, doesn't he?" I mutter, dozens of Pa Reynolds's Fenris stories rushing back to me.

"Yes. And he's right—there's a full moon in about a week, which means..." Silas drifts off.

"They're after another Potential Fenris. There must be one out there now. Here, right under our noses," I finish his sentence for him. Potentials are rare, but not unheard of. A single bite, just enough to break the skin—that's all it takes to transform a Potential into a full-fledged Fenris, according to Pa Reynolds. I shudder. I've wondered far too often what it feels like to have your soul ripped away. It's not something I want to reflect on again.

We've never been able to pinpoint exactly what makes a man—or boy—able to lose his soul and become a monster. Just that it is very specific, occurs only during certain moon phases, and is important enough to make the wolves leave their territories to find him. They're drawn to him by some unrecognizable force, like a scent that humans can't pick up on. They don't know exactly where and who the Potential is, but they know when he exists, and they'll scour the entire country for him.

"A Potential..." Silas frowns, nodding. "That makes sense. There's no other reason for so many packs to send members this far out."

"How many wolves will they send out to look for him?" Rosie asks. Silas and I shrug simultaneously.

"As many as it takes. They all want to add to their own packs, to be the pack to get a new member. And since Potentials are so rare, I bet every pack has members swarming every city in the state, or will soon. Once one of them picks up the trail of the Potential, the numbers will triple," Silas answers as we approach the picnic tables again.

"Great," Rosie says weakly.

In a big city, the pack keeps each Fenris in check to avoid drawing too much attention to itself. But when a wolf is sent out on its own, when *hundreds* of wolves are sent out... what's to stop them from feasting on every small-town girl they find?

"So we just hunt more often?" Rosie says, noting my expression. "We're already hunting all the time. We must've killed hundreds..."

"Ninety-three," I mutter, running my hand along a picnic table's mossy top. I shake my head. "We've killed ninety-three." Nearly a hundred wolves, yet with centuries of immortal wolves hunting, finding Potentials, and creating new monsters out of them, having killed only ninety-three makes my stomach writhe. The remaining Fenris probably don't even know the difference.

I shake my frustration away and continue. "All these packs are going to Atlanta, I bet—they're having a string of murders, remember? And these are huge, old packs. Bell, Arrow, Coin...and that's assuming that the smaller packs aren't hunting as well. Sparrow is getting bigger, so it would make sense for them to hunt out here—they'll have wolves all over the region. And that's *if* the packs don't combine forces to try to get the Potential—I think at the end of the day, the Fenris care even more about creating a new wolf than they do about getting him into their own pack. There's no way we can kill them all."

"We can hunt every day. And Silas is back—he can help," Rosie says encouragingly, though I can hear the disappointment in her voice at the prospect of endless hunting. Silas nods halfheartedly as we reach his car.

"The moon phase begins next Saturday," Silas says, screwing up his face as he counts off days on his fingers. "That's when the full moon hits. So for twenty-nine days after Saturday, till the next full moon, the packs will be out in droves looking for the Potential. God, I wish Pa had known more about them..." He trails off. I wish that too, more than anything. What turns a man into a Potential seems to be some crazy code that only the wolves can decipher. Sure, we know it's a certain man in a certain moon phase, but without the specifics we can't predict a Potential's emerging, figure out where he'll be, or find him before the monsters do. We might as well know nothing at all.

The sounds of the festival are loud now, invasive and far too cheery for the dark cloud hanging over my thoughts. A group of children stare at my scars. One is so entranced, she accidentally lets go of her bright green balloon, which rises and disappears into the annoyingly blue sky.

We climb into the car and sit in the stuffy air for a few moments of silence. Silas backs out of the parking lot and we weave through the crowds of people in red and green, people with no idea that a monster was in their midst. And that more are coming. Silas flicks on the turn signal and we finally escape the festival herd. We can't kill the wolves fast enough. I can't do enough. Girls will die, and a new Fenris will be changed. New Fenris hunt daily and are stronger, faster, hungrier, than any other wolf. Frustration pours over me as we turn onto our road. "So we just lose. Until they find the Potential, we just let girls die while the packs send out even more wolves every day."

"What if . . . what if we went there?" Silas says, swerving to avoid an armadillo.

"Went where?"

"To the city. Hunted them where their numbers are greater. Where they're congregating."

Yes, it makes so much sense. The perfect hunt, from their origin.

The perfect hunt. Too perfect.

"It'll never work. We can't just move to Atlanta, Silas. We can't even get an apartment. We're dead broke," I say as I run numbers together in my mind. We trudge inside; I fall onto the couch almost immediately, fingers on my temples.

"I can pay for part of an apartment," Silas says slowly, sliding into a wooden chair in our kitchen. I raise my eyebrows and Rosie makes a surprised sound in her throat.

"You want to move to the city?" I ask sharply.

"Not for good, but for a month or two, sure. I know this will kill you, Lett, if you don't go, and you're... well, you're like my family," he says quickly, glancing between Rosie and me. "I mean, I can't pay for it alone, but Pa Reynolds gave me a pretty decent inheritance. And besides, he's at Vincent's Elderly Care just inside the city. It'll give me a chance to visit with him for a while."

I rise from the couch, mind racing. It could work. It's so simple, really. But I can't believe that Silas, the one who abandoned the hunt and me for San Francisco, would be so eager to leave Ellison for the wolves. Yet he is. I am. And Rosie will go where I go.

"We still need money." But we could sell... my gaze moves to Oma March's bedroom, then to Rosie's eyes. My sister sighs and looks away, then nods at me. *Do what you need to do.* As I look at that bedroom door, a thought swims around the back of my mind: how it would feel to destroy the leader of the pack that destroyed me.

"Okay," I say breathlessly. I look at Silas. "Okay, then. Let's do it."

Silas nods. "I have a friend who I think can sublet his apartment to us. It won't be pretty, but it'll be cheap."

"Cheap is good," I reply. "When can we go?" I need to go fast, now that the decision has been made. I try to suppress the desire to get back into Silas's car and drive to the city immediately. Rosie runs her fingers through my hair in an attempt to calm me.

"I don't know—a week or so? Is that too soon? We should try to get out there before the phase starts, before the Fenris get *really* anxious," Silas says.

"No. No, a week sounds okay. A week." I sigh and turn to face Rosie, pulling my hair away from her fingertips. An unspoken message flashes between us.

"A week," Rosie answers softly, nodding.

CHAPTER SIX

Rosie

Scarlett does things now, never later. As soon as Silas leaves, she starts packing for what we begin to call simply "the move" in an ominous tone. We talk about it with the same casualness as one talks about "the table" or "the cat" because we have a silent, mutual understanding that leaving the cottage will be easier if we do it like ripping off a Band-Aid. Just go, quickly, and don't think about it too hard.

It's difficult, but possible, to back-burner the idea of leaving our home, the place where we grew up, the rooms full of memories both good and bad; it's painful, so I think my brain naturally wants to shove the idea away instead of letting me dwell on it. But there's another part of moving that I can't ignore, a part that my mind keeps coming back to because it's exciting and nerve-racking at once.

I'll be living with Silas Reynolds.

The same apartment, same rooms, same shower and kitchen and floor. Where will he sleep, in relation to me? What will he think about the fact that my hair looks like Screwtape's fur in the mornings? And most important, why do I *care* about all this so much? They're questions that I can't ask anyone — not Scarlett, certainly not Silas — and so they and a million others rotate around my head, taunting me all week while I pack my bags.

It doesn't take much packing for me to realize that my bedroom is full of *things*. Pictures and old paintings and little wooden figurines that Silas and his brothers used to carve for Scarlett and me. Old things, ancient things that I can't throw away because Oma March gave them to me or because they help me cling to my few pre-attack memories. Do those things come with me? No. Of course not. Just the essentials.

But two days before we leave, I carefully wrap Oma March's green glass mixing bowls in two of my old T-shirts as my sister mutters about maps and plots prime hunting locations.

The morning of the move, Silas pokes his head through the door. "Ready?" he asks.

"Yes," we reply, so simultaneously that even I can't tell whose voice was whose.

Silas refuses to help us cage Screwtape, who hisses loudly, having long suspected something is up. I go to pick him up, trying to act like everything is normal, but Screwtape darts away. It'd probably be easier to crate a Fenris than it is to crate Screwtape. The dance repeats until Scarlett and I are red in the face and Silas is laughing at us. We finally run the cat down, and Scarlett manages to toss the laundry basket over him when he's too busy anticipating his next dash.

"We could still leave him," Silas jokes—I think he's joking, anyway—as we load the howling basket of fury into the backseat of his car. Scarlett looks as though she might feel the same way as she nurses a batch of claw marks on top of the thicker Fenris scars. She climbs into the backseat of the car as Silas and I slide into the front. Silas hot-wires the ignition of the hatchback and pounds on the radio for a few minutes before it buzzes to life.

"We can't change the station, by the way," he says.

"Because you really like pop music?" I ask, wrinkling my nose as a bubbly song blares at us.

"Not hardly," Silas says. "I hate it. But last time I changed it, the car stopped. Oh, and lean away from your door— sometimes it opens randomly."

"Um...great," I say, leaning as far away from the door as possible. But this feels even more dangerous, because I'm leaning incredibly close to Silas, so close that I'm hyperaware of the fact that my sister is right behind me. My stomach twists as it fights my body's urge to fall against him. I shudder and try to shake the desire off.

"Well then," Silas says, and the car falls silent other than a pop singer's sexual grunting and Screwtape's low, deep growls. The three of us look up at the cottage as the car rumbles beneath us, and suddenly something tightens in my chest. I've got the sudden urge to run back and tell the cottage not to worry, we'll be back, to stay locked up and keep the garden watered.

It's just a house. But I catch Scarlett's eye in the side mirror, and she gives me a knowing sort of look.

"Go ahead, Silas," she says in a voice that's uncharacteristically gentle. I'm relieved she said it, because I don't think I could have. Silas nods and turns to back the car up, accidentally brushing a hand against my shoulders as he does so.

"Sorry," he says under his breath, like he's whispering in church. I shake my head as Scarlett settles her long arms and legs in the backseat and uses her cloak as a blanket.

Still trying to lean somewhere between the door of death and Silas's shoulder, I stare out the window as we lumber out of town. The road is smooth, hypnotic, with the dotted lines vanishing rhythmically before us. I glance back at my sister. She's fallen asleep, and Screwtape is casting her dark looks, as if she's to blame for his predicament.

I look toward Silas, trying to appear as if I'm just glancing out his window. Really, I want to study him intensely. He's wearing one of his many nearly threadbare T-shirts, jeans that are soft from washing, wavy hair...Everything about him begs to be touched...

"You're nervous," Silas says suddenly.

"What? No!" I answer sharply. Am I that obvious?

Silas raises an eyebrow and laughs.

"It makes sense. I mean, you and Lett have lived in Ellison forever." Right...right. He's talking about the trip, not my resisting the temptation to fall on him. We're silent for a moment, nearly tangible awkwardness floating around the front seats. Silas drums his fingers on the steering wheel.

"Well, it's not Ellison, but I think you'll like the place we're renting," he continues. "It's in a cool area, lots of artsy sorts of things to do. There's this community center that has dance classes and pottery classes and painting and all that stuff. It's kind of seedy but... artistic."

"Oh," I say, doing a pretty terrible job of masking some of the disappointment in my voice. I'm normally okay with not having a life outside of hunting, until I have to look at shining examples of the non-hunting world, like Sarah Worrell and company at the drugstore a week ago. And now I'll see it every day, people who don't hunt, people who don't even know the Fenris exist... and then me.

"Do you..." I begin, then turn around to make sure Scarlett is really asleep, not just faking it—her chest rises and falls a different way when it's genuine. Satisfied, I look back to Silas and choose my words carefully. "Do you think I'm a good hunter?"

Silas looks confused. "Of course. You and Lett are the best hunters I—"

"No, not me and Scarlett. Just me," I say.

Silas slows the car a tad to look over at me. "Yes. Yes, of course. You're—pardon my language—you're fucking deadly with a knife, Rosie."

I smile and shake my head, remembering all the times Silas scolded his older brothers for throwing language around

97

in front of my "virgin ears." It's sort of satisfying to know that his perspective has changed. "Right," I say. "I mean, we hunt together. But Scarlett...it's like a part of her soul."

"Dramatic much?" Silas teases, but he frowns when I don't laugh.

"You know what I mean. It drives her."

"But not you?"

"I don't know. I mean, maybe. It doesn't matter. I owe Scarlett my life, you know?"

"Yeah, but...like I told your sister, that doesn't mean she's got you locked in a cage forever. Unless you want to be locked in a cage, I mean. Wait, that sounds weird." Silas shakes his head and sighs. "I'm forever tripping on words with you, Rosie."

"I have that effect on people," I joke, but Silas's face stays serious as he nods slightly. I grin nervously.

"I'm just trying to say," Silas starts again, voice low, "that your sister didn't save your life only for you to sign it away to hunting if you want something more."

I don't answer, because therein lies the problem. Hunters don't want *more* — at least, not hunters who are related to Scarlett March. It's sort of hard to justify taking dance classes when your older sister is trying to save the world.

We ride along mostly in silence as the sun rises above us — Scarlett wakes when it's almost directly overhead. It isn't until afternoon that the city begins to hint at itself; we pass through towns not terribly unlike Ellison, then bigger towns, then rows of gas stations and car dealerships, until the tallest buildings appear on the horizon. They grow closer as though they're moving toward us as quickly as we're moving toward them, swallowing us into their steel mouths as we loop under a bridge and finally enter the city streets.

I glance back at Scarlett. She looks nervous, steely eye darting across the cityscape. She never looks nervous. Her mood makes my own nerves spike, a feeling that isn't helped by the sheer busyness of the city. People are everywhere, more people than I've seen in my entire life, more cars, more buildings as far as the eye can see, a maze of silver and gray concrete illuminated by vivid signs, flashing lights, bright yellow taxis. Scarlett sinks down in her seat slightly, lets her hair fall in front of her scarred eye, and tugs her sleeves down to cover her arms.

"Wait—there it is, Andern Street," Silas mutters, wheeling the car to the right. The street he turns down is dark, as if a thunderhead is hovering over us despite the sunny day. There's a church on the corner that's in bad need of new paint and covered in barred windows. The other buildings on Andern Street are old and crumbling, and a crowd of shady-looking men hang out on the street corner.

Silas begins mouthing the building numbers and slows the car.

"This is it," he says with an air of finality. "Three three three Andern." He looks over at Scarlett and me as we duck in our seats to look up at the building.

Nestled between two old office buildings and across from a vacant lot, it has the look of something that was once elegant, beautiful, even: white paint peels off the boards, rusted sconces swirl by the door with a sort of Victorian air, and an octagonal cupola on the roof reaches to the sky. Most of the windows have the curtains drawn, all mismatched so that the building is a bit like a patchwork quilt. It looks soft somehow, as if the entire place were constructed from the same material as a beehive and could be crushed and scattered with one heavy gust of wind or a well-aimed rock. A group of homeless men leer at us, weathered faces scrutinizing me and then moving to Scarlett, whom they stare at with looks of amazement. She adjusts her eye patch.

"We're on the eighth floor. Just stairs, no elevator," Silas says as if he's afraid we might change our minds.

"Do we have a view of anything?" Scarlett asks, ignoring the hoboes.

"Yep. The street, and we have access to the roof."

"Good," Scarlett says sincerely. "Good for a lookout-type thing, I mean."

"Right," I add, only because I feel as if I have to say something. I turn to look across the street. The vacant lot is surrounded by a dilapidated chain-link fence, tall grass, and two buildings that look like they're abandoned. In the lot I can see the frames of old cars, skeletons of a time when this street was a little more...alive. Silas does a three-point turn in the middle of the road under the hard stares of the homeless men—who I now think might actually be residents of our building—and parks in front of the vacant lot in what's barely enough space to be considered a viable parking spot.

Screwtape begins to howl again. I can't say I really blame him, if he can see his new home. I flash back for a moment to the sunny cottage, the bright flowers, the breeze that smelled like sweet hay, and the low rumble of cattle.

Silas opens the driver's door and the wail of a police siren screams nearby. He glances up at the building, then back into the car. Scarlett is hurriedly gathering her things, so Silas's eyes linger on mine, some sort of concern flickering there.

"I'm fine," I say softly. I realize only after the words have passed my lips that he didn't even need to ask the question. I pivot into the backseat and take Screwtape's basket cage from Scarlett. Silas pops the trunk, swings my duffel bag over his shoulder, and grabs a beaten red toolbox. One of the men catcalls at me, and Scarlett snickers.

"Go on, Rosie, kick his ass," she says under her breath. She's overprotective when it comes to wolves but thinks it's especially hilarious how human men assume that girls can't defend themselves.

The building is unlocked, the front door swinging open so quickly that it almost hits Scarlett in the face. The inside has the same sense of beauty gone to seed: cracked tile floors, heavily worn banisters, and a chandelier that's missing so many beads that it's practically just a ball of lights tied to the ceiling. The staircase spirals upward, each apartment jutting off a landing. Halfway up, a heavily muscled man flings his door open and scowls at us as we pass, a sickly sweet scent pouring from his apartment.

"Great. We live in a crack house," Silas says once the man has slammed his door shut again.

By the time we reach the top floor, my muscles and Screwtape are screaming at me with equal intensity. Loud music thuds at us from below, so audible that the stereo might have been right next to us. Silas sets our bags down and fumbles in his pocket for a key, but there's no need— when I lean against the door frame, the door swings open and crashes into the wall behind.

"Well then," Scarlett says. When neither Silas nor I move, she forges ahead into the apartment. Silas and I make brief eye contact before following her.

The apartment is open, no walls separating one space from another. The patterned tin ceiling is high above our heads and causes our footsteps to echo as if we are in a museum; truth is, that's sort of what it feels like. The walls are covered with tacks, to which fragments of posters still cling, and one corner is filled with magazine clippings of women in various stages of undress. The windows are huge, but several are cracked and a few panes are missing entirely. The place smells musty and damp, like a basement. Outside on a heavily rusted fire escape are a few potted plants, long dead and keeled over the sides of their containers.

There's furniture—sort of. A bed that looks to be straight out of the sixties lurks in an offshoot of the main room. There's a round dining room table that actually looks fairly decent, save the neon pink graffiti that covers the oak top. And the couch...well, the battered brown couch looks comfortable, but there's no way I'll sit on it unless it is covered with a blanket or twelve. I feel a wave of pity for Silas, having to sleep on it.

Silas looks casual, if a little disgusted by the place, and Scarlett is...well, Scarlett. Once freed from his basket, Screwtape finally stops growling and begins to stalk cockroaches and sniff around for mice as I unpack the bag of kitchen things, afraid to put anything in a drawer. Scarlett and Silas angle the mattress against the wall and take turns beating it with a broom. They hang a flowered sheet up over the entrance to the little bed area where Scarlett and I will sleep.

Three hours later, the apartment still looks terrible. But at least it's terrible without random beer bottles and cigarette ashes covering the counters. Outside, a dog barks wildly.

"I have to go pay our rent," Silas says with a halfhearted look around the room.

"I have to get you money to pay our share," Scarlett adds, rummaging through a bag. I look away; I'd rather not know which of our grandmother's items she's decided to pawn.

"You coming with us, Rosie?" Silas asks, leaning against one of the many iron pillars that break up the apartment.

I know I should go, because I know Scarlett hopes to go hunting afterward—I see her securing her hatchet to her belt. But the truth is, I don't want to hunt. I want to be at home. How long have I wondered what life would be like outside of Ellison, only to yearn for the small town now that I'm in Atlanta?

"No, I was thinking I'd stay here and finish unpacking,"

I answer, lifting myself up onto the countertop. Scarlett gives me a long stare, and I know she can see the frustration in my eyes. She nods.

"Okay. Keep your knives on you, even in here," she says and tosses me the belt that has both bone-handled knives stored securely on it.

Silas smiles gently at me, and then he and Scarlett leave, pulling the door tight until the lock pops shut behind them. Their footsteps echo loudly as they descend the stairs, and I hear the junkie's door fly open as they pass him again. I sigh and lower myself into one of the chairs. I set my feet on Silas's toolbox—I think it belonged to Pa Reynolds.

"Don't be silly, Leoni," Pa Reynolds said as he unloaded tools from the back of his ancient pickup truck. There was sawdust in his hair, and his overalls were permanently grass-stained. "A man's—or woman's—home is his castle."

"That doesn't mean I should get free labor," Oma March said, arms crossed.

"But I am your humble servant, my queen," Pa Reynolds said through a grin.

They were close in age, and there'd always been a sort of friendly flirtation between our grandmother and Silas's father. Looking back, I suppose it was normal for them to find comfort in each other. Silas's mother, Celia, had died when Silas was eight years old, and Pa Reynolds's brother

Jacob—the only one of his seven siblings that remained in Ellison—was so much younger that he was more like another one of the kids. I got the feeling Pa Reynolds longed for some companionship and understanding from Oma March, even if it came in a schoolboy tone that made us cringe.

As I stroke Screwtape's fur and look warily at the rusting pipes on the ceiling, I wonder what he would do to fix this place. Outside, the bells of the dilapidated church chime the hour—tinny, mechanical sounds that are more jarring than peaceful. Screwtape hisses at the noise, and I sigh. I'm not sure even Pa Reynolds could turn this place into a castle. But hey, maybe Silas can.

CHAPTER SEVEN

SCARLETT

I CAN FEEL THE FENRIS ALL AROUND ME IN THIS CITY, like they've touched every surface and traveled every sidewalk. All the streets are a blur of metal, glass, and people. It's so incredibly different from Ellison. People don't stare at me here. They don't stare at anyone—they look straight ahead and storm to their destinations as if they're on terribly important missions. I suppose we have that in common.

The pawnshop is dingy, overcrowded with things that smell like other people's homes: fabric softener, cigarettes, spices from cooking. I weave through to the front of the store, where a mannish, bored-looking woman watches *The Jerry Springer Show* on a tiny television. I turn over two bracelets and dip out of the pawnshop a few moments later, a thin fold of money in hand.

Twilight seems to go on forever; when the sun has set, billions of lights take over the streets. Everyone and everything is illuminated by the glow from neon signs, bright marquees, and headlights. It makes me lose track of the hours, unable to tell from the sun or moon exactly what time of evening it is. I wander down into a subway station, staring at the swirls of graffiti on the wall, searching my pockets for a coin or two to give to an older black man drumming on upturned buckets. He has a face almost as scarred as mine, though I doubt his marks are the result of a wolf.

"Hell, girl. Your man do that to you?" he says, staring at the scars on my arms and the few peeking out from my eye patch and hair. Somehow, his bluntness is comforting, more so than the sideways glances most girls give me, the horrified looks as they touch their own lovely, scar-free faces. But with this guy? It's unnecessary to hide when someone has already announced he sees you.

"Not quite," I reply and toss a few quarters into a coffee can by his feet. "And I kicked his ass anyway."

"Good for you, good for you, chickadee," he says as he taps off another intricate drum sequence.

I exit the subway to find the last few strands of twilight disappearing on the city's horizon. According to the map on the train wall, I should be only a block or so from the park. I pass the library, enormous and impressive, looking strangely classical amid all the silver and gray, and sadly realize it's already closing for the evening. I like libraries. It's a comfort that knowledge can be saved for so long. That what we learn can be passed on.

I wander a few more blocks until the trees of Piedmont Park appear at the end of the street. They seem prouder than the trees at home somehow, impressed with one another for surviving in the city for so long. Just before I reach the park, a burst of bright, pounding music rings out, then fades—a door to a club just down the street opening and shutting. I turn and walk toward it, clinging to the brick wall that surrounds an old apartment building as I watch the line of girls waiting to go in.

They're adorned in glittery green rhinestones, shimmery turquoise and aquamarine powders streaked across their eyelids. Dragonfly girls. Their hair is all the same, long and streaked, spiraling down their backs to where the tiny strings holding their tops on are knotted tightly. Their skin glows under the neon lights—amber, ebony, cream—like shined metal, flawless and smooth. I press harder against the crumbly brick wall behind me, tugging my crimson cloak closer to my body. The scars on my shoulders show through the fabric when I pull the cloak tight. Bumpy red hills in perfectly spaced lines.

The Dragonflies laugh, sweet and bubbly, and I groan in exasperation. They toss their hair, stretch their legs, sway their hips, bat their eyelashes at the club's bouncer, everything about them luring the Fenris. Inviting danger like some baby animal bleating its fool head off. *Look at me, see how I dance, did you notice my hair, look again, desire me, I am perfect.* Stupid, stupid Dragonflies. Here I am, saving your lives, bitten and scarred and wounded for you, and you don't even know it. I should let the Fenris have one of you.

No. I didn't mean that. I sigh and walk to the other side of the brick wall, letting my fingers tangle in the thick ivy. It's dark on this side, shadowed from the neon lights of the street. I breathe slowly, watching the tree limbs sway, backlit by the lights of skyscrapers. Of course I didn't mean it. Ignorance is no reason to die. They can't help what they are, still happily unaware inside a cave of fake shadows. They exist in a world that's beautiful, *normal,* where people have jobs and dreams that don't involve a hatchet. My world is a parallel universe to theirs—the same sights, same people, same city, yet the Fenris lurk, the evil creeps, the knowledge undeniably exists. If I hadn't been thrown into this world, I could just as easily have been a Dragonfly.

Footsteps approach—footsteps that I recognize, padding softly in the park's grass.

"Silas," I greet him without looking. He slows.

"You know, for a girl who can't see on her right side, you're hard to sneak up on. What is that, some sort of pirate superpower?" he teases. If anyone other than him teased me about missing an eye, I'd fight him. But Silas gets away with it.

I smile and answer, "Yep. All us pirates have superhearing. It's a side effect of wearing an eye patch." He's standing just beside the wall looking at the Dragonflies. His eyes narrow in something between disgust and intrigue, as though he's not certain if he likes looking at them or not. I want to comment, but I stay quiet. Somehow it feels important to wait for his reaction. Silas finally turns to look at me in the shadows.

"It's like they're *trying* to be eaten, isn't it?" he asks pointedly. "Can I tell you how glad I am that you and Rosie aren't like them?"

"No kidding." I grin, relieved. "Rosie could be if she wanted, though. She's beautiful like they are."

"Beauty has nothing to do with it. Rosie could never be one of them. Do you really think they'd dress and act like that if they knew it was drawing wolves toward them?"

I frown, nodding. "I never thought of that. I guess you're right, though. Knowledge does have a way of making you an outcast. Or a hunter, in her case."

"Ah yes, Scarlett March, queen of the black-or-white perspective. Isn't there something between a hunter and those girls?" Silas asks.

I shake my head as I move to the edge of the wall, then peer around. "Anyway, how am I supposed to lure a Fenris when I'm competing against *that*?" A line of Dragonflies saunters into the club, only to be replaced by a new group of sparkly girls. I try to ignore the tiny tug of pity I feel for myself and my torn-up body. *Pity is a useless emotion,* I remind myself.

"Come on. You know a Fenris isn't going to attack a crowd like that. Just be the one girl who wandered away from the group," Silas answers firmly. He's never felt sorry for me and my scars, a harshness that I've always appreciated.

"I guess," I grumble. "Rosie will have to hunt more, though. She can compete with them."

"Oh," Silas says, half question and half statement. "And you're still against Rosie hunting solo?" He shoves his hands into his pockets and joins me on the dark side of the brick wall. The moon is heavy and newly full above, bright enough to cast his shadow on the wall, even with all the city's lights.

"You know how she is. I just worry about her..." I don't want to say it, but on top of my worry that she'll let a Fenris escape, I worry about her coming out of the fight like me. Or worse, like Oma March. "She has to hunt, though, or we're dead in the water here," I continue.

"Maybe. Maybe she's just not a hunter like you are," Silas says.

I raise an eyebrow. "She's a *great* hunter, you know that. Just don't tell her I said so."

"Maybe it's not for her, though, I mean."

I sigh. "It's not *for* anybody. It's just... what are we supposed to do? Sit back and assume someone else will kill the Fenris? It's our responsibility to do good when we have the power to. I can't do it alone. It was hard enough without you. If I lost her too..." I say quietly.

"Have you considered inspirational speaking?" Silas smirks.

"They don't let pirates into lecture halls. They're afraid we'll loot everything," I bite back with a grin. Silas laughs loudly enough to earn a few flirtatious glances from the Dragonflies.

"Come on, Lett. Let's go get some sleep. And make sure Rosie hasn't been kidnapped by a crazy crack addict."

"Rosie could take that crack addict any day. And besides, I can't sleep. I have to... I have to move. Do something. Come on, Silas, hunt with me," I ask in a voice more pleading than I intended. Hunting makes things right, will make the city feel less like a strange land and more like a temporary home.

"Sadly, Lett, I am not as willing to go without sleep," he says pointedly. "Though you aren't going to start saying I abandoned you again over this, are you? Because if I have to deal with the Scarlett March you're-going-away-and-I-hate-you-for-it cold shoulder again, I might lose it."

I shake my head. "Go, get some sleep. Tell Rosie I'll be in late, I guess. Give me the key." I hold my hand out and Silas drops the apartment key in it. "And here's our part of the rent," I add and slip a hundred dollars into his hand.

"You know you two don't have to pay," Silas says seriously. "Rent isn't that bad. There's a steep discount for inhabiting crack houses, I think."

"It's fine," I say quickly, shoving my hands into my pockets before he can hand the money back.

"All right." Silas shrugs. "Be careful hunting, though. They aren't lone wolves here. Even *you* can't take on a full pack."

"We'll see." I smirk but then nod when Silas gives me

an exasperated look. He walks away as I turn my back to the Dragonflies, tugging my cloak around my shoulders and meandering into the park.

Piedmont Park is a little eerie—the proud trees cast long shadows under the street lamps. Just shadows, unless you think they're real…I intentionally walk through them, smiling to myself. I swish my cloak out a bit, peering through the landscaped flowers and shrubbery for any other signs of life.

Wait…yes.

Yes, yes! The familiar rush of adrenaline sweeps over me. On the other side of the park, huddled in a small cluster by a row of pink hydrangea bushes, are three men. Fenris—I can feel it from here. I cough lightly, nabbing their attention. Three Fenris on my first night here? My heart swells. This is what I am meant for.

I glance through my hair to size them up. I've never fought three at once before, but one looks young—well, he *looks* old, but Fenris who haven't been monsters for too long have a different sort of movement, as if their bodies are still trying to be human despite the fact that their souls are long gone. I can handle them.

The largest of the Fenris grins at me from beneath a shaggy black haircut, and they circle around behind me as I speed up. I grip the handle of my hatchet tightly and look over my shoulder with what I hope is a fearful expression. I force myself to breathe so my eagerness doesn't overtake my rationality. *Come along, come along.*

113

They've stopped.

I back up, wondering if they're just waiting for the moment to spring into action and chase me properly. But no, they've circled up and are talking casually. I squint to see the pack mark on one's wrist. Bell. Bells are always aggressive— *come on*. I give a girlish cough and pretend to be terribly interested in a swan fountain nearby.

But they don't look. Instead they turn and walk away, loping like their inner wolves.

My skin goes cold. The hand on my hatchet tightens, threatening to release the weapon at their retreating backs. I press my lips together. This doesn't make sense. I baited them! I *had* them. Everything in me shakes, and my scars burn like seams that might burst at any moment.

No, *no*. I've never lost a Fenris like that, not once I had him. This is what I *am*.

I take off after them in a dead sprint, but even as my heart thunders in my ears and sweat begins to trickle down my back, I know it's a lost cause. They're fast, so much faster than a human. Still, I run until I reach the edge of the park, where I slow to a walk and my eyes burn in anger at the line of Dragonflies before me, blond hair and bright teeth and perfect marble-smooth skin. Why did I think that I would be able to lure three Fenris when they have this kind of prey? I watch the girls glitter, sparkle, glow in the night.

I am a hunter. If I can't hunt...I'm nothing. In a flurry of frustration, I whirl around and send my hatchet whistling through the air. It strikes the base of a nearby tree, sending a shower of bark to the grass as it sinks several inches into the trunk. A few Dragonflies take notice, scowling at me before going back to their conversations. I storm to the tree, yank my hatchet from it, and start home, heart raging.

CHAPTER EIGHT

Rosie

Scarlett, you don't know it's the same Fenris you saw in the park. This is a huge city—it could have been any number of packs," I groan for what feels like the millionth time. I knew something bad had happened when Scarlett stormed in at two in the morning, dropping her hatchet so loudly that the junkie downstairs roared in distaste.

Silas rubs his neck and nods in agreement, casting the couch an accusatory glare. I'm incredibly grateful that I was too tired to pay much attention when he came in last night, though I did manage to look his way just in time to see him whip his shirt off in the moonlight. The image is burned into my eyes, which I have to admit isn't exactly the worst thing.

Come on, Rosie, get your mind together.

"It's them, I know it's them. It's like I'm being punished

or something," Scarlett growls, slamming the newspaper down on the graffiti table. "Three Girls Murdered: Killing Spree Continues," the headline screams.

"Don't be stupid," Silas says in a tone that he alone can use with my sister. "They just have more distraction here. You used to be the only bait for miles, and now they're practically living on a buffet table."

"We came here to try to do the most damage, and I can't attract a single wolf! What am I supposed to do?" Scarlett snarls. Screwtape hisses at her for waking him up.

"Be the dessert?" Silas shrugs.

"I can't do that," Scarlett snaps. She sighs and pulls her hair back into a ponytail, then drops her head into her hands for a long time, as though some great internal debate is going on inside her mind. Finally she looks up at me. "Rosie. You're the dessert."

"What?" I respond quickly, alarmed. Not only is it bizarre for Scarlett to suggest I do something so dangerous, but being the only bait means I can't mess up, not a single mistake. I can't even begin to imagine how Scarlett would react if I lured and then lost *another* Fenris.

"You have to," Scarlett says matter-of-factly. "Let's face it, Rosie, you're more dessert than I'll ever be. I can't compete with the Dragonflies"—she waves a hand toward the window when we look confused—"the *girls,* those girls with the sparkly outfits and blond hair. I can't compete with them, but you, Rosie . . . you can. You're all we've got. One girl alone is a lot easier prey than two. We'll hide, wait for them to approach you, and then we all attack." Her words are quiet but firm, as if she's battled a long time for her conclusion.

"Why do I not think I'll like this?" I grumble, sinking down onto the couch that doubled as Silas's bed, now safely covered with a sheet. "Are you saying no knives? No anything?"

Scarlett bites her lip. "You'll look more...you'll be better bait. I can't do it—it has to be you. I wouldn't let anything happen to you, Rosie," she says needlessly.

"Of course," I say quickly, waves of guilt crashing into me. "Of course, Scarlett. I'll do whatever I need to do." I nod. "It's my responsibility," I add and see Silas raise a curious eyebrow at me.

Scarlett sighs and stands, heading toward the door that leads to the rooftop deck. I went up there once this morning and promptly came back down—it's nothing more than some plywood nailed to the edge of the building. Scarlett will probably like it, though. Good lookout. My sister shuts the door as she disappears, but it drifts back open slowly so we can hear her heavy footsteps and muttered curses as she climbs the rickety stairs.

Outside, the church bells chime once; they chime for the hour and then once every quarter hour. It made sleeping even *more* difficult.

"So I'm the dessert," I say glumly, rising to put a loaf of bread away.

"Come on. Let's go get coffee, get your mind off it," Silas says soothingly as I begin to take my frustration out on the bag of bread, violently twisting the end of the plastic into a knot.

"I don't like coffee," I grumble without looking at him. Silas reaches forward and puts his hands over mine. Goose bumps erupt on my arms.

He raises his eyebrows, voice gentle. "You can get chocolate milk, then. But let's get out of here before you bend the entire loaf in half."

I sigh and look at him. Funny how he can go from being "just Silas" to *Silas* in a matter of seconds. I release the bread and follow him out the door, my frustration and the fluttery feeling fighting for control of me.

The diner Silas takes me to is just a few blocks away, a dingy but classic-looking place with black and white tile and red neon signs blinking things such as "Apple Pie!" and "Specialty Hash Browns!" We slide into a booth, and a waitress who is missing several teeth grins at us and asks us for our order.

"Just a cup of coffee for me. You, Rosie?"

"Chocolate milk," I reply with a snide look toward Silas. He laughs and the waitress hurries away. Then, silence. Silas rearranges the salt and pepper shakers, and I pretend to read a piece of paper outlining the history of the diner. *Right.*

"So," I blurt out, a little louder than I meant to, "I guess you didn't get much time at home, did you? Back from California and now stuck here with us?" *Is my voice shaking?* I think my voice is shaking.

"I'd hardly call it stuck," Silas says with a smile that's

rather dazzling. "Though you have a point. I should take a real vacation. Most of San Francisco was a blend of buying groceries for Jacob and feeling guilty over leaving you and Scarlett in Ellison all alone. I haven't had a vacation since I was...wow, since my seventh birthday, I suppose. My dad took all of us to some secluded little beach off North Carolina for a whole month."

"That sounds nice," I reply, a little jealous. I've never really been on vacation.

Silas laughs. "It was at first. But when I say secluded, I mean secluded. Having *no one* but eight siblings for entertainment gets old after about a week."

"I understand completely," I say with a smile.

"Though I will say," Silas adds, looking out the window, "I miss them more than I thought I ever could. There's a bigger difference between 'hardly seeing one another because of distance' and 'hardly seeing one another because of anger' than you'd think."

"They're just upset," I offer. "They'll get over it all, with time."

"I know, I know," Silas says. "It's because they're remembering Pa the way he used to be. Full of life and vigor and talking to tree spirits or whatever. They think I accepted a house from a healthy man. Truth is, I can't bring myself to tell them that the reason he gave me the house is that I was the last one to be forgotten. He forgot about all of them, and then...me in the end." Silas spins a napkin around on the table and exhales.

"It's like he's already...um...gone, isn't it?" I ask carefully, placing a hand over his to stop the spinning napkin. I meet his eyes and suddenly realize we're touching—I pull my hand away, but Silas smiles and answers.

"Pretty much. He's just this guy that looks like my dad and has a few of his old memories from way back in the day. It's not that my siblings don't *care,* it's just that they're so preoccupied with their own lives. But Jacob and me...I guess we weren't as busy as the rest of them."

"That's good, though," I suggest, fighting the urge to put my hand back on his. Why did I pull it away? What's wrong with me? "I mean, what if you'd gone to college with your high school friends? Who would have taken care of your dad? I mean"—I backpedal—"Scarlett and I would have, of course, but...it's not the same, I'm sure."

"True," Silas says, "my life would have been very different if I'd become a woodsman with my brothers or gone to school with my friends." He pauses. "Lucky for me, I avoided those traps and ended up fighting wolves instead."

"Lucky for both of us," I reply, smiling.

The waitress reappears and sets down a coffee mug that looks as if it could have been salvaged from our dirty apartment. Thankfully, the glass holding my chocolate milk looks as though it's been rinsed, at the very least. Silas shakes a few sugar packets into his cup and changes the subject. "So, did you see that community center I was talking about?"

"What? Where?"

"We walked right past it, just before that grocery store.

I mentioned it on the way to the city? You just drop in and take classes. They've got all sorts of stuff. I bet you can get a student rate, even."

"But I'm not a student—"

"You're young enough that they'll assume—"

"—and how am I supposed to find the time to take dance classes, now that I'm the dessert?"

"I'm starting to really regret using that metaphor," Silas says, grinning. "And let me explain something, Rosie." He takes a swig of the coffee and presses his lips together, searching for words. "I'm from a long, long, long, long line of woodsmen. My brothers are all supertalented. They all built their own rooms. For god's sake, Lucas built a freaking wooden hot tub in his bedroom with wooden monkeys pouring water into it."

"Monkeys?"

"Don't ask. Anyway, I can do some woodworking. I know my way around the forest, I can handle an ax better than most, I can make a tree grow where nothing else will, I can live off berries and hunt for my food, and I've known about the Fenris since I could crawl. I'm a woodsman, for all intents and purposes. But that doesn't mean I live for it any more than the fact that you're good at hunting means you have to live for that. So maybe breaking out of the hunting lifestyle for a few hours here and there will help you figure out if it's really for you or not."

I shake my head, confused as to why he'd even think that was possible. "I can't just not hunt, Silas. So yeah, I take a few random classes, and what if I decide that I hate hunting and want to quit? That doesn't mean I can. I owe Scarlett my *life,* and if she wants to cash in by having me spend my life hunting beside her, so be it. It'd kill her if she ever thought I wanted to quit."

"Rosie," Silas says quietly. "I'm not suggesting you drop your sister like a bad habit and take up intense ballet training."

I sit back in the booth and fold my arms over my chest. I watch the people walking outside the giant glass windows. *Innocents,* Scarlett calls them at times. People who have no idea what we do, the prices we pay for them, the price my sister paid for me. But isn't it possible that I could do something else as well?

I look back at Silas, who is adding more sugar to his coffee. "Okay. Fine. One class, but only because I might not get another chance once we're back in Ellison. And you have to promise not to tell Scarlett."

"Only if you let me pay for it," he counters.

"Silas," I say threateningly.

He shrugs. "You and Lett are broke. And besides, if you pay for it, Scarlett will know the money is missing."

"Fine," I say dismissively.

"Great. Let's go get you signed up, then," he says, rising and dropping a few crumpled dollars onto the tabletop. I remain seated, mouth open.

"Now?"

"No time like the present. I suppose I've taken Operation

Rosie-Gets-a-Life as a personal mission. It's too similar to Operation Silas-Gets-a-Life for me to ignore." He extends a hand to me and, without thinking, I take it. My heart rate quickens and I want to pull him toward me.

Oh god. What am I thinking? I pull my hand away again and smile nervously. Silas smiles almost sheepishly. Did he feel the same stirring sensation?

We backtrack down the street until we reach the community center. It's no surprise I missed it on the way; it's little more than a hole in the wall, flanked by a Starbucks and a Dollar Tree. Silas hands me thirty dollars and waits outside as I enter the center, which smells strongly of incense.

This is wrong. I am a hunter. Wasting money on a random class is wrong. I am bowing out on my responsibilities to other girls, girls who don't know about the Fenris. I peer at the board that lists the center's classes, and there's some of everything. Flower arranging, dancing, French, origami, feng shui...I almost step back from the mental overload. I can take anything I want. A flutter of joy rises in my chest.

Keep it simple, Rosie. Remember, this isn't supposed to take the place of hunting. Hunting is your responsibility. This is just for fun—don't get carried away.

"All right, it'll be a three-class series, any classes you want. They start next Tuesday and run for four weeks, and you get to skip one week. Student rates mean you owe twenty-eight dollars," the willowy receptionist says, tapping at the computer keyboard and shoving a schedule into my hand.

I hand over the money. Scarlett is going to be so angry.

"This is your class card. Just bring it with you."

I nod and take the card from her. She gives me a wary look. I leave.

"Wow," I say as I exit. Silas grins.

"Pretty empowering, breaking out of the woodsman— er, hunter—pack, isn't it?"

Yes. Yes it is. But then the guilt takes over.

"She'll be so mad. People *die,* you know? People could be eaten by a Fenris while I'm here..."

"Relax, Rosie. You aren't abandoning her. You're just taking some classes," he says, nudging me gently—but with just enough skin-on-skin contact that it sends shivers down my spine. I'm overwhelmed with the desire to link my arm in his and have to fight it away.

CHAPTER NINE

SCARLETT

MY INNER VOICE SOUNDS LIKE OMA MARCH'S, AND IT lectures me. *Yes. It'll be okay. Remember why you're here: to hunt Fenris, to stop the surge of deaths. You aren't here to be the star. Rosie deserves to try the front seat out for a while. She's a brilliant hunter. She won't end up scarred or broken, not with you and Silas to protect her. You can keep her close, you can keep her safe.*

I doubt my inner voice, to be honest.

We cut through the business district, past the darkened skyscrapers where lone security guards patrol the building lobbies. The city smells like smoke and heat from the day, but I'm cold, even with my cloak. Sounds pick up, laughing, talking, and it's almost as though we've suddenly crossed a magic line that let us into the city nightlife. Taxis fly by us, girls cry out to their friends, guys walk with bizarre swaggers and tilt their heads at ladies who swoon in response. There's a buzz with a few overheard conversations—girls recounting the recent murders, telling the details with relish. They don't think it could possibly happen to them.

I don't need to tell Rosie what to do—I've taught her well long before now. She cuts in front of us, dropping the hood from her head. Silas and I casually walk behind a row of SUVs, all customized to the point of ludicrousness, while Rosie sweeps past the pack of Dragonflies who are sipping cocktails and dancing flirtatiously on the patio of a bar. A few men turn their heads toward her. Most ignore her, but one seems drawn to her. *Way to go, Rosie.* The man—a Fenris, I can feel it—says something to the twenty-something woman he was talking to and sets his beer bottle down onto the table. They prefer their prey young. Lucky for us.

Rosie doesn't know he's there yet and keeps charging forward until she's broken free from the crowd surrounding the bar. Silas and I follow for a moment, then hang a hard right and sprint toward the park, which is better grounds for hunting, and duck behind the sign when we arrive. Rosie follows our lead and heads down one of the paved trails, raising her hood back over her head so that the Fenris sees nothing but a girl in crimson walking away. Irresistible.

The Fenris swoops around ahead of her, nothing but a shadow rushing through the dark night. My sister sees him, finally, but doesn't let on. She meanders down the trail, the trees and shrubbery blocking her from view of the street. The Fenris steps out in front of her.

"Hey — you know the park is closed this late?" he asks flirtatiously. I lean around a magnolia tree to try to get a better view of his face now that he's in the moonlight. He's young. *Very* young — Rosie's age, even. His hair is blond, cheeks round, and he's got the gangly appearance of a boy just shooting through puberty who could be in a garage band or the like.

Rosie shrugs and twirls a strand of hair in her fingers. "I'm lost, thought I'd cut through here. Aren't *you* a little young to be out this late anyway?" she asks in a voice that's equal parts sexy and sweet.

"Maybe," the boy says in a voice more mature than his baby face implies. Rosie falters a little, and I see her scan over him again. She's not certain he's actually a Fenris. She catches my eye briefly, only a flash of a moment, but I nod. He has no soul.

"How old are you, then?" she says, taking a step backward, away from the street. She lets her hips sway alluringly.

"Let's call it fourteen," the Fenris chuckles, taking a few slow steps toward her. His fingers twitch, and even from here I can see his nails inching forward into points. He busies his hand, sweeping fingers through his messy hair. It'd be enough to make most young girls swoon. Rosie plays along beautifully, biting her lip and giggling.

"Fourteen? You *are* young," she answers. I see a wave of

pity cross her face; she tends to feel sorry for the younger ones, wonders who they'd be if they weren't wolves. The Fenris laughs, his voice hoarse and lacking humor, his hair a little darker. Rosie takes another step backward. A large fountain surrounded by flowers blocks my view of her. I strain to see, but then the Fenris steps forward and they're both out of my sight.

"Damn, we have to move," I whisper.

"Wait," Silas answers, clapping a firm hand on my shoulder and pulling me backward. I glare as I almost topple into him, but then I look in the direction in which he's nodding. Across the park, out of earshot but visible in the darkness thanks to a streetlight, is a group of three guys. They fidget and dart their heads around in a very animal-like way, and I catch one lifting his nose toward the air to catch a scent on the breeze. "What do you think?" Silas asks.

"Oh, yeah. Fenris." As soon as I say it, hair starts to sprout on the arms of one of them, but he gets the transformation under control and the hair dissolves back into his skin. They begin to walk away from us, and the panicky feeling rises. More of them are getting away.

"From around here, then?" the young Fenris asks Rosie, his voice barely audible over the sound of traffic. I can't hear Rosie's answer at all. "Ellison? Nice place, I've heard. I'm from Simonton."

"Lett...you should go after them," Silas says, pulling at the leathery-thick magnolia leaves as cover. He reaches to his back and pulls the ax out of his backpack in preparation.

"Wait, what about Rosie?" I hiss.

"I'll stay with her. You're faster than me—you can take that group a lot more efficiently than I can. I'll protect Rosie, I promise."

"Silas—"

"Lett, it's *me!* Come on. Nothing will happen to your sister."

I meet Silas's eyes for a long time, warning, threatening, then nod curtly. I can't just let three Fenris walk away. Silas is my partner. He can be trusted with Rosie's life. I slink away, crouched behind some azaleas, and Silas slips through the magnolias in the other direction. The pack turns toward the sound of my encroaching footsteps, their heads tensing forward in a very canine way, but they brush the sound off and continue talking.

I'm about to stand all the way up when they move toward me, still talking, and a word catches my attention: *Potential.* I sink back down in the azaleas, curious.

"I'm just saying, he's been here, I can smell it. That means we've got to be closer than Arrow, right?" a physically old Fenris grumbles, glancing at his hands anxiously—they're covered in greasy, matted fur. He shakes them with a frustrated expression, and the fur vanishes. Without the fur, he's handsome. He looks as if he could be a doctor or a lawyer or something, with speckled gray hair and deep-set eyes that look almost steel colored in the moonlight. I wonder how many women in the midtwenties crowd he's lured away.

"That doesn't mean we can eat whenever we want to.

It's our night to look for him, not to hunt," another Fenris answers. He looks worn almost, as though he's irritated and tired—and hungry. "Come on, we've got to go get the kid. Alpha will kill him if he finds out he went after a girl on our patrol night. We can hunt tomorrow—hell, it's not like there aren't five million more where that chick came from. We're running out of time; the Potential's phase has already begun. If we miss out on this one *again*..."

"Whatever," the third Fenris grumbles, a younger one who looks about Silas's age, with sleek black hair and biceps that show through his T-shirt. "If the jackass would stop wandering around the entire fucking city...are you *sure* someone scented him in Atlanta? I'm still saying, the guys we've got out in the country think—"

"You tell the Alpha that, then," the second Fenris growls, his voice hardly human. "Want to explain that you were too busy skirt chasing and gave the Potential up to Arrow, when they're already growing? They took over Sparrow. You want them to take control of us too? Just let them get more powerful, steal our members, find the Potential for themselves?"

The other Fenris says nothing. They glare at each other, like dogs waiting for a fight, until the gray-haired Fenris turns sharply and storms away. The others follow suit, and I see the young Fenris that had been following Rosie scurry out from a side path and join them, an apologetic look on his face. His nose contorts in and out of a canine snout, and I see him glance back longingly at the spot where my sister is.

They're going to run. Any moment now, they're going to

disappear—they're going to leave me standing alone again with a hatchet and nothing accomplished. I'm not the bait, not anymore—I'm just a hunter. I stand up, my red hood falling away from my face. The wolves turn toward me, curious. I take a few strides out of the leaves and into the moonlight.

"What have we here?" one hisses. His eyes jump from the red cloak to my face, drawn to the color but repulsed by my scars. Forcing him to change out of lust won't work, but he'll change out of anger.

I charge forward, hatchet raised. The Fenris who was after my sister can't control the transformation, and he bolts forward to meet me. Before he gets too close, I release the handle of my hatchet. It whizzes through the air and slices into his arm, deep enough that he falls to the ground. He flips back and forth, human eyes becoming a beast's, always holding on to the darkness, the hatred. The other three Fenris seem to snap out of their confusion. They transform in one fluid motion.

They won't escape me—not this time. They won't fold into the night because I'm unable to bait them. The scent of their fur fills the air, and I dive forward to grab my hatchet from where it lies beside the youngest Fenris. My shoulder dips into a pool of his blood, and he lunges at me through the pain, jaws snapping. Won't be long till he's shadows, with his veins open like that.

I hear a growl behind me, followed by an angry, roarlike bark. The three Fenris gather, the largest in the center—I don't know which wolf was which human anymore. They take slow, even steps toward me, heads low and teeth bared. The two flanking the outside branch out. I grip my hatchet and unsheathe the hunting knife.

Can't let them get behind me. I take a sharp step backward, let them think I'm running. The two outside wolves jump forward, one at my throat and the other at my legs. I lean out of the way, allowing one to sail by my face, but a claw manages to sink into my shoulder with a ripping sound. I cringe, but the lower wolf is already on me, his mouth stretching open around my thigh, eyes wide and teeth yellowed and razorlike, and I barely have time to jump out of the way as his teeth chomp together. Before he can try again, I sink the hunting knife into his back.

The largest wolf slams into me on my blind side. My hatchet is knocked away, and for the first time I wonder where Silas is. *Rosie, he's with Rosie. She's safe.* I feel something crack in my chest and hear the scrambled sound of claws on pavement as the other wolves stand up. The largest wolf pants, lines of saliva dripping from his mouth onto my neck. His eyes are yellow, vibrant, and there's so much white around the irises that he looks almost insane. With a deep, low growl, he presses a paw down onto my chest and slowly begins to drag it downward, slicing through my skin.

I want to scream. But I won't, not with the way he's looking at me, with joy, with anticipation. A breathy, raspy sound chokes from his throat—a laugh? It seeps into my skin, makes me angry, makes my blood feel hot.

I swing my right fist toward the wolf's face. It makes

contact with his lower jaw, and I see several teeth flung into the night. My fingers open up, begin to bleed from the impact, but it's enough to have distracted the wolf for the tiniest moment. I draw my feet in and kick hard into his lower abdomen, a soft spot that sends him skittering off me and gasping for air. I stagger to my feet. There's only one wolf left unwounded.

Only there isn't just one wolf.

All four—even the two I hacked into—are looming before me. Their shoulder blades roll as they lurch forward. *What's happening?* They're ready to continue.

But I'm not sure if I am. I press a hand to my chest to try to stop the bleeding and try to see my hatchet and knife without taking my eye off the wolves. The wolves are actually *healing* somehow. They're stronger, stronger than me, stronger than most Fenris. I harden my stare, try not to let the all-encompassing fear show on my face. I can't take them alone.

A knife whizzes through the air beside my head but misses the largest Fenris. Rosie's knife. She and Silas run up behind me, alarmed, confused. The knife is the beginning of an avalanche of motion. The Fenris spring forward as a single unit. The youngest wolf, the one who was the blond boy, heads toward me, while the others lunge for Rosie and Silas. I kick the Fenris's back legs out from under him, buying myself just enough time to grab my hatchet. His mouth opens; he's coming for my head this time, for my face.

I wait until the last instant before his jaws will close

around my cheeks, then heave the hatchet around. It sinks into the blond wolf's neck with a cracking sound. It's severed his spine. The wolf falls to the ground, tremors for a moment, and dissolves into shadows that hurry away in the moonlight.

I turn to Rosie and Silas to see there's only one wolf left—the largest. Silas and Rosie are both fighting it, Rosie with only one knife left and Silas with the blade of an ax. The handle has somehow been broken off and thrown aside. Silas swings for the wolf, but it sidesteps out of the way. The animal paces and begins to circle them as they back up to each other, ready for a second pass.

I grab Rosie's second knife from the ground. One shot. I try not to gasp for breath despite the fact that I'm dizzy. Every movement feels as if it's ripping my chest apart. I don't have Rosie's aim, but the wolf is going to wear us down if someone doesn't get a hit. Rosie meets my eye briefly, and I see her grab on to Silas's wrist, ready to yank him out of the way should the knife near them instead of my target.

The blade spins through the air just as the wolf moves— instead of hitting his head, it slices through his ear. It's enough, though. The Fenris turns, dark eyes wide, and Silas leaps toward it. He sinks the ax blade into the wolf's head before the beast can react, and the motion throws Silas to the ground as the wolf twists in pain, jaws open and claws flecked with my blood. Its legs buckle beneath him and finally it explodes into shadows.

Silas exhales and drops his head to the ground while

Rosie races toward me, yanking her cloak off. She presses it to my chest, trying to stop the bleeding, then urges me to sit. I breathe deeply as Rosie pulls my hair away from my face, freeing it from sweat and blood.

"We need to get home," Rosie says under her breath.

"We aren't going back to Ellison until—" I choke, trying to calm my temper—every time it flares, the pain increases.

"Not Ellison," Rosie cuts me off gently. "The apartment." I hear Silas's footsteps but can't quite focus enough to look up at him. Rosie stands and the two of them help me up. I take a dizzy step forward, but the movement makes the skin on my chest feel as if it's tearing in two; I sink back to the grass. I grit my teeth, prepared to stand again despite the pain, but instead Silas's hand squeezes my shoulder.

"Let me carry you," he says lowly.

"I can make it," I mumble, pride eating away at me.

"I know you can, Lett," he says.

I mean to argue, mean to sigh, but instead I turn to him and close my eye. Silas is strong—he pulls me from the ground as if it's nothing, and Rosie takes my hand.

It doesn't take long to get back to the apartment. Silas turns away while Rosie pulls my shirt off and flushes my wounds with soapy water. The scars that were already on my chest seem to have done some good—they prevented the wolf's claws from cutting tremendously deep. Still no scars over my heart—the skin there remains smooth and perfect. Rosie bandages the four thick cuts, then wraps gauze around my body to hold them together.

"They were strong," I say, trying to pretend that speaking doesn't hurt. I lie back on the couch. Silas is sitting in one of the wooden chairs while Rosie kneels beside my waist.

"Stronger than normal," Silas adds. "Three of us, only four of them, and..." He shakes his head. "You think they were just a particularly powerful group?"

"No. Even that young one was strong. I hit all of them once. I thought they were down, but then..." I sigh. "They were talking about the Potential. I think that's it—that's how they're getting stronger, how they're staying so focused. They weren't going to attack you, Rosie. They were going to walk away, go hunt for the Potential instead of girls. Apparently they've lost this specific Potential before, and they're... motivated."

"So you're saying...we stop?" Rosie asks, shock in her voice.

I shake my head. "We've always played the part of bait before—it's just not going to work this time. We need better bait. We need the Potential if we want to lure them in."

"Scarlett," Rosie begins slowly in a voice that's meant to comfort, "I get that, but...we're only three..."

"You think we aren't up for it?" I snap at her harshly. My chest throbs in pain. "Sorry, Rosie." She nods, unhurt. She's borne the brunt of my anger before, learned to let the meaningless bits of it roll off her back. "If we can find him, we can bring them to us. We can be prepared for the new strength, and we can do more damage to the packs as a whole. But only for another twenty-eight days. And then they go back to hunting, killing like normal. Yes, the murder blitz ends, but so does our chance to really bring them in without using ourselves as bait."

I don't need to say it. They know it and I know it. Without the Potential, I'm useless in this city. Sure, I can hunt a rogue Fenris or small pack that wanders out toward Ellison, but here, where the real danger is? I am nothing. And I *need* this—I need *him,* whoever he is, to make a difference, to *be* the change I want to cause in the world. I can feel the pleading in my face, in the hoarseness of my throat, afraid I'll have to beg them to help me.

But I won't. Of course I won't. Rosie reaches up and takes my hand, squeezing it gently. We have the same heart. Where I go, she goes, and where she goes, I go. Silas looks at her and nods as well.

"Of course, Lett. We're in this together, all three of us. What can I do to help?" he says.

I sigh in relief and happiness and fear, every emotion mixed into one bursting inside me. "For starters, you can help me figure out how to find the Potential."

CHAPTER TEN

Rosie

My sister thrives on goals. The martial arts belt system was perfect for her. She set her sights on the yellow belt, the green, brown, black. When she'd learned all she could there, she trained the same way: run two miles, then three, four. And now, with the Fenris, she seems happy that she has a goal she can act on: find the Potential.

"We should start with the city. I mean, it's a decent jumping-off point, since there are more people in Atlanta than in the country. And the packs seem to be congregating here—the bigger, older ones, anyway...I imagine it won't be long before the smaller packs show up too. And if nothing else, we've got more access to information here," Silas says as we return to the apartment after a quick run to the convenience store.

"Right." Scarlett nods. "Let's start here. So how do we find him?"

It's silent for a moment.

"Okay, we can figure this out." Silas interrupts the quiet and drops down beside me on the couch. "They track him by some sort of calling or scent or something, but there still has to be something unique about this guy that *we* can find."

"We know it's a man, for starters. And we know it's a specific man, that he's got some specific trait."

"And we know he's not a child," I add. "I mean, it's not like a Potential was just born. They aren't turned till they're at least what, early teens? That's the youngest Fenris I've ever heard of, right?" I ask, and Scarlett nods.

"Great. So what is the trait that makes him a Potential during a random moon phase?" Silas asks optimistically, as though he thinks one of us will blurt out the answer.

More silence. Each of us starts a sentence, causing the other two to look on hopefully, but then we grimace and stay silent. We've got nothing. The moon phase — our deadline — ends at eleven forty-one at night in twenty-eight days.

Over the next day, my sister plunges into a flurry of research, writing notes and jotting down ideas that she leaves throughout the apartment. She can never verbalize them terribly well to Silas or me, leaving us mostly to ourselves.

Which is both good and bad.

He and I return to the diner, and then we venture to Goodwill together. He helps me hang the tropical print curtains that I found at the store, where I also managed to find an entirely too-lilac area rug and a decent clock radio as well. Scarlett immediately programmed it to the news radio stations. I keep waiting for the fluttering feelings for Silas to stop, but they merely subside a little; I still feel them whenever he brushes against me for too long or brings his face close to mine.

I've never kept a secret from my sister, and now I have two: the community center pamphlet that I keep flipping through, and the strange buzzing feeling that I get when Silas is around. I try to pretend that both are nothing she'd want to hear about anyway, but some deeper part of me reels in excitement and fear at them. The Tuesday after our failed I'm-the-dessert hunt is no exception—community center classes are supposed to start today, and the anticipation wakes me up long before my sister. Or maybe it's the tinny church bells crying out at six in the morning.

I slide out of our bed and tiptoe to the doorway in slippers—I'm afraid to walk around this place barefoot. The bedroom is lavender colored, and streaks of orange sunlight are crawling their way up the horizon. My eyes run across Silas's form huddled in blankets and sleeping soundly. I smile despite myself and slink toward the kitchen, rummaging through the refrigerator for some eggs.

The noise stirs Silas, who sits up suddenly, hair flying wildly around his eyes. Screwtape hisses at him from under the coffee table.

"Good morning to you," Silas grumbles. He lifts his eyes to mine and smiles as he rubs the back of his head. I grin back and toss the eggs around with a fork before pouring them into a frying pan.

While Silas disappears into the bathroom, Scarlett rises as well, padding out of our bedroom in a T-shirt and pajama pants. I know before she speaks that she has a plan. That bright-eyed look is back, despite the circles under her eyes and the still-fresh chest wound. She hides pain well.

"What is it, then?" I ask her before she speaks. She grins at me and lifts herself onto one of the bar stools that Silas salvaged, shivering as another draft sweeps through the apartment.

"We go back. Figure out who they were before they were Fenris. Figure out why the ones who already are Fenris were capable of becoming Fenris."

"Not before I've had eggs," Silas calls out, emerging from the bathroom slightly more shaved. He never truly gets rid of the stubble, though. I'm not certain he tries to. "Do you need help with breakfast, Rosie?" he asks.

"Almost done, actually," I reply.

"Next time, then," Silas says in the soft voice he usually uses with me only when Scarlett isn't around. I didn't even realize there was a special voice until now, but it makes me look at Scarlett nervously. She doesn't seem to have picked up on it. "So. The master plan, sergeant chief?" he continues, sliding onto a bar stool beside Scarlett.

Scarlett glares, but her excitement takes over. "Okay. So the one that Rosie almost had a few days ago said he was fourteen, and I don't think he was lying. I mean, I'm sure his Fenris age is older than that, but it looks like he probably really was changed at fourteen. And he said he's from Simonton. There can't possibly be that many fourteen-year-olds who have disappeared or died in Simonton. The place is hardly bigger than Ellison. It'd be in the papers, even if it was decades ago."

"What if he was lying?" Silas asks.

Scarlett shrugs. "He could have been. But he didn't really have any reason to, and... besides, it's not like we have anything else to go on."

"Okay... so where are these papers?" I ask, sliding the eggs onto a single plate and tossing three forks down. There's not a lot of point in washing three plates when there's plenty of room to divide one into three sections, in my opinion.

"On microfilm, at the library," Scarlett replies.

The microfilm room is freezing, as though book lovers don't heat this space out of loyalty to real pages. We've been here for hours, so long that my mind is starting to spin with newspaper articles even when the machine isn't in fast-forward mode. Today was supposed to be the first day of my community center classes, but I've pretty much abandoned the idea in order to run through ancient pages of the *Simonton Banner-Herald*.

I sigh, scanning through an obituaries page.

Joseph Woodlief

April 8, 1973–June 23, 1987

Joseph Woodlief, son of Ruth and Eckener Woodlief, passed away the evening of June 23 in his home. Joseph was an active church member and scholar recently accepted to the prestigious St. Martin's Boys' School. He excelled in rowing and was an avid lover of classical music.

Joseph is survived by his parents, Ruth and Eckener; three aunts; seven uncles; maternal grandparents; eight siblings, Stewart, Katherine, Farley, Bradley, David, Todd, Benjamin, and his younger sister, Abbygale. Services will be private; the family will be accepting social calls of mourning the evening of June 30 beginning at seven o'clock.

"Is this something? He was fourteen," I say through a yawn, pointing at my screen. The picture is blanched and hard to make out, and it looks as if it was taken when the boy was much younger, no more than five or six.

Scarlett kicks the wall to roll her chair toward me. She studies the obituary carefully, reading each word.

"It could be him. Face is similar, I think," Silas murmurs from over my shoulder, his breath on my neck dizzying.

"That 'services will be private' part is somewhat

suspicious, since if he turned Fenris, they wouldn't have a body to bury," Scarlett adds.

Silas nods in agreement. "What's the name? Joseph Woodlief? Hang on, I think I just saw that name," he says and slides his chair back to his microfilm machine. He spins the dates back and forth for a few moments, then points to the monitor. "A few months before he died—just after his birthday, actually—he got arrested for"—he spins the dial again to see the second page—"for attacking a girl at a neighborhood luncheon. She got away and told the cops."

"Well, that's even more suspicious than the private services," Scarlett says, perking up. "It takes a while for the soul to die—I bet the wolf was starting to take over the body for a few months before the family issued the official obituary." A librarian peeks in the room, smiling warmly at us, and Scarlett looks at the wall to hide her scars. She looks back once the librarian is gone, then reclines in her chair, mental wheels turning.

"So he...he was a Potential because...why?" We all turn and read the obituary again and again, until Scarlett sighs. "I thought there'd be something, some hint..."

"Well, we have nothing to compare him to. Maybe we need more information on a second Fenris," I suggest. It was the wrong thing to say, I quickly realize, as Scarlett's face darkens in frustration.

"A second Fenris will be near impossible. This one was young enough to be unique and told us where he was from. The others are just regular, nameless, placeless men. By the time we hunt them down, the Potential's moon phase will be over."

"I dunno, Scarlett...maybe it's nothing specific," Silas says. Scarlett shoots him a hard look and he shrugs. "Maybe there's no exact science as to who becomes a Potential. Maybe it's just fate or something."

"No. There has to be a reason," she wheels back. I take her hand. I can't blame her. I wouldn't like the idea of its being my fate to lose an eye either.

Silas glances at his watch. "We've been here for five hours." He gives me a meaningful look, one that translates into "you're supposed to be gone now." When did Silas and I learn to speak without words? I'd hoped he had forgotten about the classes and would let me off the hook.

"I can't leave. I wonder... you suppose there's any truth to that whole silver-bullet-kills-werewolves thing? Or maybe... that attack happened right after his birthday—maybe it's something to do with that..." she says, then rises from her chair and hurries out of the microfilm room in the direction of the restroom.

"You have class," Silas whispers as soon as she's out the door.

"Silas, come on, we have a job to do."

"Rosie, come on, you have class."

I glare at him. "This is more important."

"Scarlett and I are more than capable of handling this on our own. Go. Have fun. Experience life outside of hunting."

"If you say 'experience life outside of hunting' one more time, I'm going to knife you."

Silas grins. "Go. I'll cover for you. I'll even come get you if we find anything that has to be acted on right away. You shouldn't be chained to this unless you choose to be."

I stare at the microfilm, then at Silas, then at Scarlett's chair. I want to go to a class. I really, really want to go to a class, to not worry about hunting for just an hour, to see what life would be like if I were a normal sixteen-year-old.

"If Scarlett finds out—"

"She won't, unless you tell her. Go," he says, letting his fingers rest on my hand. He smiles as he looks at his fingertips on my skin. I want badly, so badly, to turn my hand over and intertwine my fingers with his.

He's right. I should go. I press my lips together to hide a smile, then jump up, touching Silas's shoulder briefly before racing from the microfilm room. I dart out the library's front doors, gritting my teeth until I'm certain that I'm not going to hear Scarlett calling my name in confusion and anger.

Fifteen minutes and a lot of running later, I burst through the community center's doors, getting a lot of annoyed glances from a class of pregnant women finishing up yoga in the dance studio across from the registration desk.

I can't believe I'm doing this. I scan the class board, though there's no need; I've long memorized the course offerings. *Something small, Rosie. Something simple, basic. Don't get too carried away—it's just a class.*

I force myself to breathe and hand the lady at the desk my class card.

"Which class, sweetheart?" the old woman says, her hand shaking a bit as if my card is incredibly heavy.

"Origami for Beginners."

The old woman looks at me, a bit surprised, and then swipes my card through the machine. Origami. Simple, innocent—Scarlett can't get *too* mad over my taking something as lame as origami, can she?

The pregnant women vacate the studio after lots of bowing to their instructor, and a few community center volunteers push in folding tables and chairs. We all take a seat. A woman with silvery brown hair waves me and the seven or eight other people taking origami toward her.

"New faces today," she says softly, her voice steady and calm. She passes around brightly colored paper, perfectly square and flawlessly smooth.

I spend the next hour making a rose, a crane, a ballerina. I anticipate that it will be stupid and boring, but instead... something fills me. It's not necessarily a love for origami, but rather, this amazing sensation of being *normal*.

I listen to the teacher gently talking—fold here, flip here—the paper sliding beneath my fingers for no reason other than the fact that I *want* it to be so. It feels as if I'm more than I was before I walked into the class, more than just a hunter. I'm also something silly and pointless and wonderful, doing something that isn't my responsibility, but rather just my simple desire. Somehow I get lost in the folds, each one chipping away some of the hardness that the years of hunting have built up, until I feel new and bare and wonderful.

When I slip back into the apartment, I find Silas's eyes almost instantly, as though mine are drawn to his. He smiles at me slightly, more with his eyes than his lips. Scarlett looks up at me from a pile of notes and library books.

"Hey, Rosie," she grumbles. "Look, I know you went grocery shopping and all, but I was hungry, so...we kind of ordered Chinese food." She points with a pen at the kitchen counter, where half a dozen little square boxes are lined up. "I'm sorry, though. Wait—did you go grocery shopping?" she asks, motioning toward the lack of bags in my hands.

"I"—*think fast, Rosie*—"I forgot money, actually. Made an idiot out of myself at the register."

Scarlett rolls her eye but smiles a little and retreats back into her notebooks.

Grocery shopping? I mouth at Silas. He shrugs, then turns on the radio, shuffling the dial until he finds a pop music station. I raise an eyebrow at him and Scarlett snickers. It's cheesy, but I think we all feel it's a welcome reprieve from the news stations buzzing about more murdered girls and urging us to hurry, hurry, hurry.

"It was the best I could come up with," he whispers a notch above the music, his back to Scarlett as he heaps white rice onto his plate.

"What exactly was I supposed to say when I came home without groceries?" I answer, but I can't really get angry. There's still some patterned-paper joy in my heart, I suppose.

"You're smart. I knew you'd figure it out," he answers with a bright smile. "How was it?"

"It was...nice," I say. I glance at Scarlett to be certain she's not looking, then place a folded pink rose into Silas's shirt pocket. My hand lingers on his chest, and I feel his heart beating. I smile and finally pull my hand away.

"What's this?" he murmurs, removing the flower and inspecting it.

"I took origami." I grin and turn to pick through pieces of sweet-and-sour chicken. Silas laughs under his breath.

"Origami, huh? So you're going back?" he whispers.

"Nope."

He pauses and furrows his brow at me.

I blush slightly. "I mean, I was thinking I'd do another type of class. That way I could, you know, try lots of stuff."

He nudges me slightly. "See? Nothing wrong with a little freedom," he says and retreats toward Scarlett, tucking the paper flower back into his shirt pocket. I watch him go, thinking back on the utterly strange day that's now ending in a flash of brilliant sunset outside our apartment windows. I lied to my sister. I learned how to make a paper ballerina. And I can't be certain, but I think I might have officially fallen in love with Silas Reynolds.

CHAPTER ELEVEN

SCARLETT

SOMETHING IS DIFFERENT ABOUT ROSIE.

Something small, something that I don't think anyone except the other half of her heart would notice. She picks up chopsticks and sorts through her Chinese food with an unfamiliar lightness that scares me. How is it possible that anything about Rosie is unfamiliar to me? She plops down on the floor and slides a book over, flipping through it between bites of sweet-and-sour chicken. Silas glances up at her from the book he's scanning for the second time. But I'm the only one making any headway, it seems, with a pile of notes beside me.

I shake my head and turn back to the book I'm poring over: *Myths! Legends! Monsters!* by Dorothea Silverclaw. I somehow doubt that's her real name, just as I doubt she even knows what a Fenris is. She calls them *werewolves* and draws them as cute little wolves that turn into hot teenage boys. She's all about the superstition aspect: garlic stops vampires, ghosts can't cross running water, the seventh son of a seventh son is cursed, faeries want to steal your daughters. Sure, Dorothea. I daresay that the things we learned from Pa Reynolds are far more helpful than anything I've found so far in the library's selection of werewolf lore.

But though Silas and I have written down everything Pa Reynolds ever told us about the Fenris, and I've combined it with everything useful from the library books, we *still* can't pinpoint much about the Potential.

"Maybe we're overthinking it," Rosie says, slamming her book shut.

I sigh and throw down the stack of papers in my hand. "Maybe. Or maybe this is pointless. We have to go hunting again, even if we can't kill anything—maybe we can overhear, get some information or...*something*. Anything." Even I can hear the desperation in my voice. Now finding the Potential is always in my mind, like an addiction. The thought of having to go home empty-handed physically *hurts*.

"Don't worry, Scarlett," Rosie says softly. She's used this same tone of voice to calm me dozens of times before: the first time I cried when I realized what my mangled face looked like, when we ran out of money and sold the first of Oma March's belongings, when I was certain wolves would overrun Ellison without Silas there. It's not what she says, but the way she says it—a way that makes me believe her, no matter what might be true. "We'll go hunting tonight," she adds. I meet her eyes. The mysterious change is there, shielded by a gentle, comforting expression.

Her tone is familiar, but that gaze in her eyes is still new, foreign. We need to go hunting again, and not just because we need information. Hunting brings back that feeling of oneness, the torn-apart heart recombining. Not that there's much point in it, with the Fenris being so focused, but it'll still make things *right,* not just with Rosie, but with Silas too—it binds us together no matter what sort of strange look is in my sister's eyes.

"We'll leave early this evening, then," I say.

"Okay—but I'm thinking, maybe we should change up our game plan," Silas adds, rising to set his plate by the sink. "I mean, we need information *fast.* This isn't a normal hunt."

"Any ideas?" I ask. Things already feel more right—Silas and I planning a hunt, preparing to take to the night.

Silas shrugs as he answers. "Well, we could split up. Cover more ground that way."

I frown, but what can I say? *No, Rosie can't handle going alone?* That I wanted to hunt to strengthen the bindings between Rosie and me, Silas and me? I want to say no, so badly, but the truth is, it's a good tactic and people are dying. I sigh and nod in agreement.

Several hours later, all three of us stand at the bottom of the stairwell. Light from the lampposts outside scatters over Rosie's and Silas's faces—for a moment, it's as if they're scarred like me. Rosie looks nervous, but I know she'll never admit to it. *You can hunt on your own in this city, Rosie. Probably better than I can.*

"Meet back here at what...three in the morning?" I suggest, running my finger along the handle of my hatchet.

"Two," Silas says. "Come on, Lett, some of us sleep. And besides, if we haven't found anything by two, we aren't going to."

I scowl at him but nod. "Fine. Two. Unless you know you're following one or something. In that case, stay with it. Rosie, if you find a group of them..." Rosie gives me a look of frustration and hurt. I don't want to say it—I know it hurts her to hear it—but... "Be careful, Rosie. Please." I feel a little better when Silas gives her a look that repeats my request.

"I will," she answers us with a sigh, tightening her knife belt.

"So, I'll go back toward the park where we saw that pack of three," I say, trying to hide the eagerness in my voice. Three...if only I could see those three again. I won't wait for them to transform this time. "Rosie, why don't you go down Seventeenth Street?"

"That's all businesses—there won't be anyone there this time of night. What's the point?" Rosie gripes, but she nods when I sigh in exasperation.

"And Silas..."

"I'll take the north end of the city. Probably too ritzy for many Fenris to hang out, but they'll also be easier to spot prowling, I imagine," he says, reaching back to check the ax handle and adjust his backpack straps.

"Okay. And two in the morning, right?" I finish. They nod. We hesitate for a moment, each meeting the others' eyes, Silas's lingering on Rosie. Is he worried about her just like I am?

Then we split. Silas heads in the opposite direction, and Rosie and I touch fingertips briefly before turning away from each other at the mouth of Andern Street. I feel her heart quicken as she walks away. One heart, which I'd hoped to reconnect with over a hunt. But not tonight. *Don't be selfish, Scarlett. Dragonflies need you.*

I trudge toward the park, head down and hood up. Something about the park challenges me. The site of my failure—it's as if I need to prove to it that I can hunt successfully. I head for the far end this time, where the trees fade into little bungalow houses and roads. I follow the pumping of music and the buzz of conversations until a house-turned-club appears.

One side of "the Attic" is painted with graffiti, and every time the door swings open, guitar and drum sounds sweep across the street, the notes plowing into me. There's a long line of people waiting to get in. Their shadows are sharp and well defined on the brick wall behind them. They think that *this* is what's real, that the world is just people with pretty hair and nice clothes and cars whizzing by. They haven't seen the sunlight.

Strange how seeing the light can make a person feel so

alone in the darkness, I muse as I duck behind a ridiculously large SUV. This is the perfect spot to watch them, to wait and see who follows girls when they slip away in small packs. I lower myself onto the curb and try to look bored, as though I'm waiting on someone to come take my arm and lead me into the club. A few people glance at me, but their eyes move away quickly.

Watch. Just watch. Minutes pass, maybe longer. Most of the girls who walk away seem to have cars nearby, and no one lurks after them. Maybe the Fenris aren't around this club—maybe I should try another. I rise, but as I do, a group of three girls emerges from the club. One is obviously drunk—she stumbles down the steps as if her legs are made of cloth. The others laugh and help hold her up, though they don't look to be much better off. They pause at the corner, talking and pointing toward various streets. Finally, all seem to agree on a direction, and they begin to walk away from me. I'm about to turn my attention to someone else when I see a man in a dark coat slip away from the Attic's far wall. He blends in well with the other guys, but he moves away from the blasting music and loud chatter, toward the group of three girls.

He's a Fenris. I can feel it. There's something primal in his long, striding steps. I cross to a street that runs parallel, so I can watch without his knowing he's being followed. Why do I have to wait for him to transform, to give him a chance to get away? I don't have to be the bait. I can kill him now. I take a long step closer, like a cat edging toward a mouse. I wrap my fingers around my hatchet.

And then the laughter, that damn bright, horribly bubbly laughter. They're at least my age, so how is it they laugh like children? They aren't like the sparkly club Dragonflies, but some less-adorned breed of Dragonflies in T-shirts and jeans, walking together down the city street with their arms linked and ponytails bobbing. The Fenris watches them hungrily, sniffing the air and grinning sickeningly when he catches the scent of their hair and perfume on the wind. It doesn't matter that people are all around—I can slaughter him like the monster he is, then run. They'll never find me. I *need* this.

Except that it does matter. Seeing the Fenris, seeing what they really are...it changes you. It changes everything, even if they don't take your eyes or your skin. The Dragonflies will never be the same—they'll have seen darkness; they'll *know* it exists despite their glittery eye shadow and glossy lips. They'll never look at the news the same way again, never look at a man noticing their legs the same way, never *feel* the same. I would be killing not only the Fenris, but also the girls' stupid, ignorant innocence.

Go on, monster. Transform. Force my hand. Change right here, in front of everyone. Make me fight you.

But the Fenris doesn't change. He just moves toward them, flicking his cigarette onto the city street. When he does so, the neon lights illuminate his wrist, lighting up a symbol amid the thick veins: an arrow.

I clench my hatchet so hard that my hands pinch and I feel blood vessels begin to pop. God, an Arrow. I watch the Dragonflies, certain that if I stare at him any longer, some sort of animal force will take over and I'll have to attack. As the Fenris approaches them, the Dragonflies toss their hair and sway on their feet like a row of Lipizzan horses, all refined beauty and grace, pointed shoes and glittery skin. He's smiling, grinning, shaking hands and running fingers through his lustrous hair that I know will become matted fur soon enough.

Don't fall for it. Look at his eyes. It's hunger, not desire, in them. I want to shout out, warn them...no. They'd just think I was crazy and I'd lose any element of surprise I have with the wolf.

The Dragonflies and the Fenris begin to walk away together in a chorus of giggles and chatter. I slink behind them, but they're quick and it's hard to follow without being seen. They take a sharp and unexpected turn down Spring Street, a road that's so well lit I'm afraid to follow. *It's okay. Focus.* I turn down an alley that runs parallel to the street, hoping to beat them to the far end so I can be certain of their next turn. I reach the mouth of the alley and peer around the brick corner nervously.

They're gone. Where—

A girl's scream slices through the night, terrified and shrill.

I run toward it, though it's difficult to tell exactly where the shriek is coming from as it echoes off the glass buildings. She cries out again in pain, and another girl screams. Where are they? I run down Peachtree, and a side road appears to my left, so tiny it's barely an alley. Figures loom toward the back,

158

two girls clustered together while a giant wolf circles them, snapping his jaws. There had been three girls, not two. My stomach lurches. I yank my hatchet from my waist and barrel down the tiny alley, screaming an angry war cry. *Please. I can still save you.*

The wolf roars in anger, baring glittering yellow teeth at me. I lift my hatchet—I'll never reach them in time; I'll have to throw it. The wolf's jaws snap, and one girl cries out in terror as his teeth skim her leg. I release the hatchet with so much strength and hatred that my body pitches forward onto the oily pavement as the weapon hurtles through the air.

I brace my hands to push myself up and continue, but my right hand finds something warm and smooth on the pavement. I get just enough of a glance before I'm standing again to realize what it is: a young woman's elbow. Her unattached elbow—just a small curve of skin and bone discarded in the street like a piece of garbage. The ground is awash in red. Red everywhere. Blood, matted hair, and remnants...I gag, despite all I've seen. I close my eye and force myself to stay standing.

I run toward the surviving two Dragonflies and realize with a sick, sinking feeling that they're the only life-forms left at the end of the alley—my thrown weapon missed him. The Fenris is gone into the night, once again powerful and focused after his meal. Anger rushes through me, my tongue too twisted by rage to speak. I swiftly grab my hatchet off the ground.

The girls scream. They clutch each other. Their eyes are wide and terrified, streaming with tears.

"It's gone," I say. I see them scan my body, look at the scars that cover me and the hatchet in my hand. I don't know what else to tell them. Their friend is dead—did they see the wolf devour her, or did he pick the first one off in the darkness? Someone's friend, someone's daughter, granddaughter, someone's sister...nothing more than food for a monster. My stomach tightens again and I try to vomit into the gutter but fail. I take a step closer to the girls and they scream again. I cover the scarred side of my face with my hood to settle their nerves.

"Come on. I'll walk you to a taxi. You should go home."

They tremble, afraid to move. Afraid to breathe. I know how they feel—they think it's all a horrible nightmare as they shakily walk down the alley. Is this how I looked, standing in front of my sister so many years ago? *Nothing can help you, Dragonflies. Say good-bye to the world you knew, welcome to the mouth of the cave. I'm sorry I failed you. I'm so, so sorry.*

I guide them around the dead girl's tiny, scattered body parts to the main road. I lead them to a taxi and they take off into the night. They don't look back, as though they're afraid I'm part of the bad dream as well. I think they might be right.

I consider taking the bus back to the apartment, but instead I walk, trying to ignore the deep, gnawing feeling in my heart. My mind replays finding the girl's elbow so often that I keep thinking it's beneath my fingertips. The thought mixes with memories of emerging from Oma March's bedroom, covered in the dead Fenris's blood, hoping to run into Oma March's arms only to see there was nothing left of her but a bloodied, shredded apron. It's as if the Fenris know to leave a small piece of the victim, a piece that always lurks in front of all the happy memories of the dead.

A loud stereo sings out in the night, car tires squeal, but other than that the street is empty. I trudge forward like some kind of zombie, too dead to feel anything. Well, almost anything. Self-hatred fills me. The wolf is free, when I had the chance to stop it and didn't.

I wonder if Rosie has had any luck tonight.

I know the idea of my sister being successful should make me happy, but there's some dull, disgusting feeling of jealousy swimming through my body that I think might burst out. Hunting sings to me, calms me, comforts me. I am a hunter. Or was. Now I am a failure. I yank the eye patch off and snatch my cloak off my shoulders.

The junkie is on the steps of the apartment building, but he doesn't growl at me. Instead he simply stares at the space where my eye should be and then steps out of my way with a sort of dignity that alarms me. The flickering streetlight catches the black teardrop tattoos on his face, and I can sense the shadows that my scars throw across my skin, as if they're tattooed on as well. I hit the steps slowly, feet heavy, and push open the door, trudging until I get to the top floor.

"No, they thought I was a girl, actually, up till the moment I was born. I think they were disappointed, to tell you the truth."

"Really? That explains a lot." My sister giggles in a voice that's so Dragonfly-like that it causes my cheeks to heat up in frustration. That, and what I'm seeing: Rosie is lying down on the couch, Screwtape asleep on her stomach. Silas is leaning back in one of the chairs, feet propped up on the graffiti table. Both are wearing pajamas. Both look warm. Comfortable. Bored, even. They don't look like they've been hunting, obsessing, trailing Dragonflies to protect them from monsters, trying harder than anything to make the world a slightly better place. They don't look as if they've had to deal with a slaughtered girl.

"Scarlett." My sister says my name like she's surprised and worried.

I drop my cloak and eye patch on the floor and turn around, seething, taking my time to lock the door behind me. *Breathe, Scarlett. Don't yell.*

"Lett? You okay?" Silas asks. His chair thuds to the ground and I hear his footsteps behind me.

"A girl died. I couldn't get there in time to stop it. She died. A Fenris devoured her," I say. I turn back toward them, gritting my teeth. The images of the Dragonfly, the Arrow, Oma March flash in my head.

"Scarlett," Rosie says again, jaw dropping in horror.

"I'm sure you did all you could," Silas says firmly.

I raise my eyebrows. "Of course I did what I could," I snap. "Because *I* was out hunting. Not in here chatting it up."

"Wait, Lett, you agreed to meet back here at two o'clock."

"And?" I hiss at him.

"It's four in the morning, Scarlett," Rosie says, dumping Screwtape on the ground and padding toward me with bare feet.

I glance at the clock on the radio. They're right. Four oh three. I shake my head and stomp toward the bathroom, flicking on the tap and splashing water across my face. When I come back out, Rosie and Silas are watching me carefully, lingering close to each other. Rosie still looks different, and it scares me.

"Scarlett, come on," Rosie says. "I made peanut butter cookies while we were waiting for you. Sit down for a little bit."

"Sit down?" I almost spit. Emotion bubbles through me, rises up from my toes to my head until I think my vision is doubling, tripling. "I come here, thinking I'll sleep for two hours and then go back out to try to do something, and I find you, my partner and my *sister,* just...just sitting. How can you sit? How can you just relax when you know there are monsters in this world, monsters that you have the power to stop?" My voice is high, higher than I ever remember it being, and I realize that the thick lump in my throat is from tears. I don't cry. I never cry. But I'd like to.

Don't they care? I thought we were all here for the same purpose. She's my sister — how can she not care? I took on the wolves for her, I stood in front of her, and now in exchange I *need* her to care.

Silas speaks, gently. "Because, Lett. No one can spend

163

their life fighting. Come on, sit down with us." He steps toward me and extends a hand. He has a way of talking sometimes that makes me feel as if it's only him and me in the room. I want to take his hand. More than anything, I'd like to sit down and not think about hunting for just a moment, to ignore my responsibilities like they so easily can. *They*—the two beautiful people, unmarred, an exclusive club. Of course they want to sit and talk through the night instead of hunt.

Silas and Rosie lean toward each other, like they can each shield the other from me, like I'm the outsider instead of a sister, instead of a partner. I shake my head in frustration and duck back into the bathroom, letting the door slam behind me. I turn on the ice-cold shower to drown out the sound of their hushed whispers, the sirens in the city below, and the muffled, choked sobs that force themselves up from my ugly, scarred throat.

CHAPTER TWELVE

Rosie

I don't go to a class at the community center the following week. I make ramen noodles every night, and we eat the leftovers the following morning. We barely leave the apartment. It feels as if we're standing still. Scarlett and I push the couch aside and train in the apartment. She does it because she says I'll lose my edge if we don't. I do it because I think she'll lose her mind if we don't. She counts down the days till the next full moon like a death-row inmate counting down steps to the electric chair.

Of course, I might lose my mind as well. I'm in love with a woodsman and I simply *can't* be. Scarlett has no time for love, so why should I? But it gets harder and harder not to blurt out my feelings to him; while my sister spends the days poring over notes on Fenris, Silas tugs me away, convinces me to walk around the block or the street or the entire city until we lose ourselves in a flow of conversation. I try not to touch him, not because I don't want to, but because I'm afraid that if I let my hand brush his or he puts a casual arm around my waist, I won't be able to stop. I'll want to touch him again. And again. I'll want him to pick me up into his arms like he did the night he returned to Ellison. I already want him in a way that delights and frightens me at once.

And Scarlett knows.

Well, she doesn't *know*, but she's not stupid—I see her cast Silas and me suspicious glances every now and then. I think she knows we're pulling at the ropes that bind the three of us together; I just don't think she knows that Silas and I are pulling as one.

But I am a hunter, and when we return from a walk and see Scarlett, brows knitted together in what's become a permanent frown, the point is driven home: I can't act. I have to wait for the feelings to pass. I owe Scarlett my life, and if she insists I spend it chasing Potentials and Fenris, well...it's the price I pay.

By the following Tuesday, Scarlett has brought home another giant stack of books from the library with Silas's help. They're fairly ridiculous—books on wild wolves, monsters, myths...She's getting desperate, rereading books that can't possibly help us figure out who the Potential is. I force her to eat something for breakfast, but by lunch, I feel as if I'm going to snap. Energy leaps under my skin, begging me to do something, *anything* but sit in the apartment for even another second.

Silas groans as he stretches toward the bathroom door where Scarlett is showering. "Hell, *one* wolf. If she could just bag one wolf, I think she'd relax. Is there anything I can do, anything I haven't thought of?"

"No," I sigh. "I don't think so. You know how she is."

"Yeah," Silas answers quietly, but there's new guilt in his eyes. "But she isn't always like this. She's hardly even thinking straight. Am I..." He pauses and looks down as he walks to the kitchen. "Am I pulling you away from her?"

I blink, surprised—is he asking what he means to me? He pours himself a glass of water while I try to come up with some words. When I don't, Silas speaks again.

"You know, telling you about those classes...I don't want her to feel like she's losing you. I just wanted you to be able to live a little. Maybe I should mind my own business—"

"Oh," I answer quickly. "No, Silas. Those are my decisions."

"Right. It's just..." Silas grimaces and runs his fingers over the condensation on his glass. "I don't want to play any part in breaking up the two of you. I know what it's like to be on one side of a fence while your siblings are on the other, furious with you. I can't do that to you and Scarlett. I can't... lose both you and Scarlett, to be honest. You're all I have left...She's lost weight—did you notice?"

"Lett and I will be okay. We've always been okay," I say

softly, though I'm not sure I'm telling the truth. It isn't okay to hope your sister isn't in the room with you and Silas; it isn't okay to betray her, to sneak around behind her back. If I still thought of Silas as just a friend, I might hug him for comfort, but there's that rumbling desire in my chest that is afraid I'll hug him too closely, touch him too tenderly. How can my sister and I be okay when all I want to do is *touch* her partner?

I fold my arms over my chest and lean back against the counter. I *have* noticed she's lost weight, and I've noticed the dark circles under her eyes, the way she twists and turns in the night like she never did before. The wolves haunt her, while I lie awake longing for the boy only a few yards away... I'm a terrible person.

"I'm sorry, Rosie," Silas says when he sees the sadness in my eyes. I shake my head, trying to brush the look away, but Silas isn't easily deterred. He hesitates, then leans on the counter beside me, moving slowly as if he needs verification that each move is acceptable, wanted.

"Hey," he says, resting two fingers on my arm. It starts as a friendly gesture. I press my lips together as he slides his palm up my arm and around my shoulders. Silas pauses, and though I'm not certain, I think he realizes that the touch is far more than friendly as well—a thought that makes me dizzy but practically forces me to move my own hand to the small of his back. I close my eyes and inhale, and I feel Silas's breath on my forehead, hear his relaxed heartbeats. His lips are so close to me, I could easily tilt my head back and kiss him if I were braver. It's hard to *not* sigh, like the exhausted breath is building up in my chest and I'm holding it back, though more than anything I want to release it, to truly hold myself against him—

Scarlett's shower cuts off. Silas snatches his arm away and I lean back up, head swirling from the quick change.

"Um...right," Silas says, looking startled. He looks at me. "Okay, back to studying Potentials, wolves, important stuff..." He shakes his head as if he's casting away a mental fog.

I bite my lip. I want to get out of here—I *need* to get out of here, or the thumping desire for Silas is going to consume me. There's no way Scarlett won't figure it out if I can't escape and get my mind off him. It's just for a little while—I can go get groceries or something. Silas will help her research. We can't keep paying for Chinese food. I meet Silas's eyes, dashes of sky colors in the monotone apartment.

"I'll be back," I say, then dart for the door.

"Wait!" he whispers sharply. He lunges toward the couch and tosses me the belt with my knives on it. "Just in case." I catch it with one hand and swing it around my waist. Silas gives me a sly smile—does he know the effect that smile has on me?

I manage a feeble smile in return and leave. I inhale deeply once I get outside. Have I even been outside in days? The scents of cigarette smoke and fresh air mingle in my nose. I hurry off our dilapidated block, rubbing the bills together in my pocket as I head toward Kroger. Just a few groceries and I'll go back.

A sharp breeze whips over me, swirling my hair into knots. Cars honk, traffic halts in the intersection, and I dart between taxis to cross the road. Maybe a short class—I've been hunting-focused for so long. Silas's face keeps flashing through my mind, encouraging me, supporting me.

Just one really quick class. Thirty minutes or less.

The community center is several blocks away, but I run; if I'm focusing on avoiding the crowds of people on the sidewalk, on putting my feet one in front of the other, then I can't focus on the tiny spark of guilt in the back of my mind. I dart through the community center door and hand the smiling woman behind the desk my class card.

"Which class?" she asks.

"Um..." I scan down the board. Cake Decorating, Belly Dancing, Stock Market Trading...

"Natural Drawing," I say quickly. "Wait—do I need drawing stuff?"

"No, supplies are included with the course. It's in room three and probably starting shortly. Are you eighteen, dear?"

The question throws me as I step away from the desk toward the classroom. "Um, yeah," I answer quickly. The woman nods and turns back to her desk.

Well, I'm sixteen, close enough. Scarlett is eighteen, which makes Silas...wow. What does someone Silas's age want with a kid like me? I enter the room and take one of only two available easels that are close to a chair sitting in the center of the classroom. Mostly middle-aged women chat hurriedly on either side of me, but I barely hear them. Maybe I'm misinterpreting everything with Silas...maybe the fluttery feeling is just on my end.

Two men enter the room, one old and mustached and the other young and tawny-headed, wearing sweats and a worn T-shirt. He looks like Silas, actually—god, what am I, obsessed? But there really is something of the woodsman in the younger man's face, with his full lips, his slightly curled hair that turns like tendrils around his ears...I look away before studying him too closely.

"All right, ladies, are we ready?" the older man says enthusiastically. There's a loud rustling of paper as we all flip the enormous sketchbooks on our easels until we find blank sheets. I draw a few soft lines on my page, unsure what—

Non-Silas rips off his T-shirt, revealing lightly defined muscles on his pale chest. I raise an eyebrow just as he tugs at the waist of the sweatpants. They drop to the floor in a fluid, sweeping motion.

There's nothing underneath them. At all.

My charcoal slips through my suddenly sweaty fingers.

Non-Silas steps out of the puddle of his clothes and moves to the center of the room, fluorescent lights reflecting off his slick abdomen. He's smiling as though he isn't naked, smiling as though I didn't somehow manage to get the seat closest to him. As if I can't see...um...*everything* only a few feet from my face, making my mind clumsily spiral. I squeeze my eyes shut for a moment; he looks like Silas in the face, and because of that I keep wondering if he looks akin to Silas *everywhere else.*

"All right, ladies, this will be a seven-minute pose. Ready?" the older man says, positioning himself behind the other empty easel. The roomful of housewives nod in one hungry motion. I quiver. "Go!" the older man says, starting the stopwatch. Non-Silas poses, something reminiscent of Michelangelo's *David,* only instead of marble eyes looking into nothingness, non-Silas is staring almost straight at me.

Draw. I'm supposed to be drawing. I grab a new piece of charcoal from the bottom of the easel and begin hastily making lines in my sketchbook. I can't *not* look at him, or he'll think I'm not drawing him. I glance hurriedly, trying to avoid the region my eyes continuously return to. I start to feel fluttery.

How long has it been? Surely it's been seven minutes. I try to add some tone to my drawing's chest. I wonder what Silas's chest looks like...*Stop! Stop stop stop stop stop—*

"Right, then!" the older man says as his stopwatch beeps loudly and the scratchy sound of charcoal on paper ends. *Thank you, sir, thank you—*

"Annnnd next pose!"

Non-Silas turns his head away, till all I can see is his wren-colored hair and his side, including a side view of... how many times am I going to have to draw this man's *area?* What's worse is that he looks even more like Silas now that

I can't see his eyes. *Just* like Silas, I bet. My eyes linger longer than necessary now that non-Silas isn't staring straight at me.

By the end of the class, I've drawn eight mediocre pictures of him, each one with a large white void in the crotch area. The housewives compare drawings with ravenous looks in their eyes as non-Silas tugs his pants back on and leaves the room, nodding politely. I picture him naked again.

I sprint from the class, abandoning my sketches—how could I explain them to Scarlett or Silas? *Stop thinking of Silas, stop thinking of Silas.* I dart into the Kroger, relieved when the cool air of the frozen-foods section splashes over my skin. I grab ice cream and frozen peas—anything cold. I hold the bag of frozen peas against my neck as I wait to check out. Finally, the flustered feeling drains away and I manage to go a few moments without thinking about the nude man I just saw.

I hurry back to the apartment, wondering how long I've been gone. I push the door open, then promptly drop the frozen peas.

Silas grins at me, shirtless, slightly toned chest glimmering in the sunlight pouring in through the dirty windows. His pants are slung wantonly low on his hips, and I can't help thinking about the drawings I left behind, the way non-Silas's abs looked nearly identical to real-Silas's, and therefore everything might look identical... My face flushes and I exhale shakily.

Then Scarlett kicks Silas solidly in the stomach.

Silas grunts and falls backward, grimacing. "You still have to go out tonight," he chokes out as Scarlett extends a hand to help him up. Her hair is in a tight, high ponytail that wags back and forth with her laughter.

"I still won," she snickers in response. Sweat sparkles on her stomach, droplets running down the thick scar that crosses her abdomen. She has her shirt tucked into the bottom of her sports bra, like she typically does when she's training. She tugs Silas to standing as he rubs his stomach tenderly. She never trains like that with me — neither of them does. Ever since they began training together just a year or two after the attack, they've never held back on each other. It used to make me jealous, but somehow it comforts me now. *See, I'm not tugging my sister's partner away from her. The three of us are still a team.*

"You got distracted," my sister tells Silas, mopping the back of her neck.

Silas grins at her. "Unfair. Rosie came in and surprised me."

"Yeah, yeah," Scarlett says. She knocks against his shoulder good-naturedly as she glances toward me. "What'd you buy at Kroger?"

"Uh...I bought..." It takes me a moment to collect my thoughts and remember. "I bought ice cream. And peas."

"For dinner?" Scarlett asks. Silas nods at me quickly — *yes,* the nod tells me, *say it's for dinner.*

"Yep. I thought we could use the veggies and...dairy."

Scarlett doesn't look convinced, but she turns on the

174

radio and rummages through the refrigerator for the pitcher of water.

"So how was the grocery store?" Silas asks me, so casually that I wonder if there's no double meaning to the question.

"It was fine," I say, but I can feel my eyes sparkle. Silas smiles at me and takes a long sip of water, hair falling in front of his eyes. I wonder how long I could look at him if I weren't always afraid of Scarlett catching me. Scarlett goes over to the radio, then scribbles something down on a pad of paper, sighing deeply.

"Two people died yesterday," she notes, interrupting my flowery thoughts. She shakes her head as she moves to join us in the kitchen. My mouth feels dry as guilt sweeps around me, and she continues, "Two girls. Fenris, I'm sure. They were on the opposite side of town from us, found decapitated. It's where most of the Fenris are, I think, though I'm sort of surprised they left so much...evidence. I wonder if location has something to do with the Potential?"

"No," Silas says, shaking the hair away from his face. "I don't think that makes sense. Otherwise they'd just hang out in one location instead of searching the city."

"Ah, good point." Scarlett nods and scribbles the thought down on the tattered notebook page of clues she's been working on. She digs out a spoonful of ice cream with a discouraged expression.

"Two?" I say. My voice sounds very small.

"Yes," Scarlett responds. "Both under eighteen, I think."

175

"Two girls my age," I say slowly. I sink into one of the kitchen chairs and close my eyes for a moment. Two more girls died, and I was at the community center. Scarlett trained, researched, tried to do good, and I was drawing some guy's penis. It's okay. I can make up for it. "When are we going hunting tonight?" I ask my sister.

Scarlett looks mildly surprised and very pleased, but she answers, "We're not, actually. That was what Silas and I were sparring for. He thinks I need to get out more—"

"You do," Silas interrupts.

"—so we're going bowling."

"Bowling?" I ask, bewildered that Scarlett has other plans the one time I want to hunt.

"Yeah. He said he'd train with me only if we could go bowling tonight. Though we are still hunting on the walk back," Scarlett says, brandishing her spoon at Silas.

"Of course, of course. But first, we bowl!"

Scarlett rolls her eye at him, then looks back to me. "What he said."

I nod and try to swallow the thick lump in my throat. I owe my sister everything, and she's finally relenting, finally giving us all the free time I wanted. But only after I stole it.

CHAPTER THIRTEEN

SCARLETT

"I DON'T KNOW HOW TO BOWL."

"Right, and that's a problem, since this place really screams 'professional bowling,'" Silas snips back, rolling his eyes. The bowling alley—Shamrock Lanes—is lit up in dusky yellow lamps and bright pink and green neon lights. The floor is a shabby, faded leopard-print carpet that's worn to the cement underneath in some parts, and everyone working here seems to have a mustache. Even the women.

Pitchers of beer rest on the tables by every lane, and the thunderous roll of bowling balls and clattering pins is almost deafening. I get a few odd looks from girls with brassy peroxide hair. I glare at Silas and adjust my eye patch.

"Ignore them, Lett," he says gently.

"I don't care about them," I snap back. I *do* care about

the fact that we should be hunting. But I don't think saying it for the millionth time will convince him. I turn my back on the idiots staring at me.

Rosie looks delighted, and the pink lights only make her flushed cheeks more alive, more inviting. She doesn't resemble me at all lately. Up until recently, I've always thought that Rosie looks the way I would have had I not been attacked, save for a freckle or two. Now I'm not so sure. You'd never catch me blushing. And could my face ever have lifted into that expression? Her muscles don't flex the way mine do; her eyes don't dart to assess every sound and movement in the room.

Silas doles out pairs of red and black bowling shoes that are coming apart at the soles. Rosie takes hers and meanders toward our lane—fifteen. I peer over Silas's shoulder as he opens his wallet.

"You have money," I comment.

"I have *some* money. Enough money for bowling."

"More money than we have," I complain pointlessly. I'm about to turn away when something in the billfold catches my eye. Something pale pink and out of place. "What's this?" I ask, and before he can answer, I sweep the slip of paper from the wallet. It's a paper rose, not entirely symmetrical and with creases that are a bit round.

"It's a flower," he answers casually as the clerk hands him a fistful of change. He whips the paper flower out of my fingers and places it back in his wallet.

"So what's with the flower?" I ask as we walk toward my sister.

Silas grins, and his expression is unusually sappy. "It was a gift from a friend."

"Ah. A friend," I snicker, smacking him with one of my bowling shoes. "So is your new girlfriend in Atlanta, or back in Ellison? I'm impressed, Silas. You really don't waste any time."

"No! Really. A friend," he says slowly. I don't press the issue. Silas and I have always told each other most everything, but his array of girlfriends is a topic that's off-limits. I'm not sure if it's that he's shy to tell me or if he knows I don't want to hear about the myriad of beautiful, flawless girls he wants. *Must be nice,* I think, *to have enough time to both hunt and fall in love.*

Rosie's pecking away at a keyboard when we reach her, typing LET, ROS, and SIL into the score screen. I shake my head at Silas and slide into a seafoam-colored plastic seat beside my sister. Our lane is shelved between several happy and drunk forty-somethings and a group of younger men. I try to avoid both groups' eyes, which isn't difficult with the sensory overload that is Shamrock Lanes.

At the opposite end of the bowling alley is a cover band of aging hipsters. They break into a very questionable version of some eighties song just as Rosie and Silas select bowling balls. I sigh and rise to select one as well.

"Who's first?" I ask.

"Silas is," Rosie says, beaming. It's hard not to feel rather lighthearted myself, surrounded by the two people I'm closest to, even if it's in a grimy place that reeks of cigarettes.

Silas does a goofy walk toward the lane and sends his lime green ball spinning directly into the gutter. Then Rosie, and finally me. I manage to knock three pins down, something I rub in Silas's face. He orders a beer for himself and swigs it between gutter balls, and we all—the entire bowling alley—try to sing along with the band when they put the lyrics up on the television screens. For what feels like the first time in ages, it's hard to think about hunting, as though the flashing pink lights have scared the thoughts to the back of my mind, where they linger, ever present but silent.

"Are you having fun?" Rosie asks me with a concerned look. She's been giving me that look a lot lately.

I smile despite myself. "Yes, I'm having fun. But don't tell Silas. He'll get all full of himself."

"Too late for that. Just got a spare, ladies," Silas interrupts with a buzzed-looking grin.

"I can beat that," Rosie replies, sticking her tongue out at him and approaching the ball-return bar. The young guys in the lane next to us howl with laughter as one swings the bowling ball between his legs, sending it slowly twirling down the hardwood. A few are staring at my sister. One in particular is taller than the rest; dark brown hair falls in front of his eyes, and he's got a willowy sort of build. Simply put, I can tell he's handsome despite the flashing lights and distracting sounds. I feel envious and protective all at once as the tall guy looks between Silas and Rosie. Probably trying to figure out if he has a chance with my sister. I force a low laugh at the prospect and squint my eye for a better look at his companions. They're *all* fairly attractive, with rock-star-trendy haircuts and stylishly torn clothes.

Wait. My heart beats faster as I rise and head toward the lane for my turn. Did I just see what I thought I saw? I close my eye for a moment and try to shake away the flashing lights as I approach the lane, Rosie cheering me on from the seafoam-green seats. One of the younger guys—the tallest one—stands up to bowl at nearly the same instant. I hold my bowling ball, waiting for him, and the sounds of the alley fade away. My mind clears, my eye narrows, the flashing lights dim. The guy extends his arm and releases his ball, sending it barreling toward the pins. That's when I see it: a clear, crisp black arrow, covering up a fading black bell. Almost as soon as I see it, it vanishes again, hidden underneath a thick-banded watch.

"Bowl already, Lett!" Silas shouts as the sounds of the alley career back into focus. I toss my ball halfheartedly down the lane and turn back toward my sister and Silas without even watching it.

I don't need to say it. They see my expression and their faces fall. I pretend to look toward the snack bar as I study each of the guys. Fenris, all of them. Some are wearing long sleeves so I can't see the pack signs, but I know. I was so stupid—the lights and noise distracted me. We've been sitting next to wolves this entire time.

Wolves, I mouth to Silas and Rosie as I sit down. Silas grits his teeth and nods without looking at the Fenris; Rosie's eyes flash their way. She smiles sweetly—I suppose one of them caught her gaze for a moment.

Silas and Rosie glance at each other, a sad look passing between them. A private look. They wanted to have fun tonight and think I can't imagine that. But our purpose comes first.

"Get them to the parking lot. I'll wait there," Silas says quickly. He stands and slips his bowling shoes off, making a big production of it, then hurries across the leopard-print carpet and out the door. The tall Fenris watches Silas leave, then turns a casual eye back to my sister and me, watching every move, waiting, wanting. I look pointedly at Rosie.

"Me?" she asks. What, she thinks I'm going to hit on them, now that they've seen me with the crazy eye patch and giant scar? Sure. Rosie nods when I don't answer and stands. She exhales like an actor beginning to focus, then grins and flips her hair, running on her toes toward her pink bowling ball. She dips low to throw it, arching her back so her curves are silhouetted by the neon green shamrock-shaped lights. The Fenris stare at her lustfully. Jealousy stirs up in my stomach again, but I force it back down.

"Nice throw," the tall one says, nodding at Rosie as she heads back to her seat. I get up to bowl my turn but try to listen in as Rosie talks to the Fenris.

"Come here often?" she asks.

"Often enough," the Fenris answers, voice gruff yet melodic. You'd never suspect he was dangerous. "You come here often?" He repeats my sister's question, flexing his biceps to show off a barbed-wire tattoo.

"No...this is my first time."

"Virgin," the Fenris teases, and the others snicker. He seems to be the leader of this small group, though he's no Alpha, I'm somehow sure. Rosie smiles demurely.

"So how old are you, sweetheart?" he asks, flashing a white grin. Those teeth plan to rip her apart in just minutes.

"Sixteen."

"Old enough to drive! You know, I have a sweet car just outside. Brand-new convertible, bright red."

"Hey, man," another Fenris says under his breath. "You know we aren't supposed to...tonight."

"Man, go bowl; it's your turn," the barbed-wire Fenris says dismissively. A few turn to stare as a crowd of younger teenage girls bop by.

"So how old are *you*, then?" Rosie asks quickly, trying to get their attention back. She lounges in the chair and twirls her hair between her fingers.

"Twenty-eight," he answers with a smirk, shoving his hands into his pockets. To hide the transformation, I think. His eyes are so gentle, so full of kindness...It's disgusting.

"Aren't you a little old to want to show me your...car?" Rosie asks, raising an eyebrow. The Fenris grins hungrily.

"I'm not too old to show a lady a good time. Twenty-eight just means I have more...experience."

Twenty-eight. He *might* have more experience—I wish there was a good way to tell how long a Fenris has actually been a wolf, instead of just his age when he changed. Twenty-eight doesn't tell me much; neither does fourteen or forty-nine. The numbers race through my mind as I punch them in on the scoreboard. *Twenty-eight. Fourteen. Twenty-one. Forty-nine.* Seven years. They were all changed on a seventh year.

"That's it. That's it," I whisper. My heart thunders and my lips actually crack a smile. Rosie glances at me, eyes questioning, and I lean closer to her. "The ages are all multiples of seven," I whisper. "Potentials can be changed only on their seven-year birthdays, between the full-moon phases..." I pause, my mind practically clicking, and then remember a detail from Joseph Woodlief's obituary. "*After* their birthdays. It's the full-moon phase after their birthdays. Joseph had just turned fourteen. That's why it makes them go from a normal guy to a Potential, because they've just turned the right age. That's it."

Rosie gives an almost unseen nod and I catch a look of amazement glimmer through her eyes, almost totally obscured by the black lights.

"You want to see the car?" the Fenris with the barbed-wire tattoo asks, motioning with his head toward the bowling alley door. Rosie smiles shyly and shrugs. *Yes, Rosie, yes, get him to want you.* There's some warmth in my heart, some energy that I haven't felt since leaving Ellison. One step closer to finding the Potential, a pack of Fenris in hand. We are hunters again.

"Man, come on, we're not supposed to be..." another Fenris says to the first. A waitress sets another pitcher of beer down onto the wolves' table, but their eyes are all on Rosie.

184

A few shove their hands into their pockets, I'm certain in an effort to hide the claws that are beginning to grow.

"Come on," the barbed-wire Fenris urges again, all charm.

"Okay. Real quick. And my sister has to come too. You know, to protect me from you guys," she says with a giggle. Rosie is doing this flawlessly. I ignore the Fenris's sneer as he regards me, eye patch and all.

"Of course," he says in a forced tone, then holds out his arm. Rosie links her arm through his, sticks her chest out, and tosses her hair. I follow them, and the rest of the pack follows me, one stopping to tell the attendant not to reset our lanes. They'll want to play a few more frames after they feast on us, I imagine.

The Fenris sweeps my sister past the gum-ball and toy machines, past a pack of scrawny teenage boys who try to hide the joints they're smoking as we pass. Cool air rushes over us as the Fenris throws open the bowling alley door. I don't see Silas, but I'm certain he's here, watching. The pack ignores me, huddling behind my sister while the barbed-wire wolf prattles on about horsepower and car engines. He points at a spot in front of him.

And then he freezes. The other Fenris halt in place as well, and a few lower their heads like scolded dogs. It's not that the car the barbed-wire wolf is pointing to isn't impressive; it's bright, glaring red, like a stripper in a parking lot full of beige and silver nuns. It's not the car.

It's the Fenris standing in front of it.

The monster is in human form, but his eyes are colder and more wolflike than the eyes of any Fenris I've ever seen. He's wearing a button-down white shirt, but it does little to hide his biceps or the shadows of tattoos swirling over his chest. His jaw is square, firm, and though he's perfectly, deadly still, fury radiates off him. He cocks his head at the barbed-wire Fenris and smiles, a cruel, sadistic sort of grin. He's leaning on the car, and from here I can see the mark on his wrist: an arrow. An arrow with a crown around it. The Arrow pack's Alpha.

"Having a fun night out?" the Alpha asks, running his thumb across his nails casually.

The pack trembles. Monsters, and they're terrified. I step closer to my sister, and her fear is almost palpable through the wolves that stand between us. *Don't be scared, Rosie. I'm here.* I tighten my grip on my hatchet and reach to grab my hunting knife as well. *Silas is here. We are* hunters, *I will protect you.* Is it terrible that I suddenly feel something akin to relief in the midst of this mess? That being able to protect my sister makes me feel useful, almost normal again?

"Just a break. Then we're back to looking for him," the barbed-wire Fenris says quickly, nodding his head as though that'll help him prove the point. A group of normal teenagers pours out of the bowling alley. They turn sharply and fall silent when they see us, then hurry toward their cars without many good-byes — even they can tell something isn't right in the air.

The Alpha grins, and it's *terrifying*. "Right. Right. Because, to me, it looks like you guys are having a wild night. Beer, bowling, lovely young ladies," he says, letting his eyes wander up and down Rosie's body. I feel her shudder even from a distance, and I'm not sure if it's sincere or part of her act. "You know, I realize you're new to Arrow. But I am fairly certain that even in Bell, orders were orders."

"This, uh...your brother or something?" Rosie says in a meek voice. *Good job, Rosie; keep talking. Keep talking until I can figure out how to fight the leader of a pack on his own turf, with his wolves to back him up.*

"Or something," the Alpha says. "He was showing you the car, right?" Rosie nods. "Why don't you come over here and let me show you this puppy?"

Rosie and I tremble together. She can't fight the Alpha. She can't take him. I stutter-step forward, desperate to run to my sister, though I probably can't take him either. At any rate, I won't be able to make it through all of them. They'll hold me back long enough for him to hurt her. For me to watch him kill...*Breathe, Scarlett, breathe.* Rosie lingers back for a moment, looking like she longs to stay with the lesser of the evil Fenris. I could hit the Alpha with my hatchet, maybe, with a well-aimed toss...but Rosie is right there — she's taking his hand, and I could hit her. I...

The Alpha leads Rosie toward the car like a proud parent. The pack shifts, waiting for a command. The barbed-wire Fenris falls back with the rest of them.

"All custom-painted, of course. You want to go for a ride?

187

I can take you around the town, sweetheart. Pick up some laundry? Groceries? Liquor?" the Alpha says with a wicked grin. He takes a step closer to Rosie, and he's so tall that my sister has to practically look straight up to meet his eyes. I can see her hands shaking. Worse yet, I can see the Alpha enjoying her fear.

"Oh, I'm good, actually. Just stopped by Kroger this morning," Rosie says. It's *her* voice, not the character voice, and she's trying to keep from crying out. She searches for my eye through the pack, but just before she would have reached me, the Alpha raises a hand and turns her head toward him, his nails long and yellowed, eyes glinting ocher in the moonlight.

"Now, come on. Don't be impolite," he says in a low hiss. Strands of thin, stringy hair sprout around his neck.

A streak of motion catches my eye nearby. I don't see the person, but I recognize something about the movement. Yes—Silas. Okay. Three versus...six. Still.

"It's just that...I-I don't like to get into cars with strangers," Rosie stammers. The Alpha closes his eyes, as though he's drinking in her terror. Rage begins to replace the worry in my heart, begins to fill my chest with power. *Come on, Rosie, you're the one calling the shots on this.* I see Rosie fold her arms over her chest as if she's nervous.

"Then we should be better acquainted," the Fenris says, and his voice dissolves into a growling howl. A sharp, crunching noise breaks into the silent night as his spine lurches forward, his nose lengthening as he opens his dripping mouth

188

in another deep, wild howl. The wolf lunges for Rosie, still-somewhat-human hands grasping for her shirt.

But my sister is quicker. She flicks a knife out of its sheath and lashes it across the Alpha's abdomen as deftly as an artist with a brush. The Alpha leaps backward, the last few traces of humanity vanishing as he rears around to see what she's done. When he sees the trickle of thick blood clumping his fur, his lips curl back in a snarl. His eyes flicker toward the rest of the pack, and they drop to their knees, their spines crunching. I draw my weapons—they still don't seem to realize I'm behind them.

Rosie flicks out her second knife and takes aim. It spins out of her hand like a star, straight at the Alpha's chest. But the Alpha knocks it away easily. He raises a clawed hand at my sister and I feel a scream erupting in my throat, recognizing the motion from seven years ago. The swing will take my sister's eye. I storm through the still-transforming Fenris, swinging my hatchet as if I'm hacking at tree limbs. Rosie's eyes widen in horror as the Alpha's claws begin to descend. I grit my teeth and force my body forward, now ignoring the other wolves, desperate to reach her.

A roaring scream, all human but as fierce as any Fenris howl, echoes through the parking lot. My head snaps to see its source: Silas is running toward Rosie, hunting knives in one hand, ax aloft in the other. His eyes burn brighter than any hellfire. He swings out just as the Alpha's claws are about to reach Rosie's face, knocking the monster out of the way.

Which means it's my turn. The fear and anger melt away,

and I'm all confidence. I flip my hatchet in my hand and turn back to the pack. They've all transformed and are creeping low to the ground, snapping their jaws like bear traps. I lash forward. The hatchet makes contact with the nearest Fenris's jaw, and I hear it crack. The others leap toward me in one swift motion, but I spin wildly, hacking at whatever I can hit. The Alpha howls behind me, but I don't look back. I can't look back.

"Go! Go! We have what we need!" the Alpha snarls frantically. He's the leader of Arrow . . . surely he isn't this easily startled? No matter—as long as he dies.

I leap into the air, landing hard on one Fenris's spine. I duck another Fenris's leap for my throat and sink my hatchet into the one under my feet. He almost instantly becomes shadows, lowering me enough that a few more fly over me. I turn to see one's jaws closing in toward my face, but he suddenly jerks backward. When he falls, I can see my sister standing behind him. She picks up the knife that's left on the ground when the wolf shadows.

A low howl rings out again—the Alpha, I'm somehow certain. I wheel back around and brandish the hunting knife, but I am surprised to see the remaining three Fenris backing away. Their heads are low and they're growling, deep, thunderlike growls that vibrate my bones. The Alpha howls again, and I suddenly realize that the howl is far away, only an echo. One of the Fenris snaps at me, then turns and dashes away. *No. Come on, not again.* I run forward, but the other Fenris follow him. My feet slam into the pavement, and I narrowly avoid a few cars as I race after them across the street, cloak swinging behind me.

The Fenris are faster, far faster than me. They are only dots on the horizon now. *No, no...but yes.* They dart into the woods. I follow, but finally my feet slow to a stop. My lungs burn as I turn around, gasping. Dammit! I had the *Alpha* even...

I jump as I hear faint footsteps behind me, but it's only Silas. He moves through the trees like water, feet making little noise on the ground.

"They were fast," he says with a frown as he reaches me. I nod and we stand side by side, scanning the forest. There's nothing—just the sound of trees swaying in the breeze and moonlight spotting the forest floor. Silas steps into the ray of moonlight I'm standing in. I tug my eye patch off, tired of the sweat that's running underneath it.

"The Alpha," I sigh, exasperated. I was so close this time. I just wasn't fast enough, strong enough. I swallow the guilt. "I don't suppose you could track him out here?"

Silas looks past me, into the darkness. "I can try, but unless they double back, they're probably long gone."

"Please," I say, looking down.

Silas puts a hand on my shoulder. "I already said I'd try. You don't have to say please," he reminds me gently.

Silas kneels to the ground, rubbing dirt between his fingers and brushing the edges of plants with his palms. We walk deeper into the woods, but we make it only fifteen minutes before he turns to face me, eyes apologetic.

"Look, Lett, I'm sorry, but…it's dark. Really dark. Maybe Lucas or Pa Reynolds could track in this, but I'm not the woodsmen they are."

"It's okay," I say, though I think my voice gives it away that it isn't. If we don't follow the trail immediately, there's no point. We both know the wolves will be long gone by daylight.

"We'll find him again," Silas says seriously, lifting a low-hanging branch to my right—my blind side. I wouldn't have seen it.

"What makes you so certain?" I ask, eyebrows raised as we step back onto the road.

Silas laughs lightly. "It's what you *do*, Lett."

I shrug, agreeing. "It's what *we* do," I correct him with a sideways glance. Silas rolls his eyes good-naturedly and nods as we make our way back to Rosie.

CHAPTER FOURTEEN

Rosie

Nothing," Scarlett sighs. "That's it. I've gone through every book at the library that has anything to do with werewolves or Fenris. I've printed out seven dozen pages from the Internet—nothing there either. Nothing." Scarlett looks out the window. The sky is packed with rain-heavy clouds, casting the apartment in a cold, pale blue light. I fold some of Scarlett's old notes into origami frogs, hoping my sister won't ask where I learned the trick.

It's been three days since the bowling alley. At first, Scarlett seemed happy to have killed at least two Fenris. But then she became even more driven, more motivated to find the Potential and face off with the Arrow Alpha again. I still sit bolt upright in the night occasionally, seeing the wolf's claws above my head, feeling as if there is nothing to do but take the blow. If it hadn't been for Silas...

"We're running out of time," Scarlett says, rising to pour herself a glass of water. She picks at the broken remains in a bag of animal crackers. As if to mock her, the church bells chime out once for the quarter hour. She sighs. "There has to be more we can do. Without the Alpha, we could have taken the group at the bowling alley. Maybe we should try something like that again."

"Not with the Arrow pack, though," Silas interjects from where he's lying on the couch, tossing a tennis ball to himself. "I imagine the Alpha will have warned the entire pack about the three of us. And besides, weren't we really hunting mainly to gain information about the Potential?"

"We can't just ignore a pack of wolves," Scarlett says, shaking her head with a note of desperation in her voice. "And besides, there's still Bell. And Coin. Their Alphas don't know who we are..."

"Yeah, and they're probably being absorbed into Arrow as we speak," Silas says glumly, sitting up. "They're organizing. Better to unite into one pack and get the Potential than lose the Potential and keep the smaller group. One unified pack is going to be a lot harder to fight than three."

"So *what,* then, Silas? Do you have a suggestion?" Scarlett snaps, slamming her glass down onto the counter so hard that Screwtape flees the room. Silas sighs.

"I don't know, Scarlett. I'm not trying to piss you

off — I'm just saying, we've been here for almost three weeks and all we know is that the Potential is a specific person, that he can be transformed only during a specific time, and that he has an active moon phase only every seven years. That's half the planet, and the whole full-moon-after-the-birthday thing doesn't really help unless you plan to start stalking people's birthday parties. This might be too big a job for us, Lett. Maybe we should focus on hunting instead of baiting them with the Potential," he says in the firm voice he seems to save especially for Scarlett.

"Hunting with what, Silas? You? Me? Is Rosie supposed to bait an entire city on her own? We can't even make a dent in the population if we don't have the Potential!"

"So, what, you weren't even making a dent before this? Before we threw the Potential into the mix, you were per-fectly happy to hunt the outlying wolves!" he answers. He isn't afraid to fight with her — but then, she isn't afraid to fight with him either.

"With knowledge comes responsibility!" Scarlett snaps, her face turning red with anger. "We know we can use the Potential, so it's our job to do it. We don't take the easy way out, Silas."

Silas mutters something under his breath. My sister's face is bright, anger boiling right under the surface of her skin.

"What did you say?" she says, voice dangerous, and I can tell she picked up the words that I did not. I consider stepping in during the quiet, but I'm not sure I can—whom would I agree with? The sister I'm part of or the boy that I love? I clamp my lips shut.

"Forget it." Silas shakes his head and reaches for a book.

"Tell me!"

Silas exhales and looks at Scarlett. "Lett, maybe it's *your* job. That doesn't mean it's mine." His eyes flicker toward me for just a moment as he says this, but I look away. I can't say that to my sister. Luckily, Scarlett's rage erupts and she doesn't catch the glance.

Her voice jumps. "Not yours? Not *yours?* You know what? Fine. Go to San Francisco and have a lovely time." She exhales, words snaking off her tongue. "But it's their blood on your hands, Silas. All the girls whom you could save but won't. I hope their lives were worth a guitar lesson to you. I hope you think about how it would feel to be their mothers and fathers and sisters. I wonder if you could tell them that their little girls died because you wanted to learn how to fucking play 'Twinkle, Twinkle, Little Star.'"

"Lett, come on—" Silas begins, and I see guilt replace the frustration on his face. Scarlett raises her hands and shakes her head. She looks at me.

"Rosie, it's just me and you, it seems," she says. Her words are aimed at Silas, but they cut through me. I nod, afraid to look at Silas, blinking back tears of frustration. Scarlett spins on her heel, grabs her hatchet, and leaves, slamming the door, which bounces back open on the doorjamb.

It's silent for a moment. I swallow the lump in my throat

and hurry toward the kitchen, tossing breakfast dishes into the sink so hard that I hear a plate crack. I have to hunt. She's my sister. I have to hunt—girls are murdered, *eaten,* and I can stop it.

"Rosie," Silas says with a sigh.

"No," I snap. "You shouldn't have said that to her, Silas. She's right—it's our job."

"Rosie, you don't want to spend all your time hunting and studying wolves any more than I do. I don't want to hurt Scarlett, but I can't live the way she lives...and neither can you," Silas says. I'm not sure if he's apologizing about Scarlett or pleading with me.

"She's my *sister!*" I scream, face hot. My frustration will dissolve into weeping before long, I'm sure.

"Your sister," Silas repeats, eyes deep and shining, drops of obsidian in the blue-lit room. "Not you. You're your own person, Rosie." His words aren't necessarily kind, but stern.

I laugh sarcastically and a few teardrops escape from the cage of my lashes; they splash down my face and join my hands in the dirty dishwater. "We have the same heart," I mutter, shaking my hair from my wet face. The same heart, torn apart so that I could stay safe in our mother longer while she put her body in front of mine. Her body in front of mine so that I could stay safe longer instead of face the mouth of a monster. Always her body in front of mine, always her to be wounded, to be cut into pieces and hacked away at while I see with both eyes and can think of a life beyond hunting.

I am so selfish, so petty and selfish. Thunder crashes

suddenly, so loudly that the shoddy windowpanes shake with its force. I can already see strips of lightning in the distance, blending in with the perfect lines of light from the downtown skyscrapers. It won't be long now before the storm.

I turn to snap at Silas again, to ask him how he would dare to even question why I would give up everything to hunt with Scarlett. Before I can say anything else, I see a flash of gray fur slip through the door. I drop the silverware I'm holding and cry out.

"No one shut the door!" I dash past Silas, yanking my cloak off the chair as I run. I double back in a giant bound and snatch one of the woven laundry baskets off the countertop—Screwtape can't be caught; he has to be *trapped*. I slide the crimson cloak over my shoulders, take the stairs two at a time, and fling the building door open into the street, shouting Screwtape's name like a lunatic. Why is every single thing in this city the same pale gray shade of Screwtape's fur? Stupid cat, stupid, stupid cat.

"He can't have gotten far." Silas runs up behind me, a concerned look in his eyes. I don't reply, worried my voice will come out in a pathetic squeak. So much movement around me, and none of it is familiar; everything is harsh, choppy corners and elbows and cars screeching to a halt at a stop sign. None of it is the slow, languid movement of my cat. My eyes race across the city street to the empty lot. Gray movement behind a chain-link fence.

"There!" I shout so suddenly that a bike messenger almost skids into a fire hydrant. I ignore him and bolt across the street, cloak flying out behind me. I know I saw him. I run along the fence until I find a loose section. Silas appears beside me and takes the basket out of my hands, then holds the section of fence up for me to slide through. He throws the basket through after me, then clambers through himself.

The chain-link rattles down as Silas rises. It's somehow quieter in here, as though the thick brush and junker cars that are rooted against the fence are blocking the sound of the street beyond. The buildings on either side look all but abandoned, their old wooden balconies leering at us, jagged teeth on the crumbling brick walls, a few forgotten scraps of laundry and sheets whipping around in the stormy breeze. A drop or two of fat rain runs through my hair. I fall to my knees in the dirt, peering underneath the rusted cars. I'm startled back to standing for a moment by a junkyard dog that barks angrily, taunting me with yellow eyes from behind the fence of an adjacent lot.

"You're sure you saw him?" Silas calls from the other side of the lot, where he's picking through the giant weeds. I nod and my throat aches as a horrible black ball of fear lodges itself under the roof of my mouth. I cry Screwtape's name again.

And then I just cry.

His name, Scarlett's name, Silas's name, in one desperate stream of *s* sounds that I can't separate from one another. I want someone to make things right; I want someone to make me not feel as if I'm constantly being pulled different ways by my heart and my head. Most of all I want someone to just tell me what to do, to find my cat in the rain and restore some sense of normalcy to *everything*. Silas rises and looks at me, hair dusting around his face in the wind and his T-shirt covered in mud.

"Stop," he says forcefully. I shake my head—I can't stop. "Come on, Rosie. You're in control here; you don't need to be rescued," he says, reading my thoughts. "Come on."

I nod tearfully, and without so much as a step toward each other, we turn back around. I breathe heavily but stop crying. I continue picking my way through the dirt, peering into the cobweb-filled seats of old Volkswagens and rattling the chain-link fence again.

"Wait!" Silas shouts, his voice followed by a loud crash. I leap from the ground and turn to see Silas running the length of the far wall, where the lot meets the dilapidated apartments. He dives into the weeds and jumps back out, following a gray streak that flits between cars and old appliances and underneath brush. I dash to Silas to join him just as another crash of thunder breaks through the sky and rain begins to fall so hard that it shakes debris onto us from the apartments' rotting balconies.

"Go left!" I call to him. Silas cuts in that direction and I move forward, leaping over a rusted engine block and part of an old pinball machine. Screwtape darts out from under the pinball machine, but as soon as a few drops of rain hit him, he doubles back.

"Toss me the basket!" Silas shouts, but I've already thrown it. He catches it and swings it to the ground in a single swift motion, and it clatters over Screwtape before he can slide back under the engine block.

"Ha!" Silas shouts, grinning as he puts a foot on top of the laundry basket to hold it down. Screwtape flings himself against the sides. I laugh and exhale in relief, tears streaming down my face despite the grin that feels permanently stamped on my cheeks.

"Oh god. Screwtape, I hate you." I cry and laugh in the same breath as I trudge toward them. My clothes are covered in dirt and my hair is matted, but I don't care. I peer through the basket bars at Screwtape, who looks at me as though I've betrayed his trust. I rise and meet Silas's gaze. "Thank you, Silas," I say, though the words are quieter than I mean. Something buzzes within me, stirs around in my chest enticingly.

"Of course," he murmurs. His eyes are heavy on mine, his gaze pulling me in. He licks his lips nervously and runs a hand through his hair. Screwtape howls out as the rain increases, droplets clinging to Silas's lashes and running over his lips. Why am I noticing his lips? I brush my hair behind my ears as the heavy rain drowns out the sounds of the city on the other side of the fence.

"Rosie," he says, or maybe he just mouths the word. He takes hold of my fingertips, and this time I move my hand and interlace my fingers with his. Silas inhales, as if he's going to say something else, like he wants to say something else, but instead he pulls me to him, closing the distance between us until his chest brushes mine with every breath. His body is warm, and the feeling of being against him and feeling heat from his skin makes me light-headed.

"I'm sorry," he mumbles, but doesn't break away from me.

"Why?"

"Because there's something I have to do," he says, voice velvety soft. Silas unwinds his fingers from mine and reaches up, wiping the raindrops off my face with the palm of his hand as the stirring in my chest spreads through my whole body, pounds in my veins, begs to be released. I put my hands against his chest as if I know what I'm doing, and he finally leans forward and tilts my chin upward gently.

His lips meet mine, tentatively at first, then hungrily, and I clutch at his shirt as if holding on to him will keep me from floating away into the thunderhead above. His hands run down my back, and one rests on my hip while the other tugs me closer, until I think I could melt into him because nothing has ever, ever felt so right.

CHAPTER FIFTEEN

SCARLETT

I WALK FOR MILES AIMLESSLY. I CAN LIVE UP TO MY responsibilities. This isn't a pointless game. Silas is wrong. Thunder crackles overhead.

I turn down an alley that I think leads to a sketchy row of projects and beaten-up basketball courts. A rough-looking school stands on the corner, looking defeated by neighborhood crime. My mind is so tightly wound that I feel as if it might explode from pressure. Wolves hang around schools sometimes. It's worth a shot.

I slink around the school gates just as the first drops of rain fall, and by the time I'm next to the crumbly building, it's a full-blown storm.

School must be out—the parking lot is empty, save one beat-up brown station wagon parked near a row of thick hedges. There's an older, heavily bearded man in it, and he motions an unseen person toward the passenger-side door. I creep closer and peer around the corner to see whom he's calling for. It's a middle school–aged girl, clutching her books to her chest nervously underneath a plaid umbrella.

"I just need directions!" the man calls out, something of a chuckle in his voice. The girl shakes her head and takes a step away from his car, putting several yards between them. *Good girl,* I think to myself. I sprint from the edge of the school to the hedges, ignoring the rainwater in my eye. The man calls for her again.

"Look, I don't drive. I can't give good directions. Wait till my mom gets here — she'll know," the girl calls back. The man nods and puts the car in park, then gets out, his steps slow and deliberate. The girl's face blanches, and she frantically tries to open the massive double doors of the school, but they're locked. The familiar rush of adrenaline sweeps through me, the love of the hunt, the love of my purpose. The man strides toward her, hands in his pockets and a dark glare in his eyes.

In one swift motion, I leap toward them and flip my hatchet in my hand. I dash behind the man and raise the blade of my weapon to his throat, snickering at the man's surprise. He fumbles to turn around and face me. *Transform, monster. You can be my second successful hunt.*

"Hey now, missy," he croaks at me, taking a step back. Behind him, the girl seems frozen with fear and confusion.

"Hey now, wolf," I whisper back. He looks at me for

a long time, then darts to my left. I'm faster—I swing the hatchet around and let it slice into his arm, leaving a deep crimson red line. The man screams and grasps the wound, dropping to his knees.

"You bitch," he snarls at me, voice echoing off the school and through the sheets of rain. I step closer and raise my hatchet. *Transform. Fight me.*

The man's face goes as pale as his would-be victim's. He raises his hands up in protest.

"Look, I didn't mean nothing. I'm sorry. I'll leave her alone," he pleads.

Fenris don't beg. I let my eye run down his age-spotted arms and to his wrists.

They're bare. No tattoos, no pack marks. Only a scattering of freckles.

I furrow my eyebrows and lower my hatchet to my side. The man quivers, blood from his wound seeping through his fingers. I look back up at the girl, who is regarding me with a sort of terrified appreciation.

I was wrong. He's just a man, a dark man, a monster but not a wolf. I'm really losing it.

"Go," I whisper, taking a step away from him. The man leaps up and runs to his car, peeling out of the parking lot in a hiss of tires on wet asphalt.

I stand still, letting water run down my clothes and off my hatchet. I was wrong.

I can't do this alone. I need my sister. I need my partner—I just got him back; I can't let him disappear again.

And—I sigh and close my eye—I need them for more than just hunting.

I turn and look at the girl, who is still pressed against the school doors.

"Are you okay?" I ask the girl.

She nods. "Who are you?" she asks, tiny voice barely audible over the storm.

I don't answer. I turn and trudge back through the bushes and around the school.

I can't do this alone—I can't do anything without Rosie and Silas. But I have to get them to focus. I have to keep them from abandoning the hunt.

From abandoning *me*.

When I return to the apartment, Rosie is sitting at the dining table, towel wrapped around her head. The shower is on, indicating where Silas is. I glance across the room—Screwtape is soaked, licking at his fur indignantly by our bed.

"What happened to you?" I ask flatly. I strip off my clothing and leave it in a wet pile outside our bedroom.

"Screwtape got out," Rosie explains. There's something in her voice, a singsong tone that sounds a little like the voice of some animated princess. I raise an eyebrow at her, but she doesn't look up from the book she's leafing through. I nod and pull on a dry T-shirt and jeans.

"I've already looked through that one. Twice," I tell her.

"Sorry. Just trying to help," Rosie says, closing the book.

"I know." I'm trying to lose the bitter edge to my voice,

but it's hard—the frustration at Silas still bubbles beneath my surface.

"Think of anything new?" I ask my sister, sitting down beside her at the table.

"No. We might as well be back to square one," Rosie says with a small sigh. She tosses the book onto the floor and doesn't reach for another. "Silas says he's going to visit Pa Reynolds. I'll stay and research with you, though," she says. Rosie props up her legs on a stack of books in front of her, and I see that her calves are slathered in pink calamine lotion.

"What's all that for?" I ask.

Rosie shrugs. "Apparently when we were chasing Screwtape I ran through a patch of poison ivy. I think I washed it off and put the calamine on in time, though."

"I hope so," I say, peering at her flawless skin. "Poison ivy sucks. Remember when we got it when we were little?"

"No," Rosie corrects me. "You got it first, and then I got it later. I remember that you accidentally rolled around in it when we were playing, and your face got all swollen. But— you know how I got it, like...a week later?"

I nod.

"I did it on purpose. I went out and rolled around in that same patch of poison ivy."

"What are you, stupid?" I ask, laughing.

Rosie shakes her head. "Mom let you sleep in her bed. And then I had to sleep in our bedroom all by myself, and I was lonely."

"So you rolled in poison ivy?"

"I just was so jealous of you. And I would've done anything to be like you, even something stupid…" She trails off.

Silas interrupts us by stepping out of the bathroom, wrinkled clothes sticking to his still-damp skin. He ignores me and begins rifling through his suitcase until he pulls a pair of socks from the mound of clothes. I notice he's got calamine lotion on his forearms.

"Rosie said you're visiting Pa Reynolds?" I ask. The words are a peace offering, in a way.

"Yep. I've gone only once since we've been here," Silas says, tossing his wet towel over the back of a chair. "I'll be back around eight or nine, I guess. We're hunting tonight?"

I nod. "We can leave without you if you want, though. You can always catch up to us and start hunting later." Another peace offering, but one I have to force from my lips.

Silas looks impressed, and I think I see something like guilt flicker across his eyes. He glances at Rosie, then back at me with an apologetic smile. "That sounds good, Lett."

Silas slides his shoes on and rustles his fingers in his hair, gives Rosie and me a quick wave, and leaves. He's still mad, at least a little. It's always taken Silas a while to cool down. But I need him, I need Rosie. I don't want to be alone. I hesitate, then hurry after him. He's on the second flight of the stairwell when I reach the door.

"I can go with you, if you want?" I offer.

Silas looks up at me, and a sad sort of smile tugs at his lips. "It's okay. We can go another time together."

"Okay," I answer, but he doesn't move. I look down. "You *are* coming back, right?"

Silas looks surprised. "Just because you're a pain in the ass doesn't mean I'd abandon you," he says. "Besides, Lett— where else do I have to go?"

I exhale. "Right." Silas continues down the staircase and I turn to go back inside. He needs us, and I need them.

CHAPTER SIXTEEN

Rosie

Scarlett is at city hall because, as it turns out, figuring out who in an entire region is turning a multiple of seven is pretty complex. Silas and I are supposed to be reading the newspapers, which are still headlining the murder spree, looking for the tiniest clue as to the wolves' plans.

But that really just isn't happening.

"We're supposed to be researching," I say through laughter. Silas grins and runs his fingers up my side again, dissolving me into another fit of giggles. The notepad that I'd been writing on topples to the floor beside the couch. He wraps his arm around me and urges me closer to him. Our lips find each other's and I'm curled in his lap, hands around his shoulders. The smells of oak and forest fill my lungs, as though he's breathing them into me as we kiss. I push closer against him until he circles his arms around me and hugs me to his chest. It feels natural, right, as if the change in our relationship was as simple as sliding into new clothes.

We pull away, both flushed, grinning like crazy people. "Okay. Now we focus. Werewolf birthdays," Silas says with fake intensity.

We turn back to our mostly empty notepads for a moment, but Silas's hand creeps over and pokes me in the side again, and I dissolve in hysterics. Our day of research is pretty hopeless. In fact, the last four days of research have been hopeless.

The light in the storm of Fenris researching and empty-handed hunting attempts? Silas. My heart still jumps out of my chest when we're alone together, but at least now I know that if I put my arms around him, the world won't end and he'll put his arms around me too. It gives me the same sense of normalcy, the same rightness, that taking lessons at the community center does, only magnified a thousand times.

It's been almost four weeks. Four weeks of taking community center courses, four weeks of the Potential's moon phase, four weeks away from Ellison. Almost a whole month in love with Silas.

"You could sign up for more," Silas says when I tell him today is the last day of classes.

I shake my head. "No...I can't keep lying to Scarlett. Either I tell her I'm taking them, or I quit."

"I'm sort of relieved to hear that, actually," Silas says,

running his fingers through my hair. "Scarlett somehow makes me feel guilty without even knowing about..." He pauses and runs a hand down my cheek. "Classes. So which will you do? Tell her or quit?"

I sigh. "I don't know. I probably shouldn't do either until the Potential hunt is over."

"Fair." Silas nods. "Or we could just...you know, find the Potential."

"Yeah, good luck," I murmur. I sigh and stand. "I should go take my class. If you wait until too late in the day, there aren't any good ones left."

"Want some company for the walk?" Silas offers, kissing my hand before releasing it. I grin and blush—he can still make me blush.

"You can...I mean, is that...are you offering to be nice, like before, or are you offering as...as..."

"Your boyfriend?" he finishes, raising an eyebrow. I turn so red that even my hands are mottled. Silas smiles.

I sigh. "Don't laugh. I'm just...this is new for me. You've done all this before."

Silas reaches forward quickly, then pulls me against him, his arms hard with muscle from wielding the ax. "Rosie," he says accusingly. "Believe me when I say, I have never done all *this* before."

"Oh," I muster, the only sound that my mouth seems capable of forming. Silas grins and pulls me down on top of him. Our legs tangle and I rest my head in the crook of his neck, kissing his skin lightly as I try to get even closer to him, though it seems impossible. He runs his fingers along my side, then moves to kiss my forehead tenderly.

"Maybe the class can wait after all," I mumble as I stretch upward to kiss him on the lips. My hand creeps up the front of his T-shirt, running along the lines of the muscles underneath.

"I promise," he murmurs in a tone so velvety that it makes me shiver, "there are plenty more chances for us to... well, to do this," he finishes, though I know there's more to "this" than my hand pressed against his chest and his lips on mine. I lie against him while he strokes my hair.

"As long as you promise," I whisper, grinning. Silas laughs quietly and kisses me again, then nods. I finally pull myself away and hurry to get dressed for class.

Tango lessons.

It's the only class available that doesn't sound totally lame, such as Real Estate Investing or Artificial Flower Arrangement. There's a painting course, but after the madness that was the drawing class, I'm done with art for a while. Mostly couples have shown up for the tango class, and I watch the way they act with each other as we wait together in the hallway outside the dance studio. They let their fingers rest on each other's arms, kiss cheeks, and smile softly. I wonder if I look the way these girls do when Silas puts his arms around me.

A man brushes past us, swishing his hips and sliding

around the ladies departing a yoga course. We file into the room, the couples holding hands, the scattered rest of us lingering shyly in the back. For all his praise of doing things that are "non-hunting-centric," Silas would *never* be up for this, so I'll have to find another partner today.

"All right, ladies and *gents,* I'm Timothy," the swishy man says, sashaying to the front of the room and taking off his jacket to reveal a bright orange dress shirt. "Remember: stay on your toes, let your hips move, ladies, and above all—this is a dance of love! Passion! Sex!" The room giggles and Timothy wiggles his eyebrows up and down. "Right, then. Let's see—those of you without a partner, raise your hands." The back of the room obeys. "Perfect. Mmm, let's see..."

Timothy glides toward us, hips weaving back and forth, and begins pulling people together, apparently by height. He gets to me and tugs on my biceps to move me.

"Ooh, strong girly," he says when he feels the muscles beneath my T-shirt. I blush and allow him to tug me over to someone in the corner of the room. The guy is facing the back of the classroom, inspecting a poster that displays various dance positions. When Timothy taps his shoulder to turn him around, the guy's long ponytail swings across his face. His eyes are deep and dark, and his nose is sharp and pointed. He's astonishingly beautiful, like something carved from stone and polished to perfection.

"Annnnnnd...that's it!" Timothy says as the guy and I regard each other.

"What's your name?" I ask.

214

"My name? Um…Robert," he says, voice songlike. He pauses before saying the name, as if he's having trouble remembering it. He licks his lips and gives me a weighty look that makes me shiver.

"Chests closer than hips, embrace, keep your musicality, people!" Timothy says, holding up his arms to an invisible partner. "Ladies, one hand on his shoulder. Gents, one hand on her rib cage, just above the waist." The class shuffles as everyone moves into the position awkwardly. I try not to put my entire hand on Robert's shoulder, but he clamps his hand onto my ribs to the point that it hurts a little. I try to wiggle away without being too obvious. "And your other hands come together, like this." Timothy moves to the nearest couple and clamps their hands together, then lifts their arms to shoulder level.

I raise my right hand and wait for Robert to take it. When he does, his sleeve slips back from his wrist.

And I see it. A simple tattoo of a coin, overlapped by an arrow. He's a Fenris. He's a Fenris and I'm dancing with him. They're literally *everywhere* in Atlanta.

"You like the tattoo?" Robert says with humor in his voice. I feel his nails grow a little on the hand that's by my ribs. Still, he keeps the transformation under control. *Focus, Rosie, focus. No need to panic.* Dear god, I didn't bring my knives. Scarlett always tells me to keep them with me at all times, but I didn't bring them.

"It's interesting," I say, damning myself when I hear a slight tremble in my voice. Robert smiles darkly. Does he

215

know who I am? Did the Arrow pack tell him when they took him from Coin?

As Timothy cues up the music, my mind races back to all the hand-to-hand combat skills that Scarlett and I learned in tae kwon do classes back in Ellison. He's just one Fenris. He hasn't even been a Fenris that long, given the look of that tattoo.

"And ladies, forward with the right; men, back with the left. Feel the beat!"

No. I can take him. I'm a hunter. He's just a wolf. A strong wolf, but a wolf.

We step forward, moving together in awkward, forced rhythm as Timothy claps and directs everyone's feet. Timothy commands us to snap our heads away from each other, and I hear Robert inhale, relishing the scent of my skin, of my fear.

"We're supposed to be closer," he whispers in my ear and forcibly yanks me toward him. He grins. "Sorry, but I'm the youngest of seven boys. I have a need for a lady's touch."

Focus. Be the bait. The music swirls, high-pitched violins and the low, groaning sound of cellos plucked in a dark, violent rhythm.

And I smile, the flirtiest, sexiest type of smile I can muster, batting my eyelashes for good measure. Robert looks delighted in the most horrible way, and his hold on my waist tightens. I release my hips, let them roll with each step. I flip my hair over my shoulder and lean back to reveal my throat when Timothy teaches a low, lunging step. He won't hurt me here—he can't risk it. When we rise, I roll my shoulders back. Robert's nails grow longer; his teeth have sharpened to tiny points and yellowed. And his eyes—god, his eyes— they've darkened so much that I can't believe he isn't a full-fledged wolf by now. Our hands snap toward the sky, slam down on my waist, spinning out, in, knee to the ground. I'll have bruises on my sides and wrists, I can tell. I dig my hand into his shoulder. He'll have bruises as well, if I have any-thing to say about it. Until I kill him, at least.

"Back step, side step, feel the rhythm, people, don't be afraid of the sexiness!" Timothy cries over the music, but I barely hear him, as if I'm drowning in the sound of violins and fear. The room whirls around me as we spin, as Robert's hand tightens on my spine. He's resisting the change, despite the fact that his hair has grown, clumped together like a wolf's fur is. He clenches his jaw. *Come on, you want me, you want to devour me.* If I can make it through the class, I can get him to follow me out, I can fight him. I can do this. I'm a hunter. We dip again, spin in circles. The song quick-ens, violins struggling desperately to keep up with the tempo, cellos being wildly plucked as though the music moves along the musician's very life. Our feet stomp, snap, flick, heads turn, turn back, he grabs my wrist and he snarls, the sound almost lost in the string instruments as Timothy increases the volume. Stomp, turn, twist, head pop.

I cry out and leap away, surprised when I suddenly feel claws in my skin. I push Robert back, shocked. We're in front of so many people. I look down at my waist in the mirrors that surround the room and see four dots of blood expanding through the fabric of my shirt. Other dancers gasp. Timothy raises his eyebrows and runs to turn the music off. I stare at Robert in amazement.

And then he leaps for me.

He doesn't change, but there's nothing human about the look in his eyes. He slams into me, throwing me backward. My head bounces off the wooden dance floor like a doll's and my vision goes blinding red for a moment. The other dancers scream. A few men bolt toward me, but I've got this. I brace my feet under him and kick backward with all my strength. He flies over my head, crashing into one of the mirrors. It shatters, a rain of glass that reflects me and the other horrified dancers a million times before scattering over Robert's body. I dizzily try to stand but fail; he hit me harder than I thought. I rub the back of my head tenderly.

He doesn't move. More screams. What am I doing? I have to get up, fight him. No, he hit the wall as a human. He wasn't strong enough to take that kind of blow. Several people help me off the ground while Timothy ushers us out of the room. I can't just leave him there. I should sneak back in and kill him. Fragments of conversation whirl past my ears as one of the center volunteers brushes past me and locks the door to the dance studio. My head throbs, and someone lifts me up to sit on the registration counter.

"We'll get you cleaned up—"

"Ambulance is on its way—"

"Don't you worry, honey, he's locked in there—"

"Her side is still bleeding."

"I'm *fine*," I finally say. I lift up my shirt a little to inspect the wounds. "I won't even need stitches."

"Honey, how can you possibly know that?" a volunteer asks, shaking her head. I jump up as she presses an ice pack against my head.

"Trust me. I've had a lot of stitches." I glance back at the studio door. I can't possibly get back in there now. Several people are standing in front of it, and there's practically a mob around me. Damn. Another one will get away. "Scarlett is going to kill me," I mumble.

"Don't you worry about whoever Scarlett is, sweetheart. I was right, though, you are a tough girly," Timothy tells me. His voice is shaking a little, as are his hands. "Oh, good! The cops are here!"

Outside, an ambulance and two police cars pull up. The EMTs rush in, and despite the protests from the center volunteers and the other dancers, I convince them that I don't need help. They just hand me a few more ice packs and move on to the dance studio. I tense my legs, ready to fight the Fenris, anticipating he'll be waiting just on the other side of the door. But no. When the EMTs emerge with the stretcher, he's attached to it. Blood is streaming down his face, and bits of glass peek out from his skin and hair—hair that is still mangy and somewhat furlike, though I doubt anyone else will notice. His eyes creak open as he passes me. Timothy hisses at him in a very catlike way, and the wolf's eyes close again.

People are surrounding the police officers, eager to explain what happened. I try to leave, but Timothy insists that I stay and explain. Just as I'm giving the officer a very vanilla version of the story — "He just attacked me; I kicked him" — a Lexus screeches into the parking lot. A man in a business suit leaps out, straightening his tie as he bolts through the community center doors.

"Officer! I'm Robert Culler Senior. There was an incident involving my son?" he says, holding out his hand to the police officer taking my statement.

"Yes, Mr. Culler. Perhaps we can talk to you in just a moment? Your son is on the way to Grady hospital —"

"Of course," Mr. Culler says. He looks at me carefully, then tilts his head for me to follow him away from the crowd. "Did my crazy-ass son hurt you? I can write you a check," he says quietly, yanking a checkbook out of his pocket. "What's your name?"

"I, uh..." I shake my head, wondering if I'm mishearing. "Rosie March. But it's fine. I'm fine."

"Nonsense," Mr. Culler replies. "He's sick, you see. Has been for about a year. It's not his fault he's like this." Mr. Culler glances at the ambulance as it pulls away, then turns back to me. "We tried to institutionalize him, but it made him worse, so we have a full-time caregiver now. Guess he gave him the slip..." Mr. Culler signs the check with a big swirling motion, folds it, and tucks it into my hand so swiftly that I get the impression he's done it quite often. "Did he give you that stupid line about being the youngest of seven boys?"

I nod.

Mr. Culler rolls his eyes. "Yeah, he tells everyone that. It's bullshit. I'm the youngest of seven boys, and I'm not a lunatic. He's like having a twenty-nine-year-old child."

"I can't believe you've managed to keep him...human." I say the last word mostly by accident, but Mr. Culler shrugs.

"It's taken a lot of cash and a lot of care. But look, you've got your money—don't think I don't have a lawyer who will take you—"

"Oh, uh, no," I say quickly. "It's no problem."

"Right. Well then. Officer, you wanted to talk to me?" Mr. Culler says, turning to the cop. While they're engaged, I slink away and out the door, dropping the ice packs at the exit. The sunlight is blinding and my head is still throbbing a little. I rub it tenderly as I unfold the check. I curse under my breath when I see the amount—two thousand dollars. Two *thousand* dollars? For getting thrown to the ground? I suppose it would've cost him more in court. And Culler must know I could have been killed. I wonder if other girls have been. Keeping a Fenris caged like that, trying to maintain him as a member of the family...I wonder if that's why he was able to keep a human appearance when his mind was taken over by the wolf. Years of practice, probably. Does his father even know what he is? I sigh and crumple the check back into my pocket as I trudge the last few blocks to the apartment.

"Where have you been?" Scarlett asks when I stumble through the door. Her eye runs down to the drops of blood on my shirt. Silas appears from behind the refrigerator door. His eyes widen and he steps toward me. I bite my lips, resisting the urge to move toward him, let him fold me into his arms. Scarlett rises from the couch, concerned. "Rosie? Are you okay?"

"Yeah. Yeah, I'm fine. I got hit in the head, that's all. Oh, and I made two thousand dollars."

Silas and Scarlett exchange worried glances—I see Silas take a quick step, as though he wants to run toward me, but he holds himself back.

"She's got a concussion," Silas says. Scarlett nods and they begin to usher me toward the couch.

"No! No! I mean, maybe. But look." I pull the check from my pocket and smash it into Scarlett's hand. She unfolds it and her eye widens. She hands it to Silas, who looks from the check to me no less than four times.

"Okay. So how did you make *two grand*, Rosie?" Scarlett asks.

I walk the rest of the distance to the couch and collapse on it. Scarlett and Silas crowd around. "Right. Well, I was... um..." I sigh and look at Scarlett. My head has finally stopped spinning, and I suddenly realize that I'm going to have to explain the dance class. "I was at this tango lesson," I say quickly, "and there was a Fenris—"

"Wait—at a what?" Scarlett asks.

"A...um...a dance class," I say meekly. Silas grimaces.

"A dance class? Since when do you take dance classes?" Scarlett demands, voice already rising.

"I just...I signed up for three classes at the community center, and today I took a tango course."

222

"Three classes? You...you think we have time for dance classes?" Scarlett asks. She looks shocked, then hurt, then furious, and her eye sears into mine.

"They weren't long, a half hour, hour each..." My words trail off as Scarlett leans back, away from me.

"I've...I've been living, *breathing* hunting. We're running out of time and..." She seems at a loss for words and crosses her arms over her chest. She won't even look at me.

"Look, Scarlett, I'm sorry, I just—"

"Did you know about this?" she snaps at Silas. Silas looks away, then nods grimly. Her mouth drops open and she shakes her head. "Forget it. Just forget it. Explain the money," she says flatly.

I run through the story quickly, Silas looking both angry and protective, Scarlett's eye cold and expressionless. "His dad gave me the money," I finish. "I guess he's afraid we'll sue or something. It won't be long till they can't control him anymore, though. He's already a monster..."

"You don't suppose he's the changed Potential, is he?" Scarlett asks, more to herself than to Silas and me.

"No." I shake my head. "I can't see how that's possible. He had too much self-control for a newly formed Fenris. Besides, his father said that he's been this way for a year now—I guess he turned twenty-eight last year and was bit during his phase? He was a Coin, by the way, but he's an Arrow now..." My sister's face darkens.

"Did he say anything else, though? Anything that might give us another hint as to who the new Potential is?" Silas

223

asks gently. I can tell he's trying to get both of us back on Scarlett's good side.

I shrug sadly. "Not really. That he had a bunch of brothers, and so did his—" I freeze. My eyes scan the room. I jump up, ignoring the burning, dizzy feeling in my head, and stride across the room to grab *Myths! Legends! Monsters!* I leaf furiously through the book. *Come on, where is it?* Surely it isn't this simple. I finally find the page I'm looking for. I look up to meet Silas's and Scarlett's curious gazes, holding the book in triumph.

"He's the seventh son of a seventh son." I fold my legs beneath me and sit on the floor. Silas and Scarlett rise and hurry toward me, looking from me to the page.

"So? I'm the sixth son and ninth kid in my family, you're the second one; what does—" Silas begins, but Scarlett cuts him off with a steely glance.

"The seventh..." She trails off and then darts across the room to grab a stack of papers. She tosses several onto the floor before holding up the printout of Joseph Woodlief's obituary. "So was Joseph. Seventh son of a seventh son."

"The seventh son of a seventh son, every seven years," Silas murmurs with a bit of pride in his voice that I think is directed toward me. We meet each other's eyes and I slowly flip *Myths! Legends! Monsters!* closed.

"Do you suppose that's it? That's all there is to it?" Scarlett whispers, collapsing backward onto the couch.

"Even if it isn't, how many seventh sons of seventh sons can there be in this city?" Silas says. He takes my hand, and

224

even though Scarlett is watching, I can't bring myself to pull it away. "We...we have it. We just need to find him."

We don't speak. I squeeze Silas's hand and he smiles at me as Scarlett stands and begins pacing, deep in thought.

"Good job, love," Silas whispers to me. When Scarlett's back is turned, he pulls me toward him and kisses my forehead adoringly.

CHAPTER SEVENTEEN

✦

SCARLETT

THE SEVENTH OF SEVEN. I STILL CAN'T BELIEVE IT'S that simple. Actually, no—I can't believe *Myths! Legends! Monsters!* was right. Well done, Dorothea Silverclaw. I wonder if that thing about salt on the windowsills really will keep demons away. I guess it never hurts to be careful.

I can't sleep. My head swims with thoughts that feel as if they could eat me alive. I turn over in bed and look at my sister resting like Sleeping Beauty, hair splayed around her face. She figured it out, the last key to who the Potential is.

And she lied to me. She kept secrets from me. No, she *and* Silas kept secrets from me. Have I really been left out? Deemed unworthy to know something as simple as my little sister taking dance lessons? I'm losing her. I've practically lost hunting.

What will I have left, other than a face full of scars to remind me that I'm worthless without my sister or the hunt?

She's lucky she had vital information, or I would have yelled. But she and Silas—it's as though they have some connection that I can't be a part of . . . I raise my arm and watch the moonlight reflect off my scars. I sit up on my elbows and peer through the crack in the curtain at Silas. His chest rises and falls in slumber, mouth slightly open and one leg kicked off the couch.

I sigh. The Seventh of Seven. Focus on that, not on the fact that Rosie lied. If we can just find him, *use* him, then we can go back to Ellison. Back to living in Oma March's cottage, back to hunting together in the woods behind the little town, back to the way things were with my sister, when there were no secrets.

And what if she doesn't want to go back? The thought stings with cold possibility. Rosie kept secrets because she didn't *want* to quit the classes. I'm not stupid—I'd choose tango over werewolves any day—but I have no choice. I'm scarred, tied to the hunt. But Rosie . . . she's half Dragonfly.

I research during the day. Recopy my notes. Stop by the library twice. Rosie sits for most of the day with a bag of ice taped around her side, cooling the slightly swollen wounds on her waist, and a cup of hot tea. Its vapors seem to stave off the cold rain that's been pattering outside. I come up with three names, pulled from the phone book, public records, and newspaper articles—though none of my research extends far past the Atlanta city limits. Still: Neal Franklin, James Porter, and Greg Zavodny. A bubble of hope swells in my chest as Rosie and I review each of the three.

"I don't think Franklin is the Seventh of Seven," Rosie says, readjusting her ice pack. "They mention six older siblings, but I get the feeling one of them is a girl. Otherwise, why not just say 'six older brothers'?"

I reread the article and reluctantly cross his name off the list, knowing Rosie is probably right.

"And Zavodny...I don't know, Scarlett. The man is really, really old."

"The wolves must find them and change them early on, before they have a chance to get into their eighties," I mumble. "I don't know if this guy could have eluded them all these years."

"Right." Rosie sighs in agreement. The hopeful feeling in my chest is sinking quickly.

"So...Porter. The guy we have the least amount of information on." We have a high school graduation announcement that mentions six siblings—but doesn't specify their ages as older or younger. In fact, the only reason we have his name to begin with is that Silas and Rosie started searching the paid birthday ads in the newspaper and saw he just turned twenty-eight.

But no address. Unlisted in the phone book. Doesn't appear on any search engine.

I sigh. "I've got to get out of here." The drive to hunt runs through me until it feels as if I might erupt. Silas is out paying our rent for month two when I leave, and Rosie looks so pitiful with the bag of ice, surrounded by books, that I let her off the hook despite myself — maybe being insanely kind and understanding will bring her back to me?

"So, wait, are you just going to walk around looking for Porter?" she asks as I quickly sharpen my hatchet.

"Porter. A wolf. *Anything.* I've got to do something, Rosie," I mutter as I fling open the door, then storm down the steps.

I wander the streets of the business district, cloak fluttering in the wind and hatchet strapped tightly around my waist. It's a shame I can't go to the hospital and take out the Fenris from Rosie's class. It won't be too much longer till his soul is completely gone and he can't be contained. But something tells me hospital staff wouldn't be too cool with a scarred-up girl with an eye patch coming in and hacking up one of their patients, criminal though he may be. It's probably not worth the risk of their strapping me down and pumping me with drugs.

A few businessmen are leaving their offices late and cast me wary looks as I glare at them with my good eye. Homeless people, the occasional couple walking home from something or another. But no Fenris. Not even a Dragonfly. When I begin to seriously consider shouting James Porter's name into the streets, I realize I should probably go back. I trudge toward the apartment, frustration bubbling inside me.

The junkie below us is clearly brewing up a new drug cocktail; the smell hangs over the stairwell like a thick cloud. I hurry past his door to my own, where I tug off my eye patch as a puddle of rainwater forms beneath my feet.

The door is cracked the tiniest bit, releasing a pale golden strip of light into the otherwise dark landing. I hear Rosie—I think it's Rosie, anyhow, but the voice is different. It's older, more mature, and softer, like a woman's voice instead of my baby sister's. I frown and press my back against the wall by the door, running my fingers over the ridges of peeling paint as I crane my neck and try to peer inside to see the cause of the change in her voice. I know that spying on my sister isn't exactly moral, but I can't help being curious.

I can't see much except a sliver of the kitchen and a tiny ceramic lamp that's struggling to illuminate the entire apartment. Beyond it, out the window, the Atlanta skyline glows in the darkness. Rosie's voice again—it must be her—fumbles through the silence, but I can't make out the words. Another voice, this one deep and honey-toned...Silas. He speaks with a gentle, melodic rhythm that makes him seem far more than three years my senior. I lean farther toward the crack of the door, inhaling the delicious scent of the orange blossom tea that's brewing on the stove. I begin to reach for the glass doorknob, wondering what they're talking about that makes their voices seem so foreign.

Silas steps into my line of sight and leans against the kitchen counter, and in almost the same instant, Rosie comes into view, black hair fluttering around her heart-shaped face.

She pulls the teapot off the stove and wipes her hands on her jeans, laughing at something Silas has said. He smiles broadly with a strange look in his eyes. I grab the glass door-knob, nearly charging in and demanding to know what's up, but something stops me.

Something is different, something that goes beyond the change in Rosie's voice, something that feels heavy in my mind and makes my stomach writhe. I can't pinpoint what exactly it is until Silas steps behind my sister and delicately runs his fingers through her hair, his hand gentle as if he's touching a priceless jewel. Rosie blushes as he leans into her and whispers something in her ear that makes her lips curve up in an elegant smile. I recognize the look in Silas's eyes — adoration. I furrow my eyebrows and try to shake away the feeling of being punched in the face.

I must be mistaken. I'm not seeing what I think I'm seeing.

But worse yet: it doesn't shock me. Because somehow, somewhere deep, I *knew*.

I squeeze the knob so tightly that its faceted surface cuts into my palm. He's my best friend; she's my *little* sister. No. This isn't her. This isn't us. We aren't silly girls who flirt with boys and laugh at their terrible jokes and touch like Rosie and Silas are doing right now, their fingers intertwined as she turns around to face him.

Rosie laughs. She reaches around Silas's neck — he looks taller, older than normal — and twirls the hair at the nape of his neck around her fingers. His arms circle her waist protectively, one hand half hidden beneath her silk shirt as it rests on the tiny, smooth small of her back. Everything about them is silky and gleaming, all smooth skin and shiny hair and languid voices. I can feel the scars on my body more than ever before, thick ropes working to strangle me. I swallow hard.

Silas leans in. My chest tightens and I beg for him to stop, but no one hears me — I'm not even sure if my pleas are spoken aloud. Rosie tilts her head back. His arms draw her closer, encasing her slight frame. *Stop, both of you — we're hunters; we're in this together, remember? We promised one another; we promised one another ages ago. We're in this together.* Their lips meet.

And I am more alone than ever before.

The door creaks open, loose on its hinges, and I make no effort to stop it. Rosie's and Silas's heads turn toward the noise, and then their faces pale when they see me standing in the door frame. Screwtape runs from the kitchen and dives under my and Rosie's bed, as if he senses my anger, the storm brewing in my heart. Rosie doesn't speak, though her mouth opens as though she's trying to form words. She unwraps herself from Silas's arms but takes his hand into hers. I don't move. I don't think I can move, not when I can still see the places on her neck where Silas kissed her.

"Lett," Silas finally says, his voice hoarse.

"No," I whisper in response. "No, no, no..." I scarcely hear my own words over the sound of my heart, *our* heart, pounding.

"Lett, listen to me," Silas says, stepping in front of my sister. She clings to his hand as if he can protect her. "This is not a big deal. We were afraid you'd be mad, that's all."

"Afraid..." I step into the room and turn to close the door behind me, inhaling for strength as I lock it. *Breathe, Scarlett. Just breathe.* I turn back to them, trying to maintain control of my emotions, trying to keep the two of them from seeing that I'm shaking in sorrow and anger and hurt.

"You lied to me. You both *lied* to me."

"We... we just didn't tell you. Oh, Scarlett, please," Rosie begs, releasing Silas's hand and rushing toward me with tears in her eyes. I knock her away with all the strength I'd use when fighting a Fenris. Rosie stumbles aside but regains her balance. She rubs her arm where I struck her.

"You didn't tell me. You kept it a secret, because... because I..." I look down at my scars. "Because I'm an outcast. A freak because I hunt. Because I do what's *right*. Because I...I fight. I don't let people die, while you two are here, like this...taking dance classes and...and kissing and..." I'm losing control.

I shake my head and raise my voice more than I mean to, fighting back tears. "You're both selfish children. You know what exists in this world. You have the power to stop it. And you...you abandon me so I can fight it on my own."

"We're all hunters, Scarlett. But there's more in the world—you have to know that you can't fight—" Rosie pleads.

"Yes," I snap at her, my voice nearly a growl, "I *can* fight.

Because it's the right thing to do, Rosie. How many girls could we have saved had you not spent god knows how long in dance classes or here with him?"

"I'm sorry," Rosie chokes out. Tears are streaming down her face. Silas gives her a pained look.

"Scarlett, we—" Silas interjects.

"Ah yes!" I cry with false enthusiasm. " 'We'! You and my *baby sister*, Silas. You're a happy little couple, aren't you?" I shake my head. "I can't...I *won't* stay here," I say through gritted teeth. Rosie reaches toward me, but I yank my hand away. "No," I snap. "Don't touch me."

The three of us stare at one another, our faces pictures of hurt.

Then I turn sharply, fling open the door, and leave.

CHAPTER EIGHTEEN

Rosie

Scarlett slams the door shut behind her, and I dissolve into broken sobs. Something aches in my chest, as if my heart has died within me. Maybe our hearts have finally become two instead of one. I fold my arms over my waist and cry, gasping for air and ignoring the burning of tears on my cheeks. Silas turns to look at me but doesn't move.

"Rosie," he says softly. That's all it takes; I fall forward and let him wrap his arms around me, pressing his cheek against my forehead.

"We shouldn't be doing this. We shouldn't have done this. She's my sister."

"Don't say that," Silas murmurs into my hair, voice genuinely pleading. "Please don't ever say that."

"We're hunters," I choke.

"Yes. Of course we are. We're...we're more...but..." He shakes his head and pushes me out to arm's length, lowering his head to look me in the eyes. "I didn't mean for us to hurt her, Rosie, but I wouldn't take any of it back. I couldn't take any of it back—I love you too much."

I try to agree, tell him I love him, *anything*, but I can't find the words. Silas pulls me back against him, my tears dampening his shirt.

He lowers his head and speaks softly, running his fingers through my hair. "I'm going to go after her. We can't just let her go. Are you coming?"

"I..." I think of the dark, tragic look on Scarlett's face when she saw Silas and me together. I shake my head, about to lose it again. "I can't. She hates me."

"She loves you," Silas says firmly. He pulls me to him and kisses my tearstained cheeks. "Come on. We'll split up; she can't have gone far."

I struggle to gulp down the last of my tears and nod. Silas puts his lips to my forehead and hugs me tightly.

"Okay. Come on, let's go. I'll go north, you go south? I promise, we'll bring her home."

I nod again. Silas steps away slowly, like he's worried I may topple over if he doesn't steady me. I wave my hand and signal for him to go; with another worried look in my direction he throws the door open and pounds down the stairs two at a time. I strap the knife belt around my waist and take a deep breath.

If we were in Ellison, I would know exactly where to find my sister. Here, I feel lost, like someone screaming out a missing dog's name in the middle of the night. I head toward the business district. My eyes are swollen and my nose is running to the point that anyone I pass averts his eyes. What kind of person am I? I traded my sister in for dance classes and kisses. But even as I think that, I can't help but realize how badly I want to be with Silas. Just an hour ago I was in his embrace, feeling more beautiful than I ever had before. And would I trade that in, give it away for the hunt? I stumble down the stairs of the subway. No. I couldn't trade it in again. Not now that I know what it is to be loved. Not now that I've stepped out of the cave and into the sun. But that doesn't make it feel any more fair, or make me feel any better that my sister hates me.

I brush through the subway turnstile, eyes scanning the poorly lit station for Scarlett. There's just the usual assortment of vagabonds and tired-looking waitresses. I move to leave.

"You lost, chickadee?" a voice says. I turn around to see a ragged-looking man packing up several buckets, a pair of beaten drumsticks in his dirty jeans pocket.

"No," I answer. "I'm looking for someone who is."

"No luck?"

I shake my head. "Not so far."

The ragged man nods wisely. "Maybe the trouble is, she doesn't want to be found."

"That's what I'm afraid of." I sigh. I toss the change in my pocket into the man's tip jar. He's right. Scarlett is not like me; she has never wanted to be rescued. Not from hunting, not from Fenris, and certainly not by me.

CHAPTER NINETEEN

SCARLETT

I BEGIN TO RUN AS SOON AS I HIT THE SIDEWALK. TEARS stop up my throat, wrap around my neck as if they're trying to choke me. People stare, but for the first time I don't care that I'm not wearing the eye patch in public. I dash through traffic, push through crowds, trying to outrun the hurt that's chasing after me.

Everything blurs except the hollowness in my chest and the feeling of my feet pounding against the pavement. I'm not sure how long I run, only that it doesn't seem as though it's been long enough when my body finally pleads with me to stop. Sweat rolls down my face and back, and I can feel painful blisters beginning to rub.

I grab the handle of my hatchet as I collapse onto the ground underneath an oak tree, and only then do I realize

I'm on the outskirts of Piedmont Park. I lean my head back against the tree, panting so hard that my lungs burn for oxygen, the world spinning. *Breathe. Just breathe.* I focus on the breath entering and leaving my lungs so my mind can't wander back to Rosie and Silas. The moon steadily rises into the sky, but I hardly notice. *Breathe.*

"Lett?" a quiet voice says. How long have I been sitting here?

I grit my teeth. *No. Not you.* I'm breathing.

"*Go away*, Silas," I say firmly without looking at him. I hear his footsteps in the grass and look down as he appears in front of me, then drops to his knees.

"Lett, please. You're my best friend. You're my partner," he says gently.

"And she's my sister, asshole."

"That's not..." He sighs. "We didn't mean to lie."

It must be nice to be part of a "we." Anger rolls through me. I look up at him, eye burning. Silas tenses and holds his hands up, as if he's calming a wild animal.

"You'll never understand," I hiss.

Then I lunge at Silas before I can stop myself, hitting him in the shoulder.

He offers little resistance; I doubt he was expecting me to attack him. We roll backward down the small incline and spin apart in the grass. I'm up before he is, and I swing forward, left hook to his weak side. Silas blocks my punch, so I kick back, striking him in the ribs. He tries to say something but can only cough as I swing again. Fist to nose—his nostrils begin to bleed. He growls and swings back at me, catching my shoulder blade with enough force to knock me backward. I slide my leg out as I slam into the ground, kicking his knees out from under him. He falls, hard, and struggles to catch his breath, rolling away from me. I roll toward him and kick him in the ribs, then dash forward as he tries to roll away. We finally come to a stop at the bottom of the hill. I hold Silas's chest down with my knees, breathing hard as I raise one fist. I want to hit him over and over and over again, until I hit out everything that's tearing at me, eating me alive. God, I want to hit him.

"Lett, *I-I love her,*" he stammers, though it's hardly audible due to the blood pouring out his nose. I lift my fist higher but close my eye, searching for some kind of sanity. Silas stays perfectly still, eyes animal-like and pleading.

I grit my teeth and roll off him, kicking him away just for good measure. I bury my face in the grass and rip fistfuls of it from the ground. I hear Silas cough, and when I look back at him, he's wiping the blood from his nose with the back of his hand, leaving long streaks across his face.

"Of course," I say, forcing myself to stand. "Of course you love her." I look down at the scars on my arms. "She's my sister. I took the Fenris for her. And you, you and your father taught me to hunt. I thought *surely*...you and Rosie could understand. You could know what it means to make the world better."

"We do, Lett. But we want more than the hunt. That's all. You could have more too, you know."

"Come on, Silas," I say flatly, staring at a bed of tulips to avoid meeting his eyes. "Can you really see me as a wife? A mother?" My frustration becomes desperate pleading, and I realize how badly I want Silas to have an answer to my questions.

Instead, he looks surprised. "Lett, you've got to be kidding me."

I laugh humorlessly and shake my head. "No, Silas. I'm a hunter. I thought I wasn't alone. Sure, I thought you were gone for good when you left for San Fran, but Rosie... I thought I could keep Rosie. I lost my eye, my innocence, my ignorance, but I thought Rosie..." I look away. "But of course. You love her."

"Scarlett." Silas says my full name testily. "You stupid, stupid girl."

I turn to him, eye wide in alarm. He shakes his head and steps toward me. "Scarlett, it was you. Long before it was Rosie, I wanted you."

I want to laugh, because I'm sure he's joking, but instead I feel dim-witted, embarrassed. "Why would you say that? Just to hurt me?" I whisper.

"No." Silas steps closer to me and wipes at his nosebleed again. "I had a crush on you for our entire childhood."

"Before the attack, though—"

"No, after. Before, after. The entire time. Why did

you think I was always at your house, for god's sake? Why I volunteered to be your guide to life in the Reynolds household after Oma March died? I wanted to be around *you*, Lett."

I stare at him incredulously. Would he really have the audacity to lie about something like this? I take a step back, scared by his claim. "Then why . . . you never said that, so why am I supposed to believe . . ."

"I was afraid to say it. And then I realized that you could never love me back. I'm your best friend, sure, but . . . you're in love with the hunt. You always have been."

My eye narrows. "I hunt because I *have* to—"

"Whatever." He waves a hand dismissively. "It drives you. It inspires you, it completes you, Lett. You come alive when you fight. I could never have competed with that." He steps closer to me, eyes flickering in the moonlight.

I shake my head. "No. Don't lie to me to make me feel better. Don't—"

But then Silas moves forward with the speed of an animal, closing the space between us. Before I can react, before I can realize what he's doing, his lips are on mine. I freeze. My mind stops except for the awareness of his warm kiss, the scent of his skin close to my face. When he pulls away, his eyes are searching, looking for something within me. I reach up and touch my mouth, feeling the spot where his lips were.

"I . . ." I begin, sinking to the ground. There's nothing.

No spark, no fire. Nothing. "You're right," I whisper aloud. "I didn't feel anything."

"Not like you feel when you hunt," Silas says, lowering himself to the ground in front of me. He takes my hand in his. "It's fine, Lett. But just because you can find that kind of love in the hunt doesn't mean that Rosie and I can. We're hunters, but we need something more. You don't. You're a part of it; it's a part of you."

"I can't help it," I whisper through tears. How are there even tears left in my body? "I can't help it. It's what I am; it's all I am. It's all that's left of me."

"I know," Silas says gently. He rises and pulls me to standing with him. "It's okay."

"I don't think I can change," I murmur. "I can't stop... I keep thinking about hunting and the Potential and this Porter guy and..."

Silas smiles comfortingly, then shakes his head. "Lett, I'd never want you to change anyhow." He reaches over and puts his hand over mine, squeezing it tightly. I hesitate, then put my other hand on top of his. We're partners. Always have been, even when I hate him, when he's a thousand miles away, when he loves my sister...even when it'd be easier to go it alone for good.

We're silent for a moment.

"I promised Rosie I'd make you come home," he finally says.

I shake my head, mind still whirling. "I can't, Silas. Not right now, anyway."

"I figured as much," Silas says softly. "I'll go, then?"

I nod. I don't know what else to do. Silas turns and walks away.

He doesn't look back, and I'm glad, because the tears have begun to flow again.

CHAPTER TWENTY

Rosie

I return home, cheeks now rubbed raw with tears. Only Screwtape waits for me in the apartment, though I'm not surprised. I splash water on my face and turn the lights off, then carry Screwtape to the couch in hopes he'll comfort me until someone, *anyone,* returns. He allows me to bury my face in his fur for only a few moments, though, before he leaps away to chase a bug that skitters across the floor, its silhouette illuminated by the streetlights outside.

The door opens. It's Silas. He meets my eyes in the near darkness and presses his lips together. No words are necessary. I nod as the familiar lump rises up in my throat again. Silas slips his shoes off and sinks into the couch beside me, dropping his head into his hands. Screwtape darts by him, bites his ankles, and moves on; Silas takes the most halfhearted swipe at the cat.

"No luck?" I finally ask.

"I found her. She wouldn't come," Silas says gently. My face tightens and I curl into a ball against the couch arm. She wouldn't come home. I hurt the other half of my heart that badly.

Silas sighs and moves closer to me, taking my forearms in his and trying to pull me into an embrace. I want him to hold me, I want to breathe in the scent of his skin, let my hand climb up the front of his shirt, feel the heat of his body. But something stops me, something more powerful than my own desire. I pull away and shake my head.

"I...I..." I want to say that I *can't*. I can't *touch you like this right now,* can't *hold you even though my body begs to be against yours.* I love my sister; this is what hurt her. This is what drove her away.

Silas nods sadly. "Okay, Rosie. Why don't we both just get some sleep, then?"

"Y-yeah," I stammer. "Right. And we'll go try to get her to come home in the morning," I say firmly.

"Of course," Silas answers. The bells outside toll twelve times, but it feels much later than midnight.

I grab Screwtape again and trudge to the tiny bedroom that Scarlett and I share. Behind me, I hear Silas pull off his shirt and unfold the afghan. I wonder how well he'll sleep. I don't know if there's even much point in my trying. I crawl into the bed, Scarlett's side achingly vacant. I steal her pillow and bury my face in it, inhaling the scent of her hair—it's different from mine, just the smallest bit. How can I exist in a world where she hates me? Tears burn my eyes and begin to fall again, self-hatred gnawing at me. I stop crying for a moment when light from the street steals into my bedroom as Silas gently pushes the curtain aside. He leans against the wall, arms folded across his bare chest and hair falling in front of his eyes. Almost silently, he moves to the tiny space between my bed and the wall and lowers himself to the floor. Raising his knees to his chest, he drops his head and reaches for my hand, running his thumb across my knuckles silently.

I slide off the bed, sheets wrapped around my legs, and ease into his lap, tucking my face against his neck. He cradles me against him like he's afraid to let me go. I know I should shy away, that I should climb back into my bed out of loyalty to my sister. But there's something that locks me in place, something that won't let me stray from the gentle rise and fall of his chest or from his arms, supporting me like I'm something precious as his lips brush across my forehead.

Without speaking, we finally fall asleep.

CHAPTER TWENTY-ONE

SCARLETT

I DON'T KNOW WHERE TO GO. WHERE TO GO, WHAT TO do, or whom to speak to. I don't talk to strangers; I don't chat and discuss the weather in elevators. So I wander the city, silent, stoic, as a low morning fog rolls in and covers the ground. Even the homeless avoid me, as if I'm giving off some sort of leper vibe. I try to hunt, but in a way I'm afraid to; the Arrow pack knows who we are, and I'm not sure I have the willpower or ability to stop them if they ambush me. It would be easier to just let them have me.

The next day is the same.

And the next. I wander into the library and halfheartedly type Porter's name into the computer—still no results. I sleep in the park, huddled under the coral-colored azaleas with my cloak swept over me like a blanket. A cop gives me trouble once, but when he sees me without the eye patch, I can practically feel his throat go dry. He nods at me and advises me to find a new bed in the future, then leaves me alone. I wander like a lost girl, jumping whenever I think I see Rosie or Silas. Every time I happen across a couple that resembles them, my heart leaps nervously. I don't want them to find me, but while I dread it, I also find myself hoping to see them laughing, holding hands, walking along together. Maybe I'm a masochist, but watching them together would hurt, sting with jealousy and betrayal. Hurt would be *something,* at least, some feeling to break up the dead, dull sensation I've been filled with for days now.

I take the subway in circles for most of day three, until I realize that I'm seeing the same people coming home that I saw going to the shops, the park, the diners, hours prior. I force myself off at the next stop and begin to walk. I'm surprised when I emerge from the subway station; I haven't been to this part of town before, but I recognize a logo on a sign pointing me to Vincent's Elderly Care, the hospital Silas's father is in. I linger on the street corner for a moment. I haven't talked to anyone in days. Pa Reynolds was always kind to us, took care of us after Oma March died, until our mother got there. He knows about the scars already, and he doesn't stare. At least, he didn't before the Alzheimer's. He probably doesn't remember me at all. What if he cries out? What if I scare him now?

I can't continue to be alone, though. I turn the corner to the hospital, a giant white and cream building that looks as if it's a product of the late sixties. Nurses in salmon-colored scrubs chat on benches outside while eating yogurt, and even from the sidewalk I get an overpowering whiff of that horrible hospital smell—saline and latex and rubbing alcohol. I wrinkle my nose and ignore the curious stares from the nurses as I enter through bright white automatic doors.

"Can I...um...help you?" a young girl calls out from the reception desk. Her fake smile and voice fade when she sees me, though the giant mirror behind her tells me it's not just because of my scars. My hair is a tangled mess, my clothes dotted with dirt and leaves. I grimace and yank my hair back into a ponytail as I approach her. That's better, somewhat.

"Hi," I say, but my underused voice cracks. I start again. "Hi. I'm here to see Charlie Reynolds."

"Your name is?" the receptionist says, bouncing back to her perky professionalism.

"Scarlett March."

"Oh, you're not on Mr. Reynolds's visitor list—"

"I'm visiting for Silas Reynolds. He couldn't make it and wanted someone to check on his father," I lie. The receptionist chews on her pen for a moment, then shrugs.

"Okay, then. Right this way." She slides a Be Back in a Moment sign across the desk and leads me through the hospital. We pass rooms of people in wheelchairs, pointed at televisions that I'm certain they aren't truly watching. Rooms where the curtains are drawn and doctors talk to old people in coddling, soft tones, the same voices they would use for infants. "Good job! Now eat another bite!" I frown and try to block my ears.

"He's right in here," the receptionist says, opening the double doors of a back room with a key card. We walk in and I hear them lock behind me. I fight the urge to bolt.

The room is brown. Completely brown. Brown paneling, brown carpet, brown leather furniture. The only color in the room is the patients, most of whom wear sea green hospital gowns. They have lanyards around their necks displaying their names and pertinent details. They don't even give me a second glance, and though I suspect it's not out of politeness, I'm still grateful.

"Miss March, here to see Mr. Reynolds," the receptionist calls across the room to a beefy male nurse who looks more like a club bouncer than a hospital employee. He nods and smiles, then points toward the back of the room at a small circle of wheelchairs.

Toward Pa Reynolds.

The receptionist pulls a chair up for me, but I can't stop staring. Is this the way people feel when they see me? I sink into the chair, regarding Silas's father with awe. Time has dissolved the once strong, proud man; his wrists are frail, neck small, lips loose and wet. He looks around the room in alarm, as though he's searching for something specific but can never find it. He's one of the few not wearing a hospital gown, but the gray sweatpants and white T-shirt make him look even more washed out and call attention to the age spots that cover his skin.

"Mr. Reynolds?" the receptionist says so loudly that it hurts my ears. Pa Reynolds turns to face her, bobbing a little in his wheelchair. "Mr. Reynolds, Miss March is here to visit you today. Isn't that exciting?"

Pa Reynolds glares at her. I snicker; it's a familiar glare, one that would usually accompany the words "Are you thick-headed, child?" The nurse looks exasperated for a moment, then smiles at me and walks away.

Pa Reynolds moves his wavering eyes to me. I turn my head so he doesn't see my missing eye. He smiles and reaches a delicate hand forward, and I wrap my fingers around his, soft as aged leather.

"Celia," he croaks, his voice higher pitched than I remember. "Celia, how lovely to see you, my darling."

It takes me a few moments to respond. After the shock, the hurt passes. This man doesn't know me. He made a rocking horse for me as a baby, he helped Oma March teach me to ride a bike, never once cringed at my scars, but he doesn't know me. How much harder it must be for Silas.

"I'm not Celia," I say softly. "I'm Scarlett, Pa Reynolds. Scarlett March?"

Pa Reynolds stares at me a moment, then smiles and nods. "Ah, Celia. My love."

I sigh and sit back in the chair, leaving my hand wrapped around Pa Reynolds's wrinkly fingers. Celia had been his wife, his high school sweetheart, Silas's mother, who had died when he was eight. How can Pa Reynolds mistake me for someone he once loved? I look nothing like her—she was blond, beautiful, delicate, graceful... I force myself to swallow and shake my head. This was a mistake. Even the look in his eyes is all wrong—he doesn't look like the fatherly figure I knew, the one I so desperately need advice from now, but rather like a scared boy.

"I think I should go," I whisper hoarsely.

"Oh, Celia, please, no." Pa Reynolds puts his opposite hand on top of mine, pinning it down. He looks at me, eyes full of pain. "We didn't mean it. It wasn't our fault; it just happened."

"I know," I answer quickly, though I have no idea. "I know it wasn't."

"He'll be fine there. My parents will raise him. He'll be fine."

"I'm sure he will be." I try to stand, but the old man has a surprisingly intense grip. He trails his thumb over my knuckles.

"Celia, please. There's no other way. They'll never let us get married if we keep him."

I sigh and decide to humor the old man. "Keep who, Pa Reynolds?"

Pa Reynolds reaches up and runs his fingers through the tips of my hair, apparently oblivious to the bits of leaves and grass stuck in it. "Our Jacob. Our little boy. He'll be happy, Celia. We'll be happy."

I pause, mind whirring, connections clicking together. "Our Jacob"? Jacob, as far as I knew, was Pa Reynolds's brother, Silas's uncle. Surely I'm misunderstanding. I pull my hair away from his hand.

"Pa Reynolds," I say loudly, in a voice irritatingly similar to the receptionist's, "I think you're confused. Let's talk about something else. Why don't you tell me the story about Silas getting stuck in the tree again? You loved telling that story." I attempt a warm smile, but I'm not sure it works, because instead of smiling back, Pa Reynolds's eyes narrow. His face changes, falls, lifts, falls again. He pulls his hand away from mine and, with surprising speed, moves his wheelchair so close that my knees touch the armrest.

"Scarlett. Little Scarlett March," he says softly. His face changes, crinkling up in a grandfatherly way. He presses his lips together and leans to one side to stare at my eye patch. "Oh, my child. My poor child. How are your wounds healing?"

"They're fine, Pa Reynolds. Long healed." At least he knows me now.

"Oh my...my darling. And it's all my fault..." He trails off.

"Of course not. You could never have gotten there in time," I say, cringing. Pa Reynolds had rarely talked about the attack after it happened, and to relive that time now, to hear this poor old man overcome with guilt...It's painful.

"But it is, of course it is." He shakes his head and rubs his temples with his fingers. When he looks back at me, his eyes are reddened, tears building in the corners. I sit up, scared.

"No, Pa Reynolds, you tried to get there—"

"You, and baby Rosie, and...oh god, poor Leoni!" He calls Oma March by her first name, nearly sobbing. "We tried," he says. "We tried so hard; we were just a day late leaving that year. One day! One day and they wouldn't have come. That was the key—keep him moving, and they could never find him in time."

"They..." I swallow. This can't possibly mean what I think it means, can it? "Pa Reynolds? I need you to explain to me what you mean. Please."

Pa Reynolds shakes his head as if this is something obvious, something I should know, and then his eyes change again. "Oh, Celia. They can't find us at the coast. We'll take him there again, just like we did when he turned seven. We'll take all of them to the beach for the entire month. Jacob too, even...And we'll get the triplets home from school. All our babies."

"You mean...Silas."

"We'll take them there, stay for his birthday. Silas is too gentle to saddle with this sort of knowledge." He waves his hands dismissively at the window, then leans back as if peering inside another room. "Keep him moving. As long as he's moving, the wolves can't find him."

I inhale sharply. Of course. I'm so stupid—how did I not realize? I can muster only a whisper. "Jacob was your son. Silas is the seventh son of a seventh son, isn't he?"

"We thought he would be a girl, Celia! Like the triplets, another girl! The doctors said he would be, but they made a mistake. We can keep him safe, we can take everyone away on his seventh birthdays, we'll hide him till the moon phase is over...They'll never find him, love. Never."

"Then...that's why the Fenris came to Ellison, isn't it? Silas was turning fourteen when we were attacked. Silas was a Potential." I inhale and close my eye. "No. Silas *is* the Potential." The realization crashes over me like a wave, knocking the wind out of me. He just turned twenty-one. Even though his birthday was a while ago, this is the first full phase after it. My Silas—no, Rosie's Silas. He could be a Fenris. He could be the monster I fight next. He could lose his soul. He would have already, had we not been wandering from Ellison to here and then all over this city...Silas. It's him. He is the bait I've been looking for all this time.

My eye snaps open and I look back at the old man. "Pa Reynolds, does Silas know? Did you tell him?"

Pa Reynolds looks at me, all grandfather lines again. "Scarlett. Little Scarlett March. How are your wounds healing?"

"The Fenris, Pa Reynolds!" I say urgently. The beefy nurse rises and gives me a curious look. "Does Silas know he's a Potential?"

"How do you know about Silas..." The old man's face turns white.

"Does he know?" I nearly shout.

"No. No, he doesn't. No one but Celia and I...Oh, Scarlett. Look what we've done to you. And Leoni! Oh, Leoni, it's our fault. We were a day late; we stayed in Ellison an extra day to avoid the thunderstorm. Leoni, my friend..." Pa Reynolds puts his head in his hands and begins to weep, dry, ancient sobs that sound more like gasps for air than cries.

"Is there a problem, miss?" the nurse says as he takes long, powerful strides toward us.

"No. No," I say, leaping to my feet and stepping away from Pa Reynolds. "No, but I have to leave." I have to warn Silas; I have to tell Rosie. I turn and run from the hospital, wind screaming in my ears and heart racing.

CHAPTER TWENTY-TWO

Rosie

This isn't working, is it?" Silas mumbles to me, squeezing my hand. I jolt out of the daze I was in.

"What, us?" I say quickly, chest tightening in worry.

He smiles gently and runs his palm down my lower arm, letting it rest on my fingers. "No. Hunting without her."

I nod in agreement. We've been sitting outside the Attic for hours now, waiting, watching. But we haven't seen a Fenris. Haven't seen Scarlett. Without Scarlett there's no drive, no power behind our hunting. And truthfully, I'm not hunting for Fenris anyway; I'm hunting because I hope that we'll run into my sister. I keep thinking that we'll catch her lurking around the clubs, that I'll be able to throw my arms around her and plead for her not to be mad. And of course she'll listen, and we'll go back home and order kung pao chicken, and Silas and I will...be over?

Silas draws me closer and kisses my forehead, my nose, my lips, so tenderly that I could melt against him despite my worries. I nestle my head into the crook of his neck. I can't just let this be over, not when it feels so...right. I can't be just a hunter, nothing more. Not again.

"Maybe it's for the better that we haven't seen any wolves," Silas says, hopping off the wall we're sitting on. I jump down after him. "Now that the Arrow pack knows us and all..."

"No. Fenris move quicker than this. If they were going to set up a trap for us, they would've done it already," I answer as we interlace our fingers and begin to walk back to the apartment.

"You sound like your sister," Silas says, eyebrows raised. I smile. That's comforting, in a way.

The junkie swings open his door and glares at us as we ascend the stairs. I've noticed that no matter which of us is holding the key, we always pause for a moment before opening our door, as if we're giving Scarlett time to materialize in the apartment. But Screwtape is the only one behind it tonight, just like he was when we left. Silas gets into the shower while I climb into my bed, even though I know I'll eventually join him on the couch. I can't sleep alone anymore, and his breathing, his warm body, and his assurances that it will be okay are the only things that let me rest, that let me prepare for another morning without her.

Silas is gone when I wake up. He's been slipping out in the mornings, trying to find my sister while the city crowds are still sparse. I stumble to the bathroom to splash water on my face. I consider making breakfast, but it's been so long since I went grocery shopping that we're out of everything but a can of spaghetti sauce. I suppose I should go to the store...I sigh, grab my cloak, and walk downstairs and out the building door.

I walk through the grocery store in a daze, knocking things from the shelves into my basket. Bread, eggs, pasta... I haven't been much in the mood to cook lately. Simple foods, easy to prepare. I check out without talking to the cashier, who gives me a rather cold look for my silence. She bags my groceries, smashing the bread beneath the carton of eggs, and I trudge out of the store. No rush. Not as though I have anywhere to be anyway, since Silas and I have all but given up on finding the Potential and we can't hunt.

I swing the bags of groceries absently on the way home, cloak fluttering at my heels. I cut through the park — maybe Scarlett's been here? My eyes wander across the wildflowers planted in neat patches. I sigh. Scarlett or Silas. Do I have to choose between them? Is the choice already made? I walk onto the grass, sidestepping a herd of runners on the path.

"Miss?" a male voice calls out. "Miss, you have to be careful."

I look up, realizing the voice is speaking in my direction.

One of the runners has paused in front of me, his face shadowed by a baseball hat.

"What?" I ask.

The runner steps closer and I see traces of a grin on his darkened face. "You have to be careful not to step off the path, miss."

"Oh. I'm sorry, I didn't know," I answer, but as I do so, he reaches up and adjusts his hat. My breath catches as the sunlight illuminates a tattoo on his wrist. An arrow.

With a crown around it.

Everything happens quickly. The Alpha swipes out a hand, locking it around my wrist so hard that I think I feel the bone crack. I reach for my knives, but they aren't there—how could I have left them at home, as many times as Scarlett has reminded me to always wear them? Another hand grabs my free arm. I whip my head around and realize it's one of the runners. No, it's all of the runners. They surround me, their faces contorting in and out of ferocity, teeth extending to fangs then fading back to human teeth. Their eyes flash ocher, and the Alpha yanks my body against his. I flail to pull away, to get him off me, to stop touching me, but it's useless. There are so many, more than I've ever seen in one place before, and they laugh, howl, bark. I try to scream, but a hand that's half covered in fur clamps down on my mouth. The Alpha lifts me into the air like a doll and glares at me, hunger and hatred in his eyes.

Then someone yanks my cloak around my head, twisting it until I can scarcely breathe. I feel the hem rip and fall away, and my grocery bags plummet to the grass. The Alpha clutches me close to him, digging his claws into my skin. We're running—I can feel the wind against my body, whistling against my head—but all I can see is the blood red cloak encasing me. I struggle against the Alpha's grip, but he's strong—god, he's strong—and I can barely move.

I scream again, but I know the sound is lost in the speed we must be moving with. I hear the barks and snaps of the other wolves. I'm sure they're transformed, because every now and then one bites at my legs or waist, just enough teeth to break the top layer of my skin, not enough to seriously wound me. Still, the cuts sting and ache, and I snarl as I hear their joyous howls at my expense. The Alpha's breathing is guttural, almost sexual, and we've been running for what feels like ages. I just want to cry into this suffocating cloak. But I don't. I'm a hunter. *Please, let me be a hunter again.*

We slow. I listen intently, desperate for a clue about my location. We're someplace quiet, someplace almost totally void of the blaring city noises. The breathing of the pack is heavy, and I hear the crunching noise of several Fenris turning back to their human forms. It gets darker; the inside of the cloak looks black now. I struggle again and the Alpha laughs, then holds me tighter until I feel as if I may explode in claustrophobic panic.

Just as I'm certain he'll crush my ribs if he squeezes any harder, he drops me. I hit the ground, elbows crashing against rough cement. The wind is knocked from my lungs, but I clamber backward and yank the red fabric off my face.

Not that it helps. Blackness. I'm in the complete dark.

Heavy breathing surrounds me. The scent of rotting garbage, spoiled milk. Fur brushes by my hand, my face, my legs, leaving my skin greasy and oily. Slowly, my eyes adjust to the darkness and I realize that right in front of me is a sea of ocher eyes.

There are hundreds of wolves. Some are transformed, some are not, but all stare at me hungrily, wantonly. The Alpha Fenris stands right at the edge of my toes, so close I'm afraid I'll retch from the smell, leering down at me with the most lustful grin I have ever seen.

"Hello, sweetheart. I was afraid we wouldn't see you again," he hisses. The other Fenris laugh, one maniacal sound of howls and chuckles. I look around quickly, desperate for a way out that doesn't involve running directly through a pack of wolves. We're in what I think is a subway tunnel—there are rails a few yards from me—but the graffiti on the walls and the scattered blankets make me think it's abandoned.

A Fenris rushes at me from the back of the crowd. I tense, ready to lash out at him, expecting the whole pack to swarm me. How long can I possibly last if they all attack? A minute? Thirty seconds? The wolf leaps into the air, and I see nothing but his massive claws extending toward my face.

He's thrown away, hit hard in the side by the Alpha. The wolf flips in the air and skids across the floor, transforming back to a man and groaning. His side is bleeding, the wound sticky and dark.

"Not yet. Not anyone," the Alpha hisses. He reaches

down and grabs my arm, yanking me to standing so hard that I think my shoulder pops out of joint. He strides toward a yellow metal door that has something streaked across it. Blood? Human blood? He grabs the doorknob and wrenches the door open.

"No one touches her. No one unlocks the door. Understood? She's no good to us dead, not yet." His words are dark, threatening. The pack murmurs and howls in agreement.

The Alpha whips his arm forward, throwing me into the dark room. I slam against something hard and metallic, then crumple to the floor as my head explodes in pain from the impact. The Alpha steps toward me and flicks his hand—it transforms into a claw. Incredible control. He reaches toward my face, but I can't scream. I can't move, my head hurts, I'm scared. I'm no hunter. He grabs ahold of my hair and hacks at it, his claw slicing through the strands.

Then he storms away, slams the door, and locks it.

CHAPTER TWENTY-THREE

SCARLETT

FASTER, FASTER, HAVE TO RUN FASTER. I STUMBLE wildly around corners, legs burning. I barely even know where I'm going. I should have taken the subway, but I didn't think of it in my blind panic. I could already be too late. It's been days, and the Fenris said they didn't have much time left to change him. What if he's losing his soul right now, at this very moment? The Potential was under my nose the entire time, right in front of me! The Potential. Silas. The Potential is my friend.

Or *was* my friend. He might not be anymore, after the affair with Rosie. I'm not certain what we are now, but something is driving me forward. My chest aches and pleads for me to stop, as if I'm breathing fire instead of oxygen. Finally, familiar roads start coming into view. Sweat runs into my eye and blinds me every few steps, and my shirt sticks to my chest. So close — the apartment is just around the corner. God, he doesn't even know. He doesn't even know he could be a monster.

I push through a crowd of ragged men standing on the street corner and run up the stairs, screaming Silas's name with the little power I have left in my lungs. A few doors open, people glare at me, but I ignore them. I don't have the apartment key. *Please be there.* I round up the last few steps and ram the door with my shoulder. Thankfully, it offers little resistance, crashing off the hinges and slamming into the wall behind it.

"Silas!" I shout into the apartment. No answer. I storm in, panic rising as I pant in a desperate attempt to catch my breath. He's gone, he's been taken. And Rosie? Where is Rosie —

"Lett?" I whirl around and see Silas coming up the landing. He looks at the door, then at me, questioningly. "Are you okay? God, we've been looking for you everywhere —"

"Show me your wrists," I demand. I reach for my hatchet and fear grips my heart.

"Um, why —"

"Just show me!" I scream.

Silas hesitates, then raises both hands. Nothing on his wrists. I nod and pull his face close, staring into his eyes. Gray-blue. Not ocher. I exhale. Relief. He hasn't changed. Yet.

"Lett, you're scaring me," Silas says cautiously. "What's going on?"

I sigh and step backward over the fallen door. I collapse into one of the kitchen chairs and put my head in my arms on the table. Silas kneels beside me and puts a hand on my back.

"Lett?" he says quietly.

"It's you," I say, lifting my head. I force myself to inhale. "It's you, Silas."

"What's me?" he asks.

"The Potential. It's you—you're the one."

Silas doesn't move, not even a breath, not a blink. I swallow hard and nod at him.

"Impossible," he whispers. "I have five brothers, three sisters. I'm the ninth child."

"No. I talked to your father today." I shake my head, remembering Pa Reynolds's sad state. "He thought I was your mother, and he said things. He said...your uncle Jacob. He's not your uncle. He's your father's first son. He and Celia had him out of wedlock, so they gave the baby to your grandparents to raise. You're the tenth child and the seventh brother."

"Then I...no, Lett. You're wrong." His voice is quivering, his face the pale green of magnolia flowers.

"Silas, listen to me," I say softly. "It's you. You were twenty-one last month. You're the seventh son of a seventh son. You're the Potential." I take his hand because I'm not sure what else to do. What can I say to comfort him?

When he speaks, his voice is distant, like he's not really talking to me. "They didn't tell me. Why didn't they tell me?"

"I think they were afraid they'd upset you. So they tried to take you away on the seven-year marks—"

"The beach. And then...oh god," he says, raising his eyes to mine. I see him looking at the scars, his gaze running over each one as though on a track. "Lett, that means it was me— I was the reason they came to Ellison. I'm the reason you..."

"Yes," I whisper. "You were supposed to leave town the day the wolf came. If your father kept you moving, the Fenris couldn't sense you and track you down. They didn't even know what you looked like because they had never seen you. Until now—at the bowling alley. The Fenris saw you, knew who you were, and they got away alive."

Silas reaches for my other hand, and suddenly he's pleading, a scared little boy. "Lett, what do I do?" he asks. "If I... if I bring them to me, I bring them to everyone I love, to Rosie, to you..." He pauses and seems to realize with relief that the rest of his family isn't in danger—not when they're not speaking to him.

I slide out of the chair to join him on the floor. How easy it had seemed to want to use the Potential as bait before I knew it was Silas. It had seemed simple to draw them to us, kill them...I have to admit, there's a part of me that still thinks that way. Part of me wonders just how thin a line Silas could tread luring the Fenris before he would be too much at risk. He's never been the bait before, not like Rosie and I have...

I sigh. Flipping your hair is not the same as risking your soul. "We can figure this out, Silas. Where is my sister?"

"I...oh god, if I turn, I'll want her. I'll want to..." He drops his head into my lap and breathes as if he's afraid he might hyperventilate. I touch his hair the way I would if he were Rosie, the way she says comforts her.

"Silas, where is she?" I ask again, pulling his head up.

Silas exhales and seems to regain some of his sanity. "Probably out looking for you. Maybe at Kroger?"

I want to scream at him for a glittering moment—how could he not know where she is? Doesn't he know she needs to be protected? But I shake off the need to yell.

"Let's go, then," he says. "We need to get her, lock ourselves up here, think of a plan—"

"You can't go anywhere, Silas," I interrupt him firmly. "One bite—that's all it takes."

"No," Silas says, shaking his head and springing to his feet. "No, I have to go. I can't just leave her—"

"If we can just wait this out, you won't be of any use to them—the moon phase is over tomorrow. Maybe we can even draw them out of the city—you know, lure them away from here and then just drive until your time as a Potential is up—"

"I love her!" he shouts, slamming his hands against the kitchen table. "You *know* I love her, Lett. You know I can't just stay here."

I don't know that. I don't know what it's like to be in love. But I can't possibly deny the fire in Silas's eyes, the firm set of his jaw, the knowledge that I'll never be able to keep him from going to her.

"All right," I say, nodding slowly. "Then grab a weapon."
Silas nods and grabs his hunting knives and ax off the kitchen
counter, strapping the latter to his back. We prop the door
back up and take off. I constantly scan the city around us
as we run toward Kroger. Just one bite. That's all it takes. A
Fenris could dart out, nip Silas, steal his soul away. I shiver.

"She's not here," Silas says as we arrive at the grocery
store. We dart down the aisles but see nothing save a few
bored-looking shoppers.

"Where else could she be?" I ask, frustrated, as we hurry
through the automatic doors, back to the street.

"I'm not sure," Silas mutters. He tugs at his hair worriedly.
A passerby in a suit brushes against Silas. We both lurch back,
and I nearly draw my hatchet on the businessman. No, it was
nothing, just a guy. Silas and I make nervous eye contact.

"Think, Silas. Would she have gone back to that place
where she took the classes?" I ask. I realize with a pang that
Silas knows more about Rosie's habits than I do. Silas shakes
his head. "The library? Maybe we should just go back to the
apartment and wait..."

"No. I can't just go sit, I can't...We have to find her."
Silas begins to pace, his face glistening in the midday sun
from beads of sweat.

"Let's walk, then," I say. "The park. Maybe she tried to
go hunting."

"Right. Maybe so," Silas says with fake confidence.

We walk down the main trail that winds through Piedmont Park in silence. Nothing, no sign of her, and with every

passing moment my sanity's waning. *She's fine. I'm over-reacting. She's fine.* We round the path to the flower-lined fountain in the park's center.

"Is that..." Silas's voice trails off. He points, eyes wide and jaw clenched. Grocery bags, strewn on the path. The yolks of eggs run down the path's hill; a gallon of milk sits spoiling in the sunlight. We run toward it.

"Scarlett..." Silas starts, his voice uneven. He lowers himself to the ground and runs a hand over the spilled bags, as though he's afraid to disturb them too much.

"No," I say sharply. "No...I was supposed to protect her..." My eye darts around the area, desperate for some sign that my sister is fine. *She'll come running up the trail any moment now.*

"Lett," Silas says softly. His voice is full of defeat. He walks toward the fountain and lifts something off the ledge that surrounds it. Silas clutches the object in his hand and walks back to me slowly. When he opens his palm, my heart falls, careens to some spot deep in my stomach.

It's a lock of my sister's hair, tied up with a scrap of a red cloak. There's an elegantly written note tucked into the fabric. Silas edges it out. It reads: *11 p.m. tomorrow, Sutton Station. You for her.*

CHAPTER TWENTY-FOUR

Rosie

Bait.

I'm the bait. I've always been the bait, of course, but now it's entirely different. They need me, but for what I'm not certain. To lure Scarlett, maybe, as revenge for her hunting them? Either way, they plan to kill me. The Alpha's words resonate in my mind: "not yet." They can't kill me. *Yet.*

I rub my head and look around my prison. It's a mechanical room of some sort, I think, but it's nearly impossible to tell anything in the darkness except that an enormous machine lurks in front of me. Tiny lines of light peek through from around the edges of the door, but they're not really enough to see by.

I can still hear the Fenris outside, breathing, growling, fighting with one another, shouting. I don't move for the first hour, afraid that if I do, they'll come for me despite the Alpha's orders. But eventually my muscles begin to scream, and I crawl around the machine, groping at it with my hands, trying to figure out what it is.

I'm almost certain that I'm smashing rat droppings between my fingers as I inch around the floor, but I try to put that out of my mind. The machine is huge, welded to the ground and made of cold, heavy metal—steel, I think, from the way a few bits of it reflect the door's light. There's a little door on the side, like a fuse box. I'm afraid to open it for fear of drawing attention, because I'm not sure what it would take to decide that dead bait is just as good as live bait. I think the machine is a generator of some sort, but I'm not sure. The smell of gasoline and grease hangs in the air, heavy.

One wall is covered with mostly empty shelves—the only things left on them are a few cans of chewing tobacco, a couple bottles of cleaner, some old rags, a few random nails, bits of rubber hose, three paintbrushes, and a lighter. I flick it on to see a mop propped against the shelves as well, along with a janitor's cleaning bucket. I release the lighter switch— there's not much lighter fluid left in the thing, and I should probably save it.

The walls of the room have no windows, no grates, and no air ducts. No way out except the door that leads to the most powerful Fenris pack I've ever seen.

I sigh and sit back against a concrete wall. My forehead is covered in sticky, drying blood. I pull the cloak off my shoulders and wrap it around me like a blanket. I'm probably bait for my sister, but what they don't realize is, I'm not certain she'll even come for me.

I clamber back to my knees and circle the room again, memorizing each turn, each sharp edge, each shelf. I have to save myself. Or plan to die.

CHAPTER TWENTY-FIVE

SCARLETT

SILAS PUNCHES THE WALL. HIS HAND COMES AWAY bloody, but he doesn't seem to feel it.

"They should have told me," he growls for the millionth time. "They should have told me before disappearing—"

"I don't think your siblings knew," I interject.

"Then my *father!* My father should have told me when he realized he was forgetting!" Silas yells. He grabs the alarm clock and throws it through the window; the glass shatters, raining onto the sidewalk below. I drop my head into my hands, helpless to calm him but hopefully not helpless to save my sister. This entire place feels like Rosie, as though she's in the room with us but can't speak and we can't reach her. Tomorrow. I think of all the things that could happen to her in one day. I twist a loose thread from the couch around my fingers until they tingle.

"Your father didn't want to hurt you. Sometimes you just want to protect the people you love," I say quietly, meeting his eyes, which are full of agony. I stand, starting to pace.

"Think," I say, mind racing. "Together you and I can take at least eight of them at once." It's a high number, but I'm counting on our shared adrenaline giving us much-needed strength.

"The Arrow pack has grown, though. There could be hundreds. I can't take hundreds," Silas says bitterly. "And I can't be bitten, not even a light wound, or I'm useless to you, to Rosie. I don't understand, Scarlett—how did they even know that Rosie and I..." His words drift off.

I sigh. "Remember what the Alpha said at the bowling alley? Something about them having what they need? That must have been the knowledge of who you are, how they could use Rosie."

"And they didn't try to change me then because...there were fewer of them? You could have protected me. We would have won. But now that the Alpha's fought us, he knows our strengths. He'll be more than prepared for us in terms of numbers. Especially since the moon phase is almost over— he won't want to risk anything." He raises his eyebrows hopefully. "What if we bring guns?"

"Not enough damage to kill them, most likely. And

besides, we couldn't get enough guns quickly enough." I shake my head.

"Okay, we have till tomorrow night. What else could we...Why a day, anyway? Why is tomorrow night special?" Silas mutters.

I shake my head and flip one of Rosie's knives in my hand, then send it spiraling to the door. It sinks in with a sharp crack but isn't on the mark I was aiming for— Rosie's aim is better than mine. If she'd only had these with her... "It's the end of the moon phase. At eleven forty-one, it's over. I'd bet anything they're calling in every pack member they sent out to the country, pulling out all the stops to make sure you don't get away. We could try going in early."

"But they could kill her if we try that," Silas says, defeated. He yanks at his hair until his temples turn bright red. "Scarlett...we have to do it."

"What?"

"Trade me for her."

I fold my arms. "You're saying you'll trade your soul for my sister?"

Silas breathes heavily, beads of sweat on his forehead. "Yes. Do it. Let's go, now." He moves for the door.

"Wait, wait," I say, stepping in front of him. I put my hands on his chest and force him into one of the dining table chairs. Him for her. Silas and Rosie are integral to everything that's important to me. I am an extra. I should be the one traded. I should be the one who can save her. I blink away the jealousy — there's no place for it now.

"Trade me, Lett. Then, when they . . . when they change me, just kill—"

"Shut *up*, Silas," I snarl. "They have no reason to let Rosie go even if they get you. In fact . . ." I swallow hard. "They're probably just going to hand her over to you after you're . . ." I can't say it.

Silas's face loses every trace of color, save his eyes, which glisten in fear and frustration.

I press my lips together, determined. "Listen. What if we pretend we're going through with it? You go there, act like you're going to give yourself up to them, and then I . . . I don't know. Do something. It's the only way I can see us being able to get close to her without them killing her."

Silas looks at me, understanding. "Aren't you just using me as bait? Just like you had planned to do with the Potential anyway?"

"Yes."

"And what could you do to kill them all?"

"I don't have to kill them all. We just have to get Rosie out—as soon as they hand her over, we take off," I answer.

"That sounds too easy," Silas says, shaking his head. "They knew to get Rosie to lure me; they paid enough attention to her at the bowling alley to know she shopped at that Kroger. They won't fall for a simple bait-and-switch scheme."

"I know," I answer. Which brings both Silas and me to the same question, though neither of us wants to say it. If it comes down to it, and we *have* to trade him for Rosie—an honest trade, no tricks—will we do it?

I know my answer. And one hateful, dark thought keeps running through me: Silas took Rosie from me. If he becomes a Fenris...I'll get her back.

CHAPTER TWENTY-SIX

Rosie

The screaming makes me jump to my feet, even though I know I can't help her.

It's a girl, her age difficult to tell through her sobs and pleas. She screams again. I throw myself against the metal door, gagging from horror.

"Please, please. I'll do anything you want. I won't tell anyone what you are," she begs, her words almost impossible to understand through her tears. I hear the crunching, cracking sounds of wolves transforming. I can practically see the horrible grins on their too-wide mouths.

"Please," she chokes.

When they attack her, I scream until my voice is hoarse so I don't have to hear the shredding sounds.

It was summer, and our hands and mouths were permanently stained from eating Popsicles and blackberries. The acrid smell from the junebug traps hung heavily in the air. Pa Reynolds dripped gasoline over the charcoal on the grill, then lit the fire, preparing to cook the large stack of hamburger meat. Oma March whipped a checkered tablecloth across the picnic table the Reynolds brothers had built themselves. She rushed in and out of the kitchen with bowls of macaroni salad and sliced peaches.

"You're it again," Silas called out triumphantly as he tackled me into the grass. I giggled, pulling myself up, and took off running after him, his brothers, and Scarlett. It was a variation of freeze tag that mostly involved us knocking one another down.

"Faster, Rosie, you have to run faster!" Scarlett shouted. I was the youngest and, therefore, the slowest.

I started to get frustrated that I couldn't keep up. The Reynolds brothers darted around me, holding out their hands, only to yank them away when I lunged for them, sending me toppling to the ground. Silas's oldest brothers started getting bored, waiting for me to be within inches of them only to leap away on their long legs. I set my sights on my sister instead. I knew how she played this game and could anticipate her moves.

I ran after Scarlett, our long dark hair flowing identically in the breeze, older and younger versions of the same girl.

She was faster than me, but just as I was about to give up and start crying, she finally tumbled to the ground dramatically, and I tagged her shoulder.

"Good one, Rosie!" she yelled as I used the last of my energy to hurry away before falling onto the picnic table bench, our "base," to rest. Pa Reynolds smiled at me as he squirted a bit more gasoline onto the grill and it flared up, sending black smoke spiraling into the robin's-egg sky.

I wake up so suddenly that I nearly cry out when all I see is darkness instead of blue sky and green grass. I shake my throbbing head but press my lips together to stop any sound from creeping out—after all, I can still hear the haggard, sleepy breathing of the Fenris outside. How long before they give in to their own hunger and devour me? They can still smell me through the metal door, I'm certain, and if one Fenris gives in to temptation, it surely wouldn't take long for a pack mentality to take over. That door, locked or not, couldn't hold up to the number of Fenris I saw outside.

I pull my knees to my chest, put my head in my arms, and think of Silas. What is he doing? If they're after Scarlett, where does he think I've gone? Maybe he thinks I left in search of her, just dropped him and took off. I hope not. I couldn't do that. I inhale slowly and try to pretend that I'm with him, that his arms are encircling me, that I can feel his breath on my neck and the sparse beginnings of his beard tickling my cheek. But it's hard to imagine much of anything in this cave of a room, and my eyes begin to burn. I never even got the chance to tell him I love him...

No. *Think, Rosie, think.* Scarlett wouldn't cry. Scarlett would find a way out. *Stop thinking about Silas, about origami and diner breakfasts. Think of escape.* I close my eyes again, but instead of searching for a dream to take me away, I focus on a person. My sister, the other half of my heart. The only person I know who could unfailingly find a way through a locked door and a pack of hungry Fenris.

Think like Scarlett. I push myself into her mind until I can almost feel her scars on my skin, feel the rush of energy that flows through her during a hunt. The way she felt when the Fenris attacked her. The way she felt when Mom left for the last time. The way she feels when hunting. I am Scarlett. I am confident, I am capable, and I will not wait to be rescued by a woodsman or a hunter. I will escape.

I home in on Scarlett's likes until I practically crave kung pao chicken—though I haven't eaten in ages, so that might actually be my own hunger speaking. The cottage at dawn, the way she said it felt, quiet and serene and cascaded in blue light. Philosophy...that one's tougher to focus on. I've never loved it like she does. There is that one story in particular that she recounted to me whenever I questioned hunting, the one Oma March used to tell us about the children in the cave stepping into the sunlight. How they were blinded by the light at first but had to learn to accept it once they knew it was truth. Just like Scarlett and I had to accept the existence of the Fenris once we knew they were real, not just shadows on a cave wall.

Scarlett loved the tale and said that the rest of the world lived in the cave, thought the shadows were real. Only people who know about the Fenris can really see the sunlight. And then there are those like Mr. Culler, who see the sunlight but prefer to believe in the shadows, who prefer to believe that their sons are just deranged instead of monsters. But I don't remember not knowing about the Fenris, to be honest. Scarlett remembers before the attack, but it's all a blur to me, recollections that are more a creation of her nostalgic stories than my actual memory.

Maybe I'm the opposite of her, though. Maybe the wolves are my shadows. I want to believe that they're a part of me, that they're the core of my being like they are with Scarlett. But now that I've seen this sunlight—seen what it's like to be a normal girl, felt what it's like to be kissed, to be loved— how can I go back to the shadows?

I open my eyes and I inhale sharply. Of course. The plan forms in my mind slowly, more like a tide coming in than a wave crashing over me. I am confident, I am capable, and I will not wait to be rescued by a woodsman or a hunter. I will escape.

CHAPTER TWENTY-SEVEN

SCARLETT

THIS IS MY FAULT," SILAS MURMURS, BREAKING THE silence that's hanging over us like a noose. I don't answer because I think I might agree with him. The church bells chime nine times into the morning. We've been up all night.

There hasn't been much to say, much to plan. Just what feels like endless amounts of time to wait. My body feels shredded, yanked in two directions: Half of me, the hunter half, demands I wait until the time is right to strike. The other half of me, the half that's also the half of Rosie's heart, demands I go for her immediately, throw myself in front of whatever monsters I must in order to save her. Where is she now? Is she cold? Somehow I'm incredibly concerned with her being cold. I hope she has something to keep her warm.

"Scarlett, *promise* me something," Silas begins slowly.

He sits up on the couch, making eye contact with me as I lean against the wall on the other side of the room. I toss my foot back and forth so Screwtape can chase my shoelaces.

"Sure," I mutter.

"If they...if the Fenris get me...I can't lose my soul, I can't become that. No matter what happens with Rosie, if they get me..." He looks down, then back at me as he swallows hard.

I narrow my eye. "Are you asking me to kill you, Silas?"

He nods slowly. "And tell...will you tell my brothers and sisters? Tell them I'm sorry I got the house and that I'm sorry I didn't get to see them again." He looks away.

"And Pa Reynolds?" I ask quietly.

"No." Silas shakes his head. "Don't tell him. Let him forget me. And when...if you have to do it, make it fast..."

I inhale sharply. Could I do that? "Of course, Silas. I promise."

"Good," Silas says. "Good." He sinks back into the couch, like a sick person who can't move too nimbly. We sit in silence for another few moments. My stomach rumbles, but I don't want to eat anything. How could I eat anything when my sister is a hostage?

"Do you think she's cold?" Silas says under his breath, crossing his arms over his chest. My eye shoots up at him.

"What?"

He turns his head to me. "I just...I wonder if she's cold."

I sigh and nod. "Yeah. Me too."

CHAPTER TWENTY-EIGHT

Rosie

Time to act.

At long last, the daylight fades. The tiny square of light around my door dims, and the Fenris begin to rise. They bark at one another, tousle and fight in a clattering of nails and deep snarls. A few scratch at my door but move on when the others snap in protest. I ignore them and crawl around the generator in the center of the room, groping with my finger-tips along the machine until I find the little access panel on the side. I brace my fingers underneath it and pull.

Nothing happens, and my fingers begin to bleed as the sharp rust slices into them. I hold my breath as I yank again. The door gives, sending flecks of metal raining onto the cement floor and into my eyes. I squeeze them shut and ignore the urge to release the door. I slowly pry it off; the hinges are so old that they give way and the heavy iron door falls into my hands. I ease it to the ground and blink away the dust in my eyes as the smell of gasoline overpowers my nostrils.

I grope around on the dirty shelves behind me, fingertips trailing across the cleaners and old rags until they finally wrap around the bits of hose. I turn back to the generator and run my hands across the open space. Wires, cords—I can't see anything, but I hope that my fingers will know what they're looking for when they find it. I root my nails underneath a row of cables and grab on to a tiny metal bar—it turns to the right almost too easily and lifts off to reveal the fuel tank below. I glance up worriedly. Surely they'll smell the gasoline.

I tug the wires aside with one hand and feed an end of the hose into the fuel tank with the other. How much can there possibly be left? The hose hits liquid quickly, which is promising. I glance at the door again, put my lips around the end of the hose, and inhale.

I almost instantly yank my face away and gasp for air that isn't pure gas fumes—my lungs burn and scream in pain, but it seems to have done the trick. The hose snakes in my grip, and I hear the quiet splashing of gasoline pouring onto the floor. I quickly aim the hose at the tiny crack beneath the door and watch as the liquid begins to flow out. I prop up the hose on one of the bottles of cleaner and step over the river of fuel. I tear a strip of fabric off the bottom of my shirt. Outside, I hear the wolves sniffing around the fuel.

One Fenris scratches and howls at the door, his voice half human, half animal.

> *"John and Mary were born in a cave and lived in the cave their entire lives. They always stayed far back in the cave in the near darkness, because if they tried to leave, they saw giant dark monsters on the wall. John and Mary didn't know it, but the monsters were only shadows."*

I wrap the fabric around my forehead and pull one side down so it covers my right eye. It's not as effective as my sister's eye patch, but it'll do. I tug the cloth tightly so it completely obscures my vision. The wolves gather by the door, a chorus of sniffs and growls punctuated by piercing howls. I hear the crunch of a few changing to human form and shouting for the Alpha.

> *"One day their grandmother came into the cave. She grabbed John and Mary by the hands and led them to the monsters, then explained how the monsters were only shadows."*

Oma March's storyteller voice is crisp and clear in my head, the memory of the scent of fabric softener on our fleece blankets stronger than the sharp odor of gasoline that's still pumping furiously from the generator.

"Darling, I can't promise I can hold back my pack if you

force me to open this door," the Alpha sneers through the crack. It doesn't matter; I'm going forward with my plan whether he opens the door or not. Granted, I'll die if he doesn't, but really . . . I would've died either way. I slink over to the shelves and reach for the lighter, muscles now well accustomed to navigating this space in the dark. *Here we go.*

I flick the lighter on, the little flame illuminating the dark room with what feels like a flood of light after so many hours of darkness. The wolves begin to scratch at the door, their claws cutting into the metal. The hose finally slows to a steady drip of gasoline as I stare with my uncovered eye at the flame.

My eyes begin to water as I hear the Alpha's threats again, the howls of the wolves, maniacal laughter of those in human form, crunching spines of those changing back and forth between the two. They want in; they're thriving off one another's desire for me combined with the curiosity over what I'm doing to flood the tunnel with gasoline. The Alpha gives a command to the other wolves in a low, guttural growl. I stare at the flame and in it see images: me with Scarlett as little girls with Popsicle-stained tongues, visiting her in the hospital after the attack, the first day I held the punching bags for her when she began training to hunt, the day I hunted with her and Silas for the first time, the moment I knew I loved Silas, the day he and I kissed in the thunderstorm . . .

Time moves in slow motion. I hear the Alpha unlock the door. It swings open, but I see them only for a glimmer of a moment. Hundreds of them staring at me with hungry, reddish eyes, tongues dripping saliva to the concrete floor below.

"Then," Oma March said, "their grandmother took them outside into the bright, bright sunlight."

The wolves lunge. I drop to the floor and hold the end of the lighter to the stream of gasoline. It lights up like an explosion racing out the door, flames leaping high, illuminating ancient graffiti with more brightness than the tunnel has probably ever seen. It burns my hand. I release the lighter and push forward like an Olympic sprinter bounding off her starting point.

"It hurt and burned their eyes because it was the first time they'd ever seen the sun after living in the dark for so long."

The wolves paw at their eyes, blinded by the sudden brilliance of the flames. My uncovered eye is used to it, and I run through the flames that lick at my cloak and legs, feel my skin blistering as I dart around and past wolves who snap at my ankles with their eyes closed. It's an obstacle course, a sea of flame and teeth. The Alpha is screaming orders, and the wolves are trying to follow but stumble around blindly, falling toward the fire. Eventually there is nothing but screaming and howling in my ears, one steady, horrific cry of agony.

Keep moving forward, keep going. Ahead I see the stairs,

but the Fenris by the door struggle less, their eyes becoming accustomed. I hit the steps running, legs burning from exertion and fire, and the wolves dash forward, long jaws outstretched, hunger and anger overwhelming them. I leap above one and punch both feet downward on another's jaw, whirling around to avoid teeth. I think that one nipped my side, but it's not bad. *Keep moving, keep moving.*

I break past the final line of wolves as the rush of night air hits my skin, cooling the burns lashing my body. I grab for the makeshift eye patch and yank it to the other side of my face, unveiling the eye that's been shrouded in darkness and covering the one that just saw my way through the firelight. I don't stumble, don't blink with the sudden change—I can see fine. I press forward, feet pounding the pavement of an empty street, and look back to see a few wolves stumble from the smoke-filled tunnel only to be thrown from blinding light to blinding darkness.

It doesn't matter in what direction I run—I just have to keep moving away from them as they recover. The howls and infuriated snarls of the wolves echo between the buildings on either side of me, but I have to keep moving.

Run, Rosie. You're the only one who can save yourself.

CHAPTER TWENTY-NINE

⬥

SCARLETT

YOU READY FOR THIS?" I ASK SILAS. ONE HOUR TO go before the exchange. We'll have to leave shortly.

"To lose Rosie and possibly my soul?" Silas shakes his head and manages a halfhearted grin. "Not exactly."

"But are you?" I say seriously.

Silas stands. "I'm ready."

He grabs his ax, straps knives to his waist. I sharpen the edge of my hatchet, throw my cloak over my head, and pick up Rosie's knife belt for good measure. One of the three of us is bound to need two extra knives. I hope it's Rosie.

She *will* make it out alive. My sister is the priority. I will save Silas, I will fight for Silas, but if I must, I'll take my sister and go. I have to protect her. I don't tell Silas, but I'm sure he knows—and I'm sure he'd tell me my priorities are in order. Partners know each other like that. Yet some wicked part of me is still furious with him. If he didn't love her, they wouldn't have taken her. If she didn't love him, she might have been able to focus on stopping the wolves instead of pining for Silas.

If Rosie were like *me,* she would be safe.

If she were filled with the same obsession, the same need to avenge Oma March's death and a body of scars, the same drive to stop the wolves at any sacrifice, she would be safe.

Would Silas's death be the thing that makes Rosie focus? If they take him from her, would the hunt become her passion, the way it is mine?

Probably. For a glimmer of a moment, I allow myself to imagine Rosie and me hunting together without Silas. My sister and I, side by side, equally driven, undistracted and unrelenting. A flicker of wanting shoots through me.

I shake my head. *Focus, Scarlett,* I snap at myself as guilt fills my mouth, masking the taste of anger on my tongue. *Forget that. Saving Rosie is the priority, not your anger, not Silas, not revenge against the Arrow pack, not the Potential. Rosie.*

We descend the stairs, trying to hide the fact that both pairs of hands tremble in nervous fear. I throw open the door, hoping I look more confident than I feel, and we take to the night.

CHAPTER THIRTY

Rosie

I feel them lurking behind me, closing in, even though when I look back I don't see them. My lungs are full of smoke, but adrenaline yanks me onward. I finally begin to see signs of life—hoboes and the occasional car with hydraulics rocking down the street. Can't they hear the howling? Don't they know they're in danger?

I can't keep running. I can feel the burn blisters on my legs popping, and the wet skin underneath stings as wind reaches it. The bottom of my cloak is singed and barely reaches my lower back now, and my throat is dry and pleading for water. I can't outrun them. Maybe they'll lose my scent—I slog through as many puddles as I can as I cut through alleys and parking lots, but I have to stop soon. The wolves' howls are growing fainter, but it's hard to tell if they're far away or if the metallic skyscrapers between us are merely muffling their cries. In the distance I can see the cupola that perches on top of our apartment. *Go there? Now? Where else?*

I see one of the boarded-up apartment buildings ahead, and I know the lot where Silas and I first kissed is beyond it. I duck under a rotted fence, ignoring the No Trespassing sign, and cut through the apartment's ancient courtyard, over a crumbling fountain and between long-dead hanging plants. Yes, finally. My feet force me to slow even as my mind urges me onward. Something about knowing I can slip beneath the fence, cross the street, and be back in the apartment convinces me it's safe to slow down. *Breathe. You're safe.* I slink between rusted cars, panting heavily and ignoring the furious barks of the junkyard dogs nearby.

And then I hear them.

CHAPTER THIRTY-ONE

❧

SCARLETT

I WOULD RECOGNIZE A SINGLE SOUND FROM MY sister's lips in a crowd of thousands. Which is how I know when we open the apartment door that the smallest, tiniest whimper the wind carries to our ears is hers. I signal to Silas and we hurry to the edge of the abandoned lot, like my sister's spirit is reeling us toward her. We peer through the grasses and chain-link fence.

Her back is to us, the remains of her charred cloak fluttering in the wind. Her legs, usually creamy and pale, are covered in burn blisters, and there's a bandanna wrapped around her head, tangling her long hair in its knot and covering one eye.

She looks like me.

A sound escapes from my throat, something between a plea and a cry of joy that, at the very least, my sister is alive.

Pride swells beneath fear as I realize she must have escaped on her own, but now the Fenris are closing in on her, backing her toward the fence that Silas and I crouch behind. Her hands don't tremble like they usually do when she's nervous, and I can feel her breathing slowly, trying to focus. *Good job, Rosie.* Why did I expect any less? She's a hunter.

The Alpha takes a step toward my sister, his eyes deep ocher and raging like darkened flames. The other wolves—not the full pack, but at least a dozen—cluster behind him, pawing at the ground like racehorses readying for their starting gates to spring. The dog next door howls furiously and throws himself against the fence. Apart from the dog and the heavy breathing of the wolves, the street is eerily silent. Even the street corners are empty, as though the junkies ran off like townspeople before a Western showdown.

"Lett," Silas whispers, tensing. It's not a warning but a question—Silas knows that a plan is already running through my head, building like a snowball rolling downhill.

"There are three of us again," I mutter, counting the wolves behind the Alpha.

"We can take them. We've fought nearly this many before."

"You can't get bitten. The Alpha is with them, and he wants you."

"You know what to do if it happens," Silas says seriously. I meet his eyes for a moment, and he grabs my hand and squeezes it. In unison, we break our stare and slide through the fence opening.

The wolves' eyes dart to us in one motion, as though they're a single organism. We emerge from the long grasses and stride to my sister's side. She smiles weakly, torn between happiness and fear.

"I'm sorry, Scarlett," she whispers. "They jumped me, they held me prisoner, I didn't know what to do, and I didn't think you'd come, even if you knew they had me..."

Her words slice through me. The other half of my heart thought I wouldn't come for her? I bite my tongue, afraid I'll say too much. I pass my sister the belt with her knives, which she takes without looking at me. Silas's and Rosie's fingers fumble for one another. The Alpha inhales anxiously, watching Silas with such eagerness that it's almost tangible in the air. The wolves smell of smoke and gasoline, so much so that it makes my eye water.

"They had you because of Silas, Rosie. You were bait for him," I say meaningfully.

"For Silas...? Why..." Rosie says, voice frail. I don't explain more, but I don't need to—she understands what I'm trying to tell her. She gasps for air and looks as though she might collapse, but then she grabs Silas's hand and pulls him toward her protectively.

"I'm sorry, Rosie," Silas murmurs into her hair. "I didn't—"

"It's a mistake," Rosie says, shaking her head and speaking through gritted teeth. "It *has* to be a mistake." Her face is magnolia white with fear, but her eyes are furious, demanding Silas or me to confirm her hope—that it's all a misunderstanding. That the one she needs isn't also the one the wolves need.

Silas shakes his head, and his eyes fill with pain, pity, love; he so wants to be able to tell her that he's not the Potential. He opens his mouth, but no sound comes out. His silence is more telling than words and cements Rosie's worst fear. My sister allows a single wounded noise to erupt from her throat and then entwines her fingers into his shirt. Rosie leans up and kisses Silas fiercely, as if her mouth contains the oxygen he needs to survive. He wraps his arms around her tightly, as though they're holding each other to the earth. I lose track of who is holding whom.

It's Silas's fault Rosie was held prisoner. Silas's fault she almost died. The anger at Silas that has been brewing in me was so unrelenting, so powerful, just a few minutes ago. The secret thought that if Silas is to die, Rosie would be safe. She would be a hunter again. We would be together again, in the way we were before she loved him.

But watching them kiss, I shift my anger to the pack of wolves in front of us. How dare they try to take him away from Rosie? How dare they try to turn her into something like me? I grind my teeth and turn my focus back to the pack. My sister deserves him. She deserves love, even if I can't have it. I won't let them take him away from her.

"Just don't let them touch him, Rosie," I mutter firmly, my words breaking apart their kiss. I breathe deeply to prevent my desire to destroy the Fenris from ravaging me.

Rosie exhales and steps away from Silas, teeth gritted and

a steely look in her eyes, as if she's shelved her pain for the time being. "Not a chance," she answers fiercely.

There's a swift crunch to my left as the Alpha transforms into a wolf that's enormous even for a Fenris. He ignores my sister and me, pacing in front of Silas and licking his black lips longingly. The Alpha, the goal of all of this, the reason I came to the city, is so close.

It's so simple, really. I came to kill the Alpha. So I will.

"Go," I whisper under my breath. The wolves hear me, their ears prick up, but they don't react to my words before Silas, Rosie, and I do. I throw myself in front of Silas at the Alpha.

He knocks me aside as though I'm a paper doll. Blood vessels pop, wolves growl, dust flies. I spring back to my feet just as the Alpha leaps toward Silas. My hatchet snags for a moment around my cloak, so I plunge the blade into the Alpha's side with my cloak wrapped around it. The blow severs a piece of the fabric and sinks in between the Alpha's ribs, but he brushes the injury off, his eyes maniacally focused on Silas. Rosie darts past me and I hear her knives whistling through the air. There are too many wolves—she won't have a weapon now that she's thrown them.

"Rosie!" I yell through the air. She whirls around just as I toss my hunting knife to her. It lands squarely in her hand, and she immediately turns to lash it out toward one of the Fenris. I spin back and lunge out again, a wolf's breath hot on my face, teeth grazing my ear. Silas is darting back and forth, avoiding the wolves' jaws before he brandishes his ax at them with more strength than even I knew he possessed.

A wolf approaches his other side, but Rosie kills it, then another—were there truly only a dozen? There seem to be so many more now. I look to my left and see the Alpha bounding toward Silas again. I jump in the wolf's way, preparing for him to knock me aside, and charge toward his chest. The Alpha is caught off guard and spins away from me. I charge back, but he narrowly avoids the swings of my hatchet. I duck as he leaps for me, kicking upward into the soft spot between his legs; he flips in the air and lands hard on his back. I sprint toward him, thinking there's enough time to kill him, but no—the wolves are surrounding Silas and Rosie, herding them, pinning them between their bodies. Rosie fights valiantly, her cloak a blur around her as she sinks her knives into every bit of wolf flesh she can find. It keeps the wolves just far enough away that they can't touch Silas.

But there are so many of them. Rosie stands in front of Silas, knives ready, eyes darting among the Fenris. There's fear, yes, but there's something more, something that tells me that my sister will die before she allows a wolf through to her love.

Something that reminds me of *me,* standing in front of *her,* seven years ago. But I can't allow Rosie to become what I have become. Not Rosie—they can't have her.

My sister is the priority, which is why I sprint toward the man she loves. I flip my hatchet and send it flying, slicing down the spine of the wolf closest to the woodsman. It's just enough to distract the group, and Silas downs another while the others re-form the circle around him. The Alpha bounds toward the group, but I cut him off.

"You are only delaying the inevitable," the wolf chokes through a growl-like voice, his face transforming to something slightly more human for the words.

"As long as possible," I reply under my breath.

"Stay out of the business of wolves, child," he snarls.

I shake my head, licking my lips. "I can't. I really, really can't."

He lunges for me.

CHAPTER THIRTY-TWO

Rosie

The church bells ring once behind me, the only sound audible above the roars of monsters. The closest Fenris uses my distraction to his advantage and plunges his fangs into my forearm. I scream and smash my knife into his head, pushing it through the roof of his mouth until I feel the tip of the blade against my arm, between his teeth. I kick him in the chest, and he staggers away before collapsing into a heap. He'll be shadows soon.

Blood streams down my arm, warm and sticky, but I ignore it—three wolves left. I hear my sister bellowing curses at the Alpha, and Silas is dodging the jaws of a young-looking gray wolf. The last Fenris knocks a knife from my hand, but I reach down and grab a rusty shard of metal and plunge it into his hind leg. He howls in pain as I bring my elbow down on his head. The Fenris turns to human form and staggers away, running from the scene, slipping through the fence before I can stop him. I charge toward Silas, still clutching one knife and the shard of metal. I slide in front of him, knocking him out of the way, and plunge the shard of metal into the gray wolf's shoulder. The beast roars in pain and limps backward. One left—the Alpha. Silas meets my eyes for a moment, and then we look toward my sister on the other end of the lot.

Scarlett and the Alpha are circling each other, glaring, eyes hateful and dark. Scarlett's forehead is bleeding, her hair sticking to the wound to the point that she looks almost like an animal herself. She is fierce as I will never be, but I can help her. I run forward, Silas fast on my heels.

The wolf leaps. Scarlett lowers herself to the ground, but the Fenris knows the trick and suddenly pulls himself down. His front claws pin down her arms, his jaw in front of her face. Her legs kick in protest, but he ignores the sharp strikes she delivers to his hind legs. He's too focused. I see his claws flex and pop into my sister's forearms. A long line of bloody saliva drips onto her neck and puddles. I run faster. I want to hurt him, to destroy him for her. The Alpha's eyes dart to me.

"Don't move," he growls through a partly human mouth, the words bringing his fangs dangerously close to my sister's face. He can kill her. I have to listen, or he'll kill her like the girl in the subway tunnel. I freeze. "Drop the weapons," he orders. I hear Silas drop his ax behind me. I release the bone handle, and it thuds to the ground uselessly.

The Fenris bows his head and extends his black and red tongue, then runs it up the side of Scarlett's face tauntingly. She won't give him the satisfaction of a reaction. The Alpha chuckles, dark anger underneath the laugh, then whips his head to her shoulder—the act is so quick that I don't realize what he's done until I see the giant wound on Scarlett's collarbone, so deep that I can see the muscles flexing. She doesn't cry out, doesn't move, but I scream uncontrollably. The Alpha snickers at me and snaps his head to her other shoulder as well. Finally, Scarlett grunts in pain, which the Fenris finds hilarious. He snorts, spattering blood from his nostrils. The wolf opens his mouth wide, revealing rows and rows of yellow teeth glistening in the moonlight.

Silas blazes by me.

By the time I realize what's going on, it's too late to stop him. His hair flies back, steel determination in his eyes. *This can't be happening.*

The wolf sees Silas coming, but only barely—Silas slams into the creature's side, and they both tumble off Scarlett, who lies motionless. The wolf snaps its jaws, growls; Silas leaps away, but the Alpha swipes a lanky arm under his feet and sends him tumbling into the dirt. *A weapon, I need a weapon*—I grab Silas's ax and run for him. Silas is on his feet again, but the Fenris lashes a claw across his face, flipping him back down. Silas hits his head on the ground, and I see his eyes roll back in his head. Blood begins to pool on the dirt and I cry his name. I scream, I run, but I can't stop the wolf as it steps on top of him, lowers its head to Silas's chest. *Faster, faster, I have to move faster.* But everything is in slow motion.

The bite is such a small thing. It barely breaks the skin.

But it'll be enough. It will be enough to take his soul. To take my love's soul.

A broken wail erupts from my throat, more animal than human as I hear Scarlett cry out from the ground. Suddenly time speeds up and I'm on the Fenris, pushing him off Silas's limp body. Rage seethes through me, the most deadly, hot-blooded fury I've ever known, giving me the strength to wield the heavy ax above my head. I slam it down toward the wolf. It ducks back just in time, but I sever its front toes. The Alpha howls and leaps for me, but I turn and thrust the end of the ax into the air. It slices into the animal's chest with a dull thud, and drops of its blood rain down on me. *Not enough, not enough.* I want to hack it to pieces; I want it to die fighting me. I want to be the last thing it sees since *it* was the last thing Silas—*my* Silas, not the thing Silas will become—saw.

I try to swing the ax again, but it slides out of my hands, slick with blood. I abandon it as the Alpha slowly turns back toward me, staggering to keep upright. I have no weapon, but it doesn't matter. I jump forward and knock the wolf on its back. It claws at me, its nails tearing my clothes and skin. I press my hands onto its throat. I force my body weight behind my palms and bear down as the wolf twists, trying to throw me off. I can feel its pulse, feel its throat tightening as it gasps for air. Its eyes turn dark umber; one claw rips across my back; the monster struggles, thrashes. I stare at its eyes. *Look at me — let me be the last thing you see.*

Tears begin to stream down my cheeks and fall into the Alpha's greasy fur. He took Silas from me. Took him like it was nothing, like he wasn't the one I love. How could I not make the beast suffer? I feel like someone else, like I can't be the same person who kissed Silas in this lot just over a week before. Like I'm powerful, like I'm strong, like I'm my sister. Like I can stop my pain by taking the monster's life. I tighten my grip around its neck, relishing the dullness in its eyes.

The Alpha stops struggling. Darkness explodes over the lot, blackening the streetlights, the sky. It unfurls in the air like a great black kite, then explodes into a million pieces that flee into the abandoned apartment building like scared vagrants. I fall to the ground, my body shaking from effort and exhaustion, and turn toward my love.

He's pale, so white that the blood running from his small wound looks violently red. He's perfectly still. At first I think he's dead, but then he blinks and meets my eyes. He's calm and breathes slowly, as though he's appreciating each inhale. My blood cools, the anger dissipates, and suddenly my skin feels cold. I want to close my eyes, I want to cover my ears, and I want for all of this to not be happening. I want Silas to kiss me, to wake me up from this nightmare.

Instead, I crawl toward him, unable to stand.

"It'll be okay," I lie, choked breaths distorting my words

as I reach him. I touch the wound on his chest, trembling. If only I could get the poison out, pull it from him into me. Silas struggles to sit up. I grab his shoulders and pull him forward, and blood from his chest seeps onto me. We're both wondering the same thing, I'm certain: *how long does it take?*

Silas breathes against my neck and winces as he reaches up to stroke my hair. I tighten my grip around him, as if I might be able to hold him back against the transformation. Tears run down my face and onto his shoulder.

"You have to go, Rosie," he says gently after a few moments.

I don't move.

"You have to get away from me." His voice is harder, trying to sound determined.

"I can't," I choke. It's the truth—I don't think I can pull my hands away from him. I entwine my fingers in his hair, inhale the scent of his skin. "I love you," I whisper.

"I love you too, Rosie," he says slowly and moves away so we're looking in each other's eyes. He runs his fingertips down my cheek, his thumb across my lips. He lets his hands fall to my shoulders, as though he's studying me carefully one last time.

"Stay with me," I plead. My throat is so tight from holding back cries that the words are little more than a whisper. Silas's hands tighten on me and I tense—is this the beginning of the change? I can't fight him, I can't hurt him, even if he's the monster—he can have me. He can devour me.

But no, he's not a monster yet. He pulls me against him

and kisses me, arms wrapped tightly around my body and desperation on his lips. I can feel his heart pounding through his chest as I press myself against him. We kiss as if it's the first time, and I know he's as afraid to pull away as I am because when the kiss is over, everything is over.

He pulls away first. Tears leak out of the corners of his eyes, but his jaw is firm, resolved. I can't control the cry that escapes from my lips, the garbled pleas for him to kiss me again, to not let everything end. Everything about me tangles—my words, my fingers, my tears, my mind. Silas looks solemnly over at my sister, who has pulled herself to standing in the midst of my sorrow.

"Scarlett," he says hoarsely. "You promised."

CHAPTER THIRTY-THREE

SCARLETT

MY BODY DOESN'T WANT TO MOVE; IT PROTESTS EACH breath, each tiny step toward my sister and Silas. Rosie crumples to the ground near him after he holds off her attempts to get back by his side. Her eyes are wide and wet, her body trembles, and her fingers dig into the dirt, as though she's looking to grab something that can make her spinning world stop.

"I promised," I answer Silas, though I'm saying it as much to myself as I am to him. I promised. I promised my partner. He saved my life; I can't deny him a promise. Silas moves away from my sister as best he can, closer to me. Rosie chokes on tears, as if each inch between them is making it harder to breathe. I take another step toward Silas, searching for any sign that he's already changed, that I have to move far faster than I want to. But those are still his sparkling, determined eyes.

My stomach lurches when I get close enough to see the bites in detail. Puncture wounds crescent around his chest and spit blood at me as I raise my free hand to my mouth. I'd hoped there had been some sort of mistake, that I hadn't seen what I'd thought I'd seen. But no, he's been bitten. He will lose his soul, and he will want to devour my sister like a monster. He isn't Silas, or, at least, he won't be for long.

"Silas..." I say his name softly, like a prayer.

He swallows hard. "I'm so sorry, Lett," he answers.

"You saved me," I murmur, shaking my head, throat thick with unreleased sobs.

"Don't let it bother you too much," he jokes, but his voice shakes.

I look away and close my eye against the flood of tears that begin to fall, hoping that my aim will be true even with the convulsing way I'm sobbing. I turn back to see Silas reaching into his shirt pocket. He removes a tiny folded paper rose and clutches it as if it might save him.

"I don't know that I..." I try to speak, but my voice breaks and refuses to pull itself back together. Silas shakes his head at me.

"You promised. Don't look at me. I'm just another wolf. Just another monster."

I obey, squeezing my eye shut again so that my cheek is inundated with tears.

"I can't," I protest over Rosie's sobs.

"Yes, you can. You're a hunter, Lett. I'm a wolf," he says slowly, coaxing me through it. I raise my hatchet. "Come on, Lett. Do it," he murmurs, so quietly that I'm sure Rosie can't hear.

"Silas," I plead, shaking my head.

"Do it."

"No—"

"Kill me, Lett, before I change. I don't want you and Rosie to see me changed."

"I—"

I'm cut off again, not by him, but by the sound of the church's horribly mechanical bells tolling.

Once. Twice. Twelve times, the tinny sound echoing through the lot.

"Midnight," I whisper frantically.

"What?" Silas says. I look at him, his face contorted into a worried grimace.

"Midnight," I whisper again. I release my hatchet, and it falls into the dirt with a heavy thud. "The clock rang once for the quarter hour before the wolf pinned me. It's been over for nineteen minutes, since eleven forty-one. You're not a wolf, Silas."

Silas presses his lips together and closes his eyes. "I-I..." he stutters, and his lips seem incapable of forming words. Instead he looks up at me, eyes filled with emotion. I fall to my knees and take his hand. I want to speak, want to reassure him that it's okay, but words fail me. Instead we stare at each other, hands locked together.

Until Rosie inhales, a sharp, wounded sound. I turn toward her and see her face pressed against the dirt, hands over her ears. She hadn't wanted to hear it—hadn't wanted to know the moment that I killed him. I release Silas's hands and crawl across the ground toward her.

I pull her hands away from her ears, then wrap my arms around her, pulling her up from the ground as I do so. Her eyes are squeezed shut, tears forcing through the corners and running down her face. I hear Silas stand and take several unsure steps toward us.

Rosie hears it too.

Her body freezes. Everything about her stops as she listens to him take the final step forward. She opens her eyes— they're red and longing as they meet mine, as if she wants me to confirm that what she suspects is true, that he's standing just behind her. I smile as best I can through my own tears, and Rosie whirls around.

Silas drops to his knees and he and Rosie fall against each other, as though they each need the other to hold them up. Rosie laughs, cries, speaks all at once, but I can't understand her. Silas seems to, though, and he nods as they hold each other so tightly that it becomes difficult to tell where she ends and he begins.

CHAPTER THIRTY-FOUR

Rosie

Scarlett doesn't want to go to the hospital. Not surprising, really, since we have to come up with an elaborate story about how we all got so severely wounded.

"Dogfight. We broke one up," my sister answers for us as a horrified emergency room receptionist looks at Scarlett's raw, bleeding shoulders.

"Dogs dislike us." Silas shrugs, clutching the wound on his chest. He glances down at the burn wounds on my legs. I think they might scar, but it's hard to say. The receptionist speaks into a walkie-talkie, then lets her eyes travel from the fresh wounds to the ancient scars on Scarlett's body.

"Dogs pretty much *hate* me," Scarlett says testily. The poor receptionist looks relieved when the ER doctors appear and usher us down the hall.

The doctors give me ointment for my legs, shaking their heads when I tell them that not one of us has health insurance. Scarlett is the worst off. They cover her shoulders in bandages until she looks as though she's wearing football pads, but she draws the line when they ask her to stay in the hospital overnight. By the time we've quietly snuck out without paying, it's dawn. The first few rays of hazy lavender light are fingering their way into the sky, the cool blues reflecting off the glass and concrete buildings.

Silas calls a taxi—a luxury that we can't afford but feel we deserve—and we speed through the nearly empty streets without talking. He takes my hand in his, and I meet his eyes meaningfully.

"You understand," Silas says quietly—the words are just for me, but I know Scarlett hears—"I'm...when I'm twenty-eight, Rosie. You know what this means. I'm *dangerous*, Rosie."

"You plan on loving me when you're twenty-eight?" I interrupt, uncertain if my question is serious or not.

Silas's eyes widen in surprise. He turns to look out the taxi window for a moment, and when his eyes meet mine again, there's a beautiful sincerity glistening in the gray-blue irises. "Rosie...I love you. Now, when I'm twenty-eight, when I'm thirty-five...I love you."

I exhale. "Okay, then."

"But I'm—"

I put a finger against his soft, bow-shaped lips. "Okay, then."

Silas closes his eyes and nods in relief. He's right—I probably *should* be thinking about what this will mean in seven years, what it means now, how close we all came to a very different fate, but all my fears vanish and a single warm feeling fills my body and mind: completeness. Well, that, coupled with total and utter exhaustion. I take Scarlett's hand with my free one.

"You're happy?" I ask quietly over the hum of morning talk radio. The driver takes a sharp turn and I bump Scarlett's wounded shoulder. She winces but nods in response.

"I suppose. Fenris are dead. The Alpha is gone. For now," she says, sighing contentedly. For the first time in weeks, she looks calm, as though her mind isn't on the hunt. "We're safe."

"We can go home?" I ask hopefully, visions of the cottage and long grass and streets that are more dust than garbage flitting through my head.

My sister nods, ends of bandages fluttering around her face like scarves. "I think we are long past due to go home."

Packing to leave Atlanta is a lot easier than packing to come here. We bundle most everything up in our bedsheets and cram clothing into duffel bags, leaving the rugs and thrift store findings to whoever the next tenant may be. We leave the next morning, Scarlett waving a sarcastic farewell to the junkie downstairs before we take off in the hatchback, pop music blasting and me leaning toward Silas, both to avoid the door of death and to rest my head against his biceps.

Ellison hasn't changed, unsurprisingly. Buildings here are yellow and pale gold instead of harsh steel and silver. Trees dapple the sunlight across the car. The air is warmer, like loving arms that swirl around me for comfort. It's so good to be home.

Days pass. Weeks. Silas and I steal moments together. We kiss, we touch, we let our fingers graze each other's shoulders whenever my sister isn't looking. I want to wrap my arms around him and lie on the couch for hours on end, but Scarlett…Just because she knows, just because she doesn't say anything about us, doesn't mean she doesn't busy herself whenever she sees us touch, or find a sudden reason to sprint out the screen door if we lean in to kiss.

"She'll come around, Rosie," Silas assures me one day as we watch Scarlett dig up the mostly ruined potatoes from the garden. It's evening, and fireflies blink on and off around the yard like living Christmas lights. The table outside is set — most of Oma March's old and battered dishes filled with as many of her garden recipes as I could find. Mashed potatoes with sweet butter, stuffed green peppers, watermelon cut into sugary pink squares. Even food tastes better here, as though the city food we'd been eating had been missing something integral.

"We're ready to eat?" Scarlett asks, rising as Silas and I kick open the screen door, letting it slam behind us. She ripped the bandages off her shoulders weeks ago, and now new, shiny pink scars lace her skin, as if she's only badly sunburned. My legs have healed almost completely, and I have to admit, I'm somewhat proud of the few dotted burn scars that remain. Silas and I slide onto the smooth wooden picnic bench, and Scarlett joins us on the opposite side. We don't speak, just serve our plates in silence. Scarlett glances back at the moon behind her. It's full, heavy and white in the sky. When she turns back to me, our eyes meet for a moment.

And there it is.

I knew it would return; I just didn't know when. The look, the *need* that I saw for wandering in my mother's eyes, I see for hunting in Scarlett's. I never expected her to quit, and it was only a matter of time before she wanted to begin training again, hunting in the night, buying gauze and scented soap and using our newfound knowledge of Potentials to track them. It is not a sickness, it's a passion, I now realize, a passion to hunt the same way a painter must paint or a singer must sing. It's her blood and her heart.

We don't need to speak. I drop the slice of watermelon I'm holding and Scarlett slowly rises, because we both *know*. We both know the light is there, and there's no use pretending the shadows are real. I swing my bare legs out from under the picnic table, Scarlett mirroring my actions, and we meet at the table's head, entangling our arms around each other and breathing in the scent of each other's hair while Silas watches, silent, confused.

My sister has the heart of an artist with a hatchet and an eye patch. And I, we *both* now know, have a heart that is undeniably, irreparably different.

EPILOGUE

A Fairy Tale, Seven Months After

The sisters walk slowly. Their arms are weighed down with bags, and the afternoon sun beats down on their necks mercilessly. Scarlett stops to drop a handful of change into a street drummer's bucket while Rosie pauses to count the money in her pocket. Their thoughts are on each other as they almost always are. They reach their destinations simultaneously, Rosie on the platform of a train station with her luggage in tow, and Scarlett asking one of the junkies to grab the apartment door for her.

There are letters outside Scarlett's door, and it looks as if someone has already rooted through some of the mail. She grabs what's left—the important ones almost always get left anyhow. The ones from Rosie. She kicks open the heavy wooden door and drops her bags just inside, tearing into the paper eagerly.

The cursive handwriting tells her that Silas is still learning to play guitar—and still isn't very good at it—and that Rosie is practicing all of Oma March's old recipes—and isn't very good at them. Scarlett smiles and sets the card on the dining table with the others. There are hundreds, one almost every day, filled with folded roses and swans and frogs. They come from different cities—San Francisco, Phoenix, Boston, New York. Silas sold his father's house so he and Rosie could use the money to visit and make amends with his siblings, to get purposefully lost in strange places, to eat local fare and hold hands as they explore the world together. Their lives are the eager question "Where should we go?" while Scarlett's is a resolute answer: "Here is where I am needed."

The sisters rarely call each other, because whenever they hear the other's voice, they repeat the same things into the phone: I love you, I miss you, are we making a mistake? And both know the answer to the question. No, this is not a mistake. This is a hard, and perhaps cruel, necessity.

Rosie grins as Silas catches up to her, two train tickets in his hand. He abandons his suitcase and puts his arms around her. They kiss like lovers in an old movie, two people who don't care if others are watching. She giggles as he looks at her adoringly, as though she is the most beautiful thing he's ever seen and if he blinks, she may vanish. She runs her fingers across the hair at the nape of his neck and smiles as the train pulls into the station.

Scarlett climbs the stairs to the rooftop deck. Tonight will be a good night to hunt. Already the desire to take to the streets pulls at her like an old friend. She stares out at the city. *Where to go tonight? Whom to protect, whom to defend?* She sweeps her hair back into a ponytail as she looks at the streets below. *Her* streets, *her* responsibility and passion. It's already dusk—she hurries back downstairs, preparing to leave early. The apartment isn't quite what it used to be; Scarlett has hung up the hundreds of decorations and drawings and elaborately folded papers that Rosie has sent, so many that it's like a field of flowers that bloom year-round. She runs her fingers across the crimson red cloak that hangs on the back of a chair.

Rosie takes her seat while Silas puts her luggage overhead. Her cloak is inside the battered suitcase, tattered, largely unused but still present, like a quiet friend who's waiting for a moment to join the conversation. She turns to gaze out the window as the train eases forward, uncertain exactly what it is she's looking for.

Scarlett pulls the cloak onto her shoulders in one swift, fluid motion; Rosie smiles as the landscape begins to fly by. Scarlett steps out into the city streets and Rosie reaches for Silas's arm. Matching memories swirl in their heads, memories of running through the grass and spinning in circles and holding each other in the garden, memories where they lose track of who is who and they begin to feel like a beautiful, golden link connects them. A single, shared heart.

ACKNOWLEDGMENTS

If writing my first book was hard, then writing my second—
Sisters Red—was near impossible. At this rate, I'm terrified
of writing the third, but luckily I know I can count on a few
people to help me out—people who helped give Scarlett and
Rosie voices, stories, and a heart. Thus, I'm forever indebted
to the following:

Naturally, to my sister, Katie Pearce, not only for being
the source of much inspiration but also for telling me exactly
how brutal a beating Scarlett, Rosie, and Silas could take
without breaching medical plausibility.

Granddaddy Pearce, who helped me get Rosie out of the
subway tunnel.

Saundra Mitchell, who critiqued early drafts of *Sisters*

Red in record time, marked it all to pieces, and made the book sparkle like never before.

Rose Green, for translating English into German for me and Oma March.

Cyn Balog, R. J. Anderson, and Jason Mallory, for reading *Sisters Red* when it had been "complete" for all of five minutes.

The 2009 Debutantes, for continued support, wisdom, and candy.

My editor, Jill Dembowski, for believing in the March sisters, and because not many editors would dress up in a red cloak and send you the picture.

My parents, for continued support and for taking me to the Apple Time Festival as a kid—with paper apples stapled to my clothes.

And again, to Papa, because I'm certain he had something to do with this.

DISCUSSION QUESTIONS

1. What happens to a man once he becomes a Fenris? How does he live? What causes him to transform from man to Fenris?

2. What is the significance of the different Fenris packs: Coin, Bell, Sparrow, and Arrow? How are the Fenris from different packs identified?

3. Why are Rosie and Scarlett so close to each other? How does their dependence on one another help them to survive? How does their dependence on one another hurt them individually?

4. What role does Silas play in the sisters' lives? How does his role change as the story progresses?

5. Why do Rosie and Scarlett keep their grandmother's room as a memorial to her? What causes the sisters to remove items from her room?

6. What prompts Rosie and Scarlett to move from their home to the city? How does the move affect their relationship with each other? And with Silas?

7. How do Rosie's and Scarlett's motivations to hunt differ? How does that bring about conflict in their relationship?

8. What personality traits do the sisters share? How do their similarities and differences make them such a dynamic team?

9. Scarlett refuses to feel pity for herself and her scarred body, but she imposes a sense of responsibility on herself because of it. What responsibility does she assume? How does it affect her life?

10. Why does Rosie feel so much guilt? How does Silas help her overcome her feelings of guilt? Does Scarlett's jealousy have anything to do with Rosie's guilt?

11. As the Fenris attacks become more frequent and the search for the Potential becomes more intense, how does Scarlett react? To whom does she turn seeking answers?

12. As Silas, Rosie, and Scarlett try to determine the reason a young man becomes a Fenris, what do they discover?

13. What do the Fenris hope to gain by kidnapping Rosie? How is their plan ruined?

14. What does Silas do to protect Rosie from the possible danger he could cause her? What does Rosie's reaction to the danger say about their relationship?

15. If Silas had been transformed into a Fenris, would Scarlett have really killed him? Why or why not?

NOT EVERYTHING IS AS SWEET AS IT APPEARS. . . .

Turn the page for a sneak peek at this delicious reimagining of "Hansel and Gretel," coming August 2011.

PROLOGUE

(Twelve Years Ago)

The book said there was a witch in the woods.

That's why they were among the thick trees to begin with — to find her. The three of them trudged along, weaving through the hemlocks and maples, long out of sight of their house, their father's happy smiles, their mother's soft hands.

A sharp ripping sound bounced through the trees. The boy whirled around.

"Sorry," one of the girls said, though she clearly didn't mean it. Her cheeks were still lined with baby fat and her hair was like broken sunlight, identical to the girl's standing beside her. She held up the bag of chocolate candies that she'd just torn open. "You can have all the yellows, Ansel, if you want."

"No one likes the yellows," Ansel said, rolling his eyes.

"Mom does," one of the twins argued, but he'd turned his back and couldn't tell which one. That was how it normally was with them—they blended, so much so that you sometimes couldn't tell if they were two people or the same person twice. The sister with the candy emptied a handful of them into her palm, picking out the yellows and dropping them as they continued to trudge forward.

"When we find the witch," Ansel told his sisters, "if she chases us, we should split up. That way she can only eat one of us."

"What if she catches me, though?" one of the girls asked, alarmed.

"Well, what if she catches me, Gretchen?" Ansel replied.

"You're bigger. She should chase you," the other sister told him, pouting. "That's the way they work." She was the only one who claimed to know the ways of witches—she was the one with the stories, the made-up maps, the pages and pages of books stored away in her head. She reached into her twin's bag of candy and pegged Ansel in the back of the head with a yellow candy. He didn't react, so she prepared to throw another one —

"Wait...do you know where we are?" he asked.

One of the twins raised her eyes to the forest canopy and scanned the closest tree trunks, while her sister turned slowly in the leaves. They knew these woods by heart but had never ventured quite so far before. The shadows from branches felt like strangers, the cracks and pops of nature turned eerie.

The twins simultaneously shook their heads and their brother nodded curtly, trying to hide the fact that being out so far made him uneasy. He hurried forward, eager to keep moving.

"Ansel? Wait!" one asked, and ran a little to close the space between them. "Are we lost?"

"Only a little," he answered, jumping at the sound of a particularly loud falling branch. "Don't be scared."

"I'm not," she lied. She began to wish she'd packed peanut butter and jelly sandwiches for their adventure, instead of two Barbies and a bag of candy, which Gretchen had almost finished off anyway. What if they were stuck out here past dinnertime?

"Besides," Ansel said over his shoulder, "maybe she'll be a good witch, like Glinda, and help us get unlost."

"I thought you said she might want to eat us."

"Well, maybe, but we won't know until we find her. Unless you want to go back," Ansel said. He didn't entirely believe the stories about the witch, but his sisters did and he didn't want to ruin it for them. Another pop in the woods made him jump; he shook off the nerves and sang their favorite song, one from a plastic record player that had been their father's.

"*In the Big Rock Candy Mountain, you never change your socks.*" The twins began to hum along, adding words here or there, until they got to the line all three of them loved and they sang in unison.

"*There's a lake of stew and soda, too, in the Big Rock Candy Mountain!*" The familiar words calmed them, made things fun again, as though their combined voices swept the fear away.

Ansel was about to begin another verse when a new noise came from farther in the forest—not a pop, not a crack, but a footstep. A slow, rolling foot on dried leaves, then another, then another. He grabbed his sisters' hands, one of their sticky palms in each of his. The bag of candies fell to the ground and scattered, rainbow colors in the dead leaves.

They waited. There was nothing.

And yet there was something—there was something, something breathing, something dripping, something still and hard in the trees. Ansel's eyes raced across the trunks, looking for whatever it was that he was certain, beyond all doubt, had its eyes locked on them.

"Who's there?" Ansel shouted. His voice shook, and it made the twins quiver. Ansel was never scared. He was their big brother. He protected them from boys with sticks and thunderstorms.

But he was scared now, and they were torn between wonder and horror at the sight.

Nothing answered Ansel's question. It got quieter. Birds stilled, trees silenced, breath stopped, his grip on his sisters' hands tightened. It was still there, whatever it was, but it was motionless, waiting, waiting, waiting...

It finally spoke, a low, whispery voice, something that could be mistaken for wind in the trees, something that made Ansel's throat dry. He couldn't pick out the words—they were torn apart, and they were dark. Low, guttural, threatening.

The words stopped.

And it laughed.

Ansel squeezed his sisters' hands and took off the way they had come. He yanked them along and ran fast as he could, over brush and under limbs. The twins screamed, a single high-pitched note that ripped through the trees and swam around Ansel's head. He couldn't look back, not without slowing.

It was behind them. Right behind them, chasing them.

Gretchen stumbled but held tightly to Ansel, let herself be dragged to her feet just as something grasped at her ankles, missed. They had to move faster; it was coming, crunching leaves, grabbing at the hems of their clothes.

It's going to catch us.

The twins slowed Ansel down—their joined hands slowed everyone down. They'd promised to split up so the witch could eat only one of them, but now...

It's going to catch us.

Ansel lightened his grip, just the smallest bit, and suddenly his hands were free and the three of them were sprinting through the trees. The thing behind them roared, an even darker version of the words they'd heard earlier.

Both twins knew the other couldn't run much longer. Did Ansel know the way out?

Candy.

On the ground, yellow candies. Ansel was following them, slicing around trees while the twins followed along desperately, eyes focused on finding the next piece, the trail back to the part of the forest they knew. The monster leapt for one of the twins, missed her, made a breathy, hissing sound of frustration. She dared to glance back.

Yellow, sick-looking eyes found hers.

She turned forward and sped up, faster than the others, driven by the yellow eyes that overpowered the sharp aches in her chest, her legs begging for rest. There was light ahead, shapes that weren't trees. Their house, their house was close—the candy trail had worked. She couldn't feel her feet anymore, her lungs were bursting, eyes watering, cheeks scratched, but there was the house.

They burst from the woods onto their cool lawn. *Get inside, get inside.* Ansel flung the back door open and they stumbled in, slamming the door shut. Their father and mother ran down the stairs, saw their children sweaty and panting and quivering, and asked in panicky, perfect unison:

"Where's your sister?"